# Pole Pedal Murder

Ted Haynes

Copyright 2022 by Ted Haynes. All rights reserved.
This is a work of fiction. Names, characters, and events are fictitious or are used factiously.

ISBN 978-1-7331544-4-4
Library of Congress Control Number: 2022906260

Book Design by Jim Bisakowski of BookDesign.ca

The Robleda Company, Publishers
1259 El Camino Real, Ste 2720
Menlo Park, CA 94025
www.robledabooks.com

*For*
*Andi Northcote*
*and*
*Molly Cogswell-Kelly*

# Contents

| | | |
|---|---|---|
| Chapter 1 | Sheriff's Detective Carl Breuninger | 9 |
| Chapter 2 | Sheriff's Detective Carl Breuninger | 15 |
| Chapter 3 | Sarah Chatham | 26 |
| Chapter 4 | Amy Martinez | 33 |
| Chapter 5 | Sarah Chatham | 40 |
| Chapter 6 | Sheriff's Detective Carl Breuninger | 51 |
| Chapter 7 | Amy Martinez | 57 |
| Chapter 8 | Sheriff's Detective Carl Breuninger | 61 |
| Chapter 9 | Sarah Chatham | 73 |
| Chapter 10 | Dan Martinez | 79 |
| Chapter 11 | Sarah Chatham | 86 |
| Chapter 12 | Sheriff's Detective Carl Breuninger | 93 |
| Chapter 13 | Sarah Chatham | 101 |
| Chapter 14 | Sheriff's Detective Carl Breuninger | 105 |
| Chapter 15 | Amy Martinez | 109 |
| Chapter 16 | Sarah Chatham | 117 |
| Chapter 17 | Sheriff's Detective Carl Breuninger | 123 |
| Chapter 18 | Sarah Chatham | 133 |
| Chapter 19 | Sheriff's Detective Carl Breuninger | 139 |
| Chapter 20 | Sean Wray | 144 |
| Chapter 21 | Sheriff's Detective Carl Breuninger | 148 |
| Chapter 22 | Dr. Boyd McGrath | 159 |

| | | |
|---|---|---|
| Chapter 23 | Sheriff's Detective Carl Breuninger | 165 |
| Chapter 24 | Sarah Chatham. | 171 |
| Chapter 25 | Sarah Chatham. | 176 |
| Chapter 26 | Sarah Chatham. | 187 |
| Chapter 27 | Sarah Chatham. | 191 |
| Chapter 28 | Sheriff's Detective Carl Breuninger | 197 |
| Chapter 29 | Sheriff's Detective Carl Breuninger | 201 |
| Chapter 30 | Sheriff's Detective Carl Breuninger | 214 |
| Chapter 31 | Amy Martinez | 218 |
| Chapter 32 | Sheriff's Detective Carl Breuninger | 221 |
| Chapter 33 | Sarah Chatham. | 226 |
| Chapter 34 | Sheriff's Detective Carl Breuninger | 231 |
| Chapter 35 | Skip McNulty. | 235 |
| | Acknowledgements | 243 |
| | Fact and Fiction | 244 |
| | About the Author | 246 |
| | Books by Ted Haynes | 246 |

## Pole Pedal Paddle Racing Teams

| RACE LEG | "The Pickup Team" | "Chatham Family Team" |
|---|---|---|
| Downhill Ski (1,200 yards) | Unnamed - Oregon State Student | Bud Russell – Sarah Chatham's Second Husband |
| Cross Country Ski (5 miles) | Wendy Whitlock | Lars Willemoes – Kate's Husband |
| Bicycle (22 miles) | Unnamed friend of Amy Martinez | Kurt Chatham – Sarah's Son |
| Run (5 miles) | Natasha Korel | Kate Willemoes – Sarah's Daughter |
| Kayak (2 miles) | Amy Martinez | Gwen Chatham – Kurt's Wife |
| Sprint (1 mile) | Grace Wray | Sarah Chatham – Partner at Oxton, Rath, & Flynn, Attys. |

## The Cascadians One Fly Fishing Team

**Carl Breuninger** – Deschutes County Sheriff's Detective. Wife is Estelle.

**Dr. Samuel Dee** – Wendy Whitlock's boss at Sisemore Orthopedics. Wife is Charlotte.

**Dan Martinez** – Sr. Associate at Oxton, Rath, & Flynn. Wife is Amy.

**Sean Wray** – Engineer and Investor. Wife is Grace.

Chapter 1

# Sheriff's Detective Carl Breuninger

I volunteered to drive a convict to prison in Lakeview. The man sat in the back seat, behind the metal screen. His hands were cuffed in front of him and the handcuffs were chained to a bracket on the floor. But the handcuffs were loose and the chain was long enough that the man could sit comfortably.

I felt badly for Roland Lightfeather, even if he had murdered a man. He had never been arrested before. He'd worked all his life and raised a son who was on his way to law school. And, though it didn't make it right, the man Roland killed truly deserved it. The man had murdered Roland's father when Roland was a child. Roland wasn't an evil man and he wasn't likely to break the law again. I wanted him to ride to his five-year incarceration with someone he knew and that someone was me. With luck he would serve his minimum sentence and go home.

"Stay calm in prison when you get there," I told him, "and pay attention. Act polite and considerate. Don't ask too many questions. Privacy is scarce. Don't be too quick to make friends. And stay away from the child molesters. They can seem like the most civilized people in there but nobody wants to be their friend. A lot of the prisoners were abused themselves when they were children."

I delivered Roland and started the drive back to Bend when the Deschutes County Medical Examiner, Kristen Valle, called me on my cell phone.

"I'm working a death outside of town on Route 20 that has the marks of suicide but it might not be. I think you'll need to get out here."

If it was a suicide I'd be home for dinner with my wife Estelle. If it was murder, or possibly murder, I could be out to all hours. It was three o'clock on a cold and cloudy January afternoon and I had two more hours to get to Bend.

"You got an ID?"

"Wendy Whitlock. White female, thirty-eight. Her son says he came home from school and found her hanging from a beam in the barn behind her house."

"And it might not be a suicide?"

"No note on the body and the son, Ethan Whitlock, says there is no note on the kitchen counter where she usually leaves notes. He says, for what it's worth, that his mother wasn't unhappy and she would never kill herself. The son says she competes in ski races and I can pretty well see that. If she's a suicide she's the healthiest suicide I've ever had."

"Where's the body now?"

"She's lying on a workbench in the barn with a tarp over her. I'm waiting for a hearse to take her away. Ethan cut her down."

"So he's compromised the scene," I said.

"That's an understatement," said Kristen. "He says the ladder was lying on the floor and he set it up so he could climb up and get her. He lifted her down by himself."

"What time did she die?"

"Two o'clock, give or take a few minutes. I checked her temperature and lividity. That's one good thing about Ethan bringing her down. It would have been hard to get a rectal temperature up in the air." Kristen expected the bodies she examined to be lying down. She was a small redhead, strong enough for her size but she never moved bodies herself if she could help it.

"Where is Ethan now?" I asked.

"There's a workout space in the back corner of the building. He's sitting on a bench keeping an eye on me. Shotwell is on his way to talk with him. He'll get him out of here and back in the house." Reverend Shotwell was the Sheriff's Department chaplain. The man saw a lot of grief and, God bless him, he dealt with a lot of stuff we didn't want to. He was a pastor in an evangelical church but he could comfort anybody, even an atheist.

"And Susan is on her way. I told her to bundle up. It's freezing in here." Susan McCarthy was the tech on contract with the sheriff's department. She was on call to document crime scenes—take photographs, draw diagrams, and bag evidence. Kristen must have talked the sheriff into sending Susan out despite limited evidence a crime had been committed.

"What do you think?" I asked. "Is it murder or are we just covering all the bases?"

"Suicide by hanging is common enough, even among women, but death is almost always by asphyxiation. A person can hang an extension cord over a door, put a slip knot around their neck, and collapse on the floor. If they don't get up they strangle to death."

"Like Robin Williams," I said.

"He used a belt," said Kristen, "but it's essentially the same thing—you run out of oxygen. This woman didn't suffocate. She died the instant she dropped, a real execution. She used a hangman's noose and she had to get up high, high enough to fall at least five feet and make sure her neck broke."

"So she planned this carefully, or somebody did."

"Yeah," said Kristen. "People can have suicidal thoughts for a long time but it's very often a much shorter time, ten minutes or less, from the final decision to actually going through with it. This was not a ten-minute decision. It took time to set up."

"Possibly killed first and then strung up?" I asked.

"We won't know until the autopsy but I don't think so. No signs of a struggle, no trauma except the broken neck. Her eyes would be bloodshot if she were strangled or poisoned with strychnine. They aren't. Arsenic would have made her sick and vomitous before she died. She'd smell like bitter almonds if she'd ingested cyanide. She'd smell like alcohol if she'd been drunk. There's none of that. She might have been sedated and we won't know until we get the tox screen. But if she were sedated somebody pretty strong would have to carry her up that ladder and get the noose around her neck. She weighs about one-fifty."

"Could her son have done that?"

Kristen paused, probably to take a glance over at Ethan. "Strong enough," she said softly. "You're supposed to be the judge of character, not me. But from what I've seen, I can't believe this boy would drug his mother and drag her up a ladder to kill her."

Kristen went on in a normal voice. "She's wearing business casual and a down parka, like she came straight from the office. The son says she's an administrator for a group of doctors, works in the mornings."

"Does this Wendy Whitlock have a husband? Where is he in all this?"

"The son called him. He's coming from a jobsite in Sisters. He's a landscape contractor. Name is Warren Whitlock."

"How many deputies on the scene?" I asked. One guy. "Tell him not to let anyone on the property except the chaplain and the husband. And Susan of course." Kristen said she would and we hung up. She'd be gone long before I got there, hopefully not to another death. We only had three or four murders a year in Deschutes County but we had ten times that many traffic deaths. Speed, alcohol, drugs, and cars hitting pedestrians or bicyclists. Kristen saw a lot sorrier sights than I did—more blood and broken bodies, more shocked and grieving family members. At least the dead weren't dishonest or crazy or filled with hate or desperately unhappy like the losers I usually had to deal with.

I had planned to stop for coffee and pie in Paisley, a pretty little town with the only restaurant in a seventy-mile stretch of highway. I couldn't take the time now but, crossing the bridge on the far side of town, I gazed fondly at the frozen Chewaucan River. I had camped and fished up that river for years. The sight made me wish for summer, for time off, and for fishing with Estelle.

My daydreaming was interrupted by the sight of a pickup truck a quarter mile away, coming at me, something wrong with it. The truck's license plate was hanging by a single bolt. The truck was a light blue Chevy showing the scratches and dents of hard work. Standard Oregon license plate. Last three digits were 892. Typical farmer's truck with bales of hay in the bed.

I thought of turning around and telling him he was about to lose his license plate. I'd be doing him a favor. But I didn't have time. And why would I, or any law enforcement officer, expend that much effort on such a minor problem? People had missing front license plates all the time and law enforcement hardly ever stopped them.

Curiosity, I admitted to myself, was why I wanted to stop the guy. The driver, as unexpected as the crooked license plate, was a black kid with a narrow face wearing a John Deere baseball cap. This part of Oregon was less than one percent black. Who was he and what was he doing here? Curiosity is generally a good thing if you're a detective. But how would my curiosity look to that kid? Or to an uninvolved citizen reading about it in the paper? It wouldn't look good.

Ten miles later, driving past Summer Lake, I answered my curiosity for myself. Paisley didn't have enough kids to justify having a high school of its own. But the parents didn't want their kids to ride a bus ninety miles every day to get back and forth to high school in Lakeview, especially in the winter. So they hosted kids from all over the world who wanted to learn English and experience America. That got the student population up enough to have a high school. The foreign kids adapted to small town life and the residents broadened their perspective on the world. The kid in the truck was having an experience he'd never forget. Wherever he was from, Kenya or Nigeria or Jamaica, the Oregon outback would always be a part of him.

Susan, the crime scene tech, called me as I passed the turn for Fort Rock.

"I just started here," she said. "Kristen took the body and the boy's gone over to the house with Reverend Shotwell. I'm gonna begin by dusting the victim's car for fingerprints while it's still light out then come back to the barn. I'll photograph the interior and then dust whatever seems likely, starting with the ladder. But it's a big place and I can't dust the whole building. Anything you want me to keep an eye out for?"

"The ladder sounds like the best bet. Check the temps of any machinery you find to see if any of it was used recently. Use your own judgment after that. I'll be there in a little over an hour."

Chapter 2

# Sheriff's Detective
# Carl Breuninger

The city of Bend has trees and, in the summer, lawns that are watered. The sagebrush ocean starts at the city limits, right where the apartment buildings end. You can spot the edge of the city without a sign. The road continues east for six miles, past a scattered collection of ten acre "ranchettes" before completely surrendering to the largely uninhabited high desert—widely spaced juniper trees and dry buttes for two hundred miles to the Snake River. Some of the ranchettes on the road near town had green lawns and landscaped shrubs at great expense to the owner. Others had not progressed very far beyond the rock and sand they started with. The Whitlocks lived on a dry and dusty ranchette, undeveloped except for the small house and the large steel barn behind it. Not the best showpiece for a landscape contractor.

There was one deputy parked in the driveway and the chaplain's car was gone. Susan was packing her camera and plastic bins of evidence into her car, already running the motor so the heat would be on when she drove away. She wore a powder blue knitted ski hat over her usual crew cut. She was a strong woman, with a big frame and a square face. Susan played rugby for Bend's Lady Roughriders.

"I got most of it," she said. "The sheriff's office called and said to wrap it up. It has too many hallmarks of suicide to spend any more time on it."

"Is that what you think?" I asked.

"I don't get paid to think," she said. "I collect the evidence and let the crime lab sort it out."

"Did you find anything interesting?"

"I'm taking the ladder with me. Fingerprints and glove marks all over it. The lab will have a field day figuring out who they all belong to. Some recent prints are from bare hands. Must have been cold. None of the equipment or the two space heaters have been used since at least noon."

I took a quick scan around the barn myself. No surprises, at least not so far. It seemed to be more or less what I'd expect the barn of a landscaper with an athletic wife to look like. There was a Bobcat, a riding mower, and two walking mowers lined up against the right-hand wall. Racks on the left wall held long lengths of PVC pipe. A flatbed truck was parked against the left wall, leaving empty space in the middle of the barn. Rakes, shovels, three blowers, and two sets of shelves lined the back wall with a man door, not another garage door, centered between them. There was a space heater on the floor next to a workbench but it was too small to have much effect in the dead of winter. Warren Whitlock, the husband, would still need a coat to work there. Over in the far-right corner, the weights, mats, stretch bands, a Nordic Track and a balance board were in order, presumably where Wendy last left them.

"Anything else?" I asked Susan.

"The husband was out to the barn. I wouldn't let him touch anything but he cast his eye around. Said he didn't see anything missing. Kept telling me his wife wouldn't commit suicide. Pretty adamant about it. That's it. If you want the crime lab to analyze the evidence I picked up, you better push them. Otherwise they'll assume it's a suicide and they'll sit on it." Susan locked up the barn and gave me the barn door key to give to the husband. She left while I walked around to the front door of the house.

I braced myself for talking with a family that had just lost a wife and mother. I wouldn't like doing it, seeing the pain in their faces, having little to offer them. But I'd done it enough times to know more or less to go through the routine. And, of course, I would want to know what light they could shed on Wendy Whitlock's death. I wouldn't tell them I was picking at the edges of the possibility that one of them had a hand in this.

Warren Whitlock answered the door, hunched over like a beaten man. Standing up, he would have been about five-eight, my height. "Glad you're here at last," he said. "You better find the son-of-a-bitch who did this before I do." He had dark hair, dark eyes, a short nose and a prominent chin. Ethan stood behind him, taller than his father, and watched me expectantly—a mixture of hope, doubt, and curiosity. I told them I was sorry for the loss of their wife and mother and assured them the sheriff's department would do everything it could to find out what happened and who was responsible.

"Mr. Whitlock," I said, "will Ethan be all right if you and I talk privately somewhere?" I thought Warren's talk of murder might be for his son's sake. It would be crushing enough for the boy to lose his mother. Even more so if this was suicide. Warren asked Ethan to go upstairs for a minute and we sat in two upholstered chairs in the corner of the living room near a small brick fireplace and away from the stairwell. A pinewood counter separated the living room from the kitchen at the opposite end from us. The rug and the furniture were plain, with a subdued plaid on the couch. But the room was well kept up—clean, orderly, pillows plumped and in place. The one tall bookshelf held photographs, two glass vases, about thirty hardback books, and a full shelf of trophies, medals, and ribbons. One shelf held a photo of Ethan in wrestling garb and one of a woman, presumably Wendy, in ski clothes but no hat, leaning forward on her ski poles and smiling at the camera.

I asked Warren where he was when he heard of his wife's death and who he was with in the hours before he got the call. He didn't seem bothered by the question. I was doing my job and he understood that. He told me about the jobsite in Sisters and gave the names of two workers and a driver who delivered trees while he was there.

Phone numbers too, from memory.

"What makes you think your wife was murdered?"

"There's no way Wendy would kill herself. It's not who she is. She's a woman with a purpose. Hell, you don't work hard all morning and train hard in the afternoon if you're planning to kill yourself."

"Where does she work?" I asked, careful not to use the past tense yet.

"Administrator for a group of doctors, Sisemore Orthopedics. Been there ten years. And you see all those trophies and ribbons?" Warren pointed to the bookshelf. "Wendy won those cross-country skiing. She was much too serious to go killing herself. And furthermore she loved us, Ethan and me. She watched out for us. Dedicated to Ethan going to college. I don't know what we're going to do now." He stared at the front door as if the question of how to manage his life had finally preempted finding his wife's killer.

"If Wendy was murdered, who do you think killed her?" Was I humoring him or asking a serious question? It didn't matter.

"I don't know," he said, "not an enemy in the world. People depended on her. Maybe a crazy competitor from a ski race. Some patient at Sisemore who blamed her for his troubles. More likely some guy who picked her at random and followed her home. That's what you need to find out. You need to get out there and ask questions. Knock some heads."

"We're already investigating," I said. "The crime lab reports and the autopsy will tell us a lot."

"How long will that take?" asked Warren.

"Usually three weeks or so."

"Meantime the killer could disappear. You need to start asking questions right now. Tonight."

"The county is already spending its time as effectively as possible," I said. "We've done this before." I was tempted to add, "As for asking questions, Mr. Whitlock, I'm asking questions right now. I'm asking questions of you." I also didn't add that if his wife's cause of death was murder, Warren Whitlock would be in for a good hard examination himself.

"Is this going to be in the news?"

"Better for both of us if it isn't," I said. "But that means for now we're going to leave the cause of death as undetermined. If we decide it was a murder the sheriff will tell the media. In the meantime I need to talk with Ethan."

"Take it easy on him," said Warren. He went upstairs and sent his son down. Ethan walked like a zombie but his eyes darted around the kitchen as we sat at the table. Was he on the alert for another catastrophe to hit him out of nowhere? Or was he half hoping his mother would appear and make the nightmare go away?

We sat at a little table in the kitchen and established that Ethan was at school all day. He took the school bus there and back and we went through the teachers he had and he gave me the name of his wrestling coach. He had lunch with his girlfriend but he didn't want me to call her.

"I may call her tomorrow or the next day," I said. "You call her if you want, and your friends. But only if you can trust them not to put anything about your mother's death on social media. People will distort the story, you won't like being in the middle of it, and it can make my investigation more difficult." The poor kid was going to have a tough time beyond losing his mother. What to say? What to think? What to do? How to act? He wasn't ready for it.

"Talk with your father," I said. "It's hard sometimes for teenagers to talk with their parents but he can help you and you two need to pull together on this one. He is going to need you too, you know." Ethan nodded.

"Did your mother say anything to you this morning?" I asked.

"Not really," he said. "She made me a roast beef sandwich for lunch. It's my favorite. She asked me if I'd put my pajamas in the hamper. I went back upstairs to do that before I went out to get the bus."

"Anything else?"

"She kissed me on the cheek. She kind of snuck up on me because she doesn't usually do that. I told her before I didn't like it. And then she said, 'Be good. Be happy.' She usually says, 'Have a good day' or

'See ya.'" The implications of his mother's actions hadn't hit him until this moment. He was startled. He started to cry and he covered his eyes.

"Don't feel like you had any responsibility in this," I said. "She wasn't crying for help. She wasn't hoping you'd stop her. I know this from long experience." I didn't know this at all but I said it to comfort him. Keep him from feeling guilty. "Very likely she was killed and it's my job to find out by whom." I wasn't at all sure she'd been murdered but it would do no harm to say I thought she had been.

There was another question I had to ask. And better to ask it when the witness was upset and not thinking clearly.

"Do you know the PIN to unlock your mother's cell phone?"

"Yes," said Ethan.

"What is it?" I didn't stop to say why I wanted or needed it.

"1859," he said. That was the year Oregon became a state. Easy to remember but maybe not the most secure PIN in these parts.

"And where is her phone?"

"I don't know," said Ethan, frustrated and a little annoyed.

"What does it look like? Can you find it?" Susan hadn't found a phone in Wendy's clothes or in the barn.

"It was an iPhone in a case with an old-fashioned drawing of a woman skiing. We could look for it but why don't we just call it?"

He told me the number and I called it. Four rings to voicemail. The woman's voice in the greeting was businesslike but not unfriendly, the kind of voice that would encourage you to get to the point. I hadn't heard the phone ring in the house.

"Do you know your mother's voicemail password?"

"No."

"How about her Apple ID and password?"

"No. None of my business." He either didn't know the answer or he was embarrassed at the suggestion he would spy on his mother. "What about privacy? I didn't think you could search people's data even if you are a police officer."

I tried to sound like a teacher, authoritative and concerned. "The law says citizens lose their right to privacy when they die. And if someone else had a hand in her death I think she would want us to find out about it. Her phone could tell us who she talked to and texted with recently."

"I'll keep looking for it."

"So, Ethan, what's your favorite subject in school?"

"Computer science."

"You want to be a programmer?"

"I want to develop video games, especially in virtual reality." From what I knew of virtual reality I wanted no part of it, people shooting each other for fun.

"Gonna go to college?"

"MIT, CalTech, or Carnegie Mellon if I can get in. I want to get a wrestling scholarship." The kid was motivated.

"Stay with it and I bet you will," I said. I asked Ethan to call me if he thought of anything I should know and I reminded him to be careful about sharing news of his mother's death.

My own phone rang before we stood up. The call was from the deputy at the end of the driveway. "I have a man here who wants to come in. He says he's Mrs. Whitlock's brother and his name is Skip McNulty. I checked his license."

I shouted the name up to Warren as a question.

"Ethan, did you call him?" Warren asked.

"I thought he should know. But I didn't think he would come here."

"Okay, let's let him in," came Warren's words in a resigned and reluctant tone.

"Frisk him and take a quick search of the car," I said over the phone, "then let him drive in."

"He came in a taxi," said the deputy. "I'll frisk him and send him to you." I hung up and went to the front door to wait for the visitor. Warren came downstairs to join me.

"We had a deal that Skip wouldn't ever come to this house," said Warren. "Now Wendy's barely dead and here he is."

"Who is he and why is he not supposed to come to the house?"

"He's Wendy's brother. He's a leech and a drunk. Used to ask

Wendy for money all the time. I hate the guy and both of us, Wendy and me, didn't want to remind Ethan who he is related to."

"Where was Skip when you called him?" I asked Ethan.

"At the D&D. He doesn't have a cell phone so I called him where he likes to hang out."

The D&D on Bond Street was the oldest tavern in Bend, begun when half the men in town worked in the lumber mills. It still served more locals than tourists. The portions were big and not too pricey. If you wanted a drink at 8:30 in the morning, the waitress on duty, sexy in a no-nonsense sort of way, wouldn't judge you one way or the other. They were there to do a job, not to make friends. Efficient. A good place for hangovers— creating them or getting over them.

We heard steps on the porch and a knock on the front door. The man standing outside was carrying too much weight for his short frame. He would have made a good Santa Claus if he'd covered his stubble with a white beard and replaced his faded tan jacket, lined but not thick enough for winter, with a red coat trimmed in white fur.

"I'm so sorry about Wendy," the man said.

"Don't stand there," said Warren. "Come in so I can shut the door." Skip stepped into the little front hall. "You might as well sit down." Warren spoke with resignation, not a hint of concern or sympathy for Skip and no suggestion of shared sorrow.

The rule in law enforcement is to first get control of a situation, establish your authority. But I'd learn more if I shut up and listened. Skip stepped to the biggest chair in the living room, the upholstered chair that Warren had been in. Warren sat in a wooden captain's chair that matched the one I was in.

"How did she die?"

"Murdered," said Warren. "Hung by the neck in the barn. Somebody tried to set it up as suicide but it wasn't. I'm counting on detective Breuninger here to find out who did this." This was as close to an introduction as I was likely to get.

"When you find that bastard," said Skip, glaring at Warren and not at me, "I want you to tell me who he is and I'll kill him myself."

It is not a smart move to threaten anybody in front of law enforcement. But Skip wasn't thinking clearly. He'd wobbled when he walked across the room and his pupils were open wide. His breath, I could tell from five feet away, carried an exhalation of vodka.

"Wendy and I had a special relationship," said Skip. "She was my big sister. Always watched out for me, ever since we were kids." He paused to consider the importance of what he'd said. Or maybe to admire himself for saying it. I didn't like the man but I tried to remain open-minded. "Even now, she gave me my RV and she gave me a thousand dollars every month. Like clockwork. God, I'm going to miss her."

"What RV?" asked Warren with an edge to his voice.

"She must have told you about it. You know, the RV that I drive, the Ford 250 with the camper built into it. It's the only place I've got to live."

"And how long has she been giving you a thousand a month?"

"Five years. She said it was okay with you as long as I didn't come to the house or call you."

Warren pulled his shoulders back and scanned the room, as if searching for a club with which to brain his brother-in-law.

"And where did she get that money from?" Warren asked.

"Every fifth of the month it shows up in a checking account she set up with an ATM card. I go draw from it as I need it."

Warren sat back in his chair, his hands gripping the wooden armrests. He was angry but kind of paralyzed by what he'd heard. His wife, now dead, had not been honest with him for years. What else had she not told him? And no way to ask her for the truth or for explanations.

"Can I see the ATM card?" I asked Skip. He leaned way forward and pulled a red leather wallet out of his rear pants pocket. He fumbled getting the card out and wavered when he held it out to me.

"You be sure I get it back," he said as though he were the person in authority. The blue ATM card was issued to Skip McNulty by Chime, a bank I'd never heard of, and I wrote down the card number. There was already something fishy about Wendy and her brother that I had better get to the heart of. I handed Skip back his card.

"How was your day before you heard about Wendy?" I asked.

"Okay up to that point, I guess. I worked at the car wash until three. It was cold but it wasn't too busy. Some God-awful dirty cars, though. You wouldn't believe the trash some people leave behind. We have to be very careful what we suck up with the vacuum. Then I drove to the D&D for a late lunch and I was there when Ethan called me with the news. I had to hold onto the payphone to keep from collapsing. When I sat down again I could only stare at the Keno board, watching the numbers. A waitress asked me if I needed a taxi and I said yes. I couldn't think of any other place to go."

Warren rejoined the conversation. "Where's your camper now?"

"Parked on Bond Street."

"Let's call you a cab and get you back there."

"Am I going to get my thousand dollars in February? It was always like clockwork but I don't know if it came automatically or Wendy had to do something to make it happen."

"You're not getting another dime," said Warren, "if I have any say in it. I've still got to figure this out."

"Oh, come on, Warren. Wendy would want me to have it. No matter our differences, you've got to honor that."

"If there's any consolation in Wendy being dead it's that I'll never have to deal with you anymore. Don't call me or Ethan and don't you dare set foot on this property again."

"You don't have to be so harsh, Warren." I couldn't tell if Skip was begging for understanding or mocking Warren for getting upset. "It's not Christian of you. Not Christian at all. At least invite me to her funeral."

"Hell no!"

"She was my only sister."

"The funeral will be in the paper," I said to make the peace. Actually, if Warren didn't put an announcement in the paper there wouldn't be any funeral notice. But Skip's mind wasn't sharp enough to think of that right now.

Warren took Ethan aside and sent him upstairs. "Ethan's calling an Uber for you, they'll be here in five minutes. You can wait at the end of the driveway."

"It's cold out there."

Between Skip's delays and Warren's not wanting to touch him it took five minutes to get Wendy's brother out the door. I could see the Uber car in the driveway by the house. Once Skip left and Warren turned the lock I could see the tension in Warren's body drain out of him like water out of a turned-over bucket. Ethan reappeared from upstairs.

"You need to find Wendy's phone," I said to both of them. "Call Sisemore and any other place you can think of in the morning and see if she left the phone somewhere. Let me know and I'll pick it up." I told them again I was sorry for their loss and assured them that the sheriff's department would do everything they could to find out what happened. I went out the front door, told the deputy to leave, and drove away myself. I could have stayed and asked more questions but Warren and Ethan had been through enough without me grilling them.

It was late, cold, dark, and I was starving. Glad to get away from all that sorrow and have a warmed-up dinner at home. I told Estelle about my drive to Lakeview and crossing the Chewaucan.

Chapter 3

# Sarah Chatham

How did I get involved with Wendy Whitlock? On a December morning, with snow on the sidewalks but so much sun pouring through my window I lowered the shade, our admin came to my doorway to say there was a woman in our tiny lobby who didn't have an appointment and wanted to see me. The clients our law firm wanted were businesses, not people wandering in off the street. But I wasn't busy and, even if nothing came of seeing this woman, I might build some goodwill.

"Show her in."

I was a senior partner with Oxton, Rath and Flynn, a major wood-paneled firm in Portland. I moved to Bend a few years ago to lend my title and reputation to the new branch without carrying a full workload. We had half the top floor of a four-story building on the edge of downtown. The space was furnished more like a startup than a prestigious law firm, with six modular steel desks and fabric-lined cubicles. The industrial gray carpet covered empty floor space we expected to fill as we grew.

My small corner office, the only office with a door, was strictly functional except for three paintings I'd picked for the walls. The redeeming feature of the office was a large window looking west over downtown toward the snow-topped Cascade Mountains.

The woman who came unannounced to our office that morning,

about forty and taller than my five-foot-seven, had short brown hair she didn't have to spend a lot of time on. Not much make-up either. But she was dressed for work, a long-sleeved blouse and a tweed pencil skirt. She seemed intense but not fearful, like an athlete before a competition or an actress waiting for her entrance. I rose quickly, not an old lady by any means. I was still fit and my hair remained thick and black, courtesy of my Cherokee grandmother.

The woman introduced herself with a firm handshake and a perfunctory smile. Wendy Whitlock.

"Pleased to meet you," I said. "Sarah Chatham." We sat on my guest chairs across a low round table pushed into the corner of my office. "What do you think we can help you with?"

"I can't tell you what I need until I'm sure you won't reveal it to anyone, not even the police."

"If this is a criminal matter you need a criminal attorney. I can refer you to several who are qualified."

"It's a business negotiation."

"Well, we're well equipped for that. And what is at stake in this negotiation?"

"A hundred thousand, possibly more." That was worth negotiating over. And Wendy, in spite of her reticence, appeared to be a rational and responsible person.

I reassured her. "Even our discussion of Oxton becoming your attorney is privileged. If we don't proceed I still cannot reveal what you tell me." This was true under Oregon law.

Wendy eyed me carefully. "I need you to negotiate with the company I work for, Sisemore Orthopedics."

"Worker's compensation? Discrimination in the workplace? What is the issue?" I could count on specialists in the Portland office to know more about these topics than I did.

"No, none of that," said Wendy, waving her hand as though brushing away a cobweb. She studied me carefully again. "I took their money. They don't know how much but they know some is missing. I want to negotiate a deal where I stop taking their money, I give back an amount we negotiate without telling them the total amount I took, and they agree not to tell the police or come after me for the rest of it. I want a signed agreement so they can't change their minds."

"That's quite a negotiation," I said, hiding my concerns for myself and for Oxton. We could represent Mrs. Whitlock even if she had committed a crime, but we couldn't become an accessory. We couldn't help her further a crime.

"How much did you actually take?"

"About two hundred thousand a year, two million total." Either Wendy was very clever or the doctors were simply not paying attention. Probably both.

"When did you stop taking the money?" I asked.

"Six months ago. One of the doctors talked about hiring a forensic accountant to see why they weren't making more money. I want to head them off. I got your name from one of the women I train with, Amy Martinez. Her husband works here. You can see why I need an attorney."

"We can help with that if you pledge not to continue any criminal activity while we're working with you."

"I can commit to that," she said. "I'm done. I want to put it behind me."

"Good. We should be clear, though, that the State of Oregon regards embezzlement, and I think we are talking embezzlement here, as a crime. The good news is, if your company doesn't want to press charges, the district attorney probably won't want to pursue it."

"That's what I want."

"No guarantees," I said. I wondered how and why Wendy got herself in this position. She didn't strike me as a drug user, though I'm no expert. None of the pallor I expect to go with heroin or meth. I used to see some weird-looking people in Portland. Gambling maybe. I didn't want to ask. I didn't want to know. Keep this case as straightforward as possible.

"And there are taxes," I said. "I don't imagine you paid income taxes on whatever you received and you're going to need to pay them. We'll have to get our firm's tax attorneys to negotiate with the IRS.

You'll give them numbers for income and offer a settlement. The IRS won't be happy but they'll have a hard time showing your numbers are wrong. And they'll be glad to get money they didn't even know they were owed. Same with the State of Oregon. Fortunately the district attorney won't have access to your tax records."

"Like a district attorney going after Donald Trump."

"You're lucky you're not that big a target," I said. "But all this hinges on your being able to pay these settlements with Sisemore and pay the income taxes. Do you still have the money?"

"Yes. Or enough of it. It depends on what I have to pay back to Sisemore. Frankly, and I'm going to say this believing you are my attorney, they have no idea how much is missing and I think they'll be glad to get anything back."

"And you'll have to pay my firm's attorney fees."

"First priority," said Wendy.

"So how do the doctors know the money is missing?"

"They don't exactly. This one doctor, Dr. McGrath, thinks the clinic should be making more money. But he doesn't understand the books and he doesn't have the patience to get into them. So he got Dr. Dee to handle it and Dr. Dee is asking me questions because I manage administration. No point in asking the bookkeeper I hired because she only enters transactions and does arithmetic. Sisemore could list Peter Rabbit as a client and Willy Wonka as a vendor. The accountants who certify the books don't know much more and we barely pay them enough to keep them coming back."

"Who would we be negotiating with?"

"Dr. Dee, Samuel Dee. He'll have to get the settlement approved by the other doctors but they'll go along. They'll grumble but they'll sign. They don't want to be businessmen. They want to be doctors. Besides, if they don't agree they may get nothing. We need to make them see the light." Wendy was no lawyer but she was definitely a businesswoman.

As it happened I knew Dr. Dee and I suppressed a little smile at the prospect of seeing him again. He had replaced my worn-out knee two years earlier and I could not have wished for a better doctor.

He had done the operation hundreds of times before and he exuded confidence. I felt he cared a lot about me, was glad to have met me, and was joyful about making me better. There are some people who show you how good and generous people can be and what a wonderful place the world could be if there were more of them. That was Sam Dee. Outside of our doctor/patient relationship I knew his reputation as a contributor to the community. He was the doctor on hand for multiple local sporting events. I saw him at all the top fundraising events in town. His idea of a vacation was to volunteer with Doctors Without Borders in South America. Always cheerful, always enthusiastic, and always impeccably dressed. It didn't hurt that he was handsome and kept himself fit.

"I'll need time to check the law on this," I told Wendy. "And, given the circumstances, you need to bring me proof you have the funds to pay for Oxton's legal advice."

"How about I bring you five thousand dollars cash in advance?" asked Wendy.

"A check would be better," I said.

"Cash would be better for me," she said.

"I can't accept payment out of the funds you embezzled. Can you promise me that's not where the funds are coming from?"

"Yes, I'll take them out of my savings."

"Okay," I said. "I could meet you at the bank and we'll deposit the cash together. In the meantime, before we do any work on this you need to sign an agreement to have us represent you."

"I'll sign it."

I buzzed the admin for a standard agreement and Wendy signed it.

"One more thing," said Wendy. "My husband doesn't know anything about this. He doesn't know I took the money, any of it, and he doesn't know Sisemore is coming after me. I want to make sure he's protected, that he is never charged with anything. Not my son either."

"We can take steps to protect them," I said. I walked her to the elevator and shook her hand. I had regrets about taking her business as soon as the elevator doors closed. I'd imagined, in my semi-retirement, that I'd never again feel the queasiness I'd encountered multiple times in my career. I personally wanted justice and took a quiet pride in thinking that the world was a little fairer to everyone because of my efforts. But the job of an attorney is to represent the interests of clients. And here I was, after all this time, representing a thief.

Wendy called an hour later to say she had the cash for the deposit. We met at the bank Oxton used on Oregon Avenue. Standing in line, waiting for a teller, I was embarrassed, annoyed, and amused at the same time. This was the practice of law in a small town. A senior partner would never be doing this in Portland. The teller put the hundred-dollar bills through a counting machine and printed the receipt. All in a day's work, as if the teller saw five thousand dollars in cash all the time. A cardinal rule of banking, I'd learned, was to remain unperturbed.

In the parking lot, with her parka on but not yet zipped, Wendy brought five folded sheets of paper out of the pocket and handed them to me.

"I brought you a copy of my will," she said. "Can you make sure it's done right, just in case?" The will, on a form downloaded from the internet, was signed by Wendy and witnessed by two other women.

"This isn't in the scope of work we talked about earlier," I said. "It may cost a thousand dollars or more to review the will, simple as it appears to be. I may need our wills and estates attorneys in Portland to work on it. Are you sure you want us to go ahead?" She gave me a definitive "Yes" and we parted company outside the bank.

I read the will late that afternoon. The assets Wendy claimed were a checking account, a savings account, a truck, a half ownership in her house and in the landscaping business her husband ran, and an interest in The Conclave, a resort development near Bend that happened to be Oxton's client. That was the first thing about her will that raised my eyebrows. I was sure The Conclave was not taking investments from individuals but here was Wendy claiming to own a part of it.

I asked Dan Martinez, my senior associate in the office, for a list of The Conclave's investors. There were only four—a lumber company listed on the New York Stock Exchange, a resort management company, a development company from California, and a trust called Far Away Resorts. The smallest investor, Far Away, had twenty million into the deal—far more than Wendy could possibly embezzle from a doctors' clinic. Perhaps, I decided, she imagined buying a lot in the future and had anticipated that in her will. But the will was valid whether or not Wendy had anything to do with The Conclave.

A second unusual thing about her will was that, except for the truck she left to her brother Skip McNulty, Wendy left her entire estate to her son, Ethan. Wendy was thirty-eight and I didn't think her son could be more than a teenager. Maybe she didn't trust her husband or maybe she calculated she could avoid some inheritance taxes. Or maybe she didn't expect to change her will for the next forty years.

The third and last unusual thing about the will, and most troubling to me, was that Wendy had named me her executor. She didn't need an attorney to be her executor and she hadn't asked me first as she should have done. I didn't want any part of it. I would insist she pick someone else, her husband, her brother, or a friend. And from my point of view, the statutory fee I'd receive for acting as executor, set by the state of Oregon, wouldn't make executing the will worth my time.

I left Wendy a voicemail about preparing for the negotiation with Dr. Dee and about changing her will to remove me as executor. I never heard from her again.

Chapter 4

# Amy Martinez

I met Wendy Whitlock in December, four weeks before she died, on a six-woman team my friend Grace Wray pulled together to compete in Bend's annual Pole Pedal Paddle race five months away. Grace invited me to join the team on the shortest day of the year, while she and I were on a hike, more a get-out-of-the-house-walk, around the five-mile loop in Shevlin Park. We started at one o'clock, the warmest part of the day, temperature in the thirties, no wind, sunlight spotting the ground where it broke through the canopy of full height ponderosa pines.

"It will get us in shape over the winter," said Grace. "We'll train hard, encourage each other. It'll be fun."

The race did sound like fun but it would require a major adjustment to my plans. I was going to find a new job in January. The company I'd worked for collapsed while I was on maternity leave and I'd spent the last eighteen months being a mother. Dan and I lived like a 1950's family for over a year. I was remarkably happy with it for someone who had taken her job so seriously. Dan was a senior associate at a law firm, Oxton, Rath, and Flynn, and came home every night for dinner. I spent my days keeping house with Emma. A strange but joyful interlude in my life. But I wanted to continue my career. Not to mention we could use the money.

Grace's idea picked up speed in my mind, temptation into desire into rationalization, like a runaway ski. I could put off my job search long enough to train for the race and spend a few more months at home with Emma. I might not get another chance in my life to compete like this or get as fit as the race would make me.

"Let me talk it over with Dan," I said. Dan's instinct would be to encourage me. But he thought like a lawyer. He thought about what could go wrong. He'd learned, after a few unhappy arguments, not to share his reservations with me, at least not at first. Then the risks and disadvantages would come out. At least when we did agree on something I felt confident we'd taken everything into account. No nasty surprises.

"Who else have you asked?" leapt out of my mouth. Six segments would need six racers. The race started with downhill skiing and cross-country skiing at Mt. Bachelor. That was the "pole" part. Then a twenty-two-mile-long bike ride down the mountain into Bend followed by a five-mile run, a mile-and-a-half kayak race, and a one-mile sprint. The race ran in May because there was still snow on the mountain but the ice was gone from the river. Some racers did the whole thing by themselves. You had to be really tough to do that.

"I have a terrific cross-country skier," said Grace. The cross-country ski leg of the race was considered the most difficult and the most critical, the leg that more than any other separated the winning teams from the others. "Her name is Wendy Whitlock and she races all winter in Oregon and California. Last year she won the Great Nordeen cross-country race in her age group. She works half days at Sisemore Orthopedics so she has time to train."

Grace wanted me to do the kayaking, the second most important leg of the race. I knew how to paddle a kayak, of course, but I had never raced in one. Grace said she picked me because I rowed in college. Different muscles but I was comfortable on the water and I had strong shoulders. Excellent aerobics and stamina too if I worked at it. I liked competing. Dan and I met training for an off-road triathlon.

"I thought you'd know a good bicyclist," said Grace.

"I'll ask around." My favorite sport, before Emma was born, was mountain biking—racing along dirt trails, jumping the bike over logs, navigating over rocks. I knew plenty of women who were good at it. I could surely find a woman who'd welcome the challenge of racing on asphalt. "But the women I know," I said, "probably don't have a good road bike."

"We can get them one," said Grace, "if they need it." Grace and Sean, her husband, didn't throw their money around. They wanted to fit in with their friends. But Sean had been one of the first engineers at Facebook and was worth millions. An average engineer, he said, who got incredibly lucky. He worked at home most days. When he drove the fifty minutes to the company's data center in Prineville he drove a Hummer with a custom stereo system that sounded like a concert hall. He said he liked the landscape between Bend and Prineville—green fields where there was irrigation, dry desert where there wasn't. And seeing the sun set over the mountains on the way home, he said, was more than worth the drive.

"Are you going to race yourself?" I asked. I hoped Grace wouldn't be insulted by my raising the question. She skied the intermediate slopes in the winter and swam twice a week year-round. But she had never been a serious athlete.

"I'd like to do the so called 'sprint' at the end if the rest of you will let me. I've got five months to train for it." The sprint was the final one-mile run, not really a sprint except in comparison to the other thirty miles of the race.

"Sounds good to me," I said. Grace would never be a star runner. But that last sprint would count for less than eight minutes in a three-hour race. The team would not live or die by Grace's run. I thought the other team members, whoever they were, would be happy to let Grace do the sprint in exchange for pulling together the racers, the equipment, a support team and all the organizing we'd need. With Grace managing the team, no matter how we did, we would not flounder for lack of coordination.

On the return leg of the Shevlin Park loop, where the trail ran along the side of a ridge, Grace asked, "How about a runner?" An ideal runner immediately came to mind but I didn't say her name. Grace knew who she was too but wanted me to suggest her. The woman, younger than my twenty-eight, had been on the University of Oregon cross-country team. She'd won NCAA medals.

Her name was Natasha Korel and she was a junior associate at Oxton, Rath, and Flynn, the law firm where Dan was a senior associate. She'd moved from the company's office in Portland to the little branch office in Bend because she loved the outdoors. She was a good lawyer, said Dan, very thorough and very logical. What he didn't say and what was obvious the first time I laid eyes on her was that she was also gorgeous. Tall and slim with thick, dark hair.

It bothered me, more than I liked to admit, that Dan saw Natasha every day and worked with her sometimes for hours. And every night he came home to me, not dressed for work and not engaged in anything the least bit interesting. I'd spent the day with a child who hadn't yet started to speak. I knew our marriage and our child were the most important things in Dan's life. The bonds between us were strong but they were tested.

Grace and I walked single file past the lava outcrops along the forested hillside. Thinking of Natasha, I tripped over a rock and leapt forward three steps to catch myself. At least I was quick enough to stay on my feet. "Whoopsie," I said, as though talking to Emma.

"If you break a leg, of course, you're off the team. Are you okay?"

"If I break a leg," I said, "you'll have to carry a kayak to the water with me in it. I'm fine for now, though. I'll try looking where I'm going for a change."

I didn't want to be on a team with Natasha Korel. Small-minded of me. I told myself to grow up. If I wanted our team to do well, how could I sabotage it by not getting the perfect runner?

"I've got your runner," I said, and I told Grace how perfect Natasha would be. I didn't say how I felt about her.

The winter shadows were growing longer and the day was already colder when Grace and I reached the park entrance. We threw our parkas in the back, climbed into Grace's Mercedes, and got the seat warmers going.

Training for a race would be, in a way, irresponsible, a distraction from real life—finding a job and caring for Emma. I rationalized, soundly or not, that racing would give me time to gather my strength for true adulthood. I had the trappings of being an adult—college degree, a career I could go back to, a solid marriage, even a child. But I felt I was playing at it instead of taking full responsibility. The thing about a race, as opposed to real life, is that the race is eventually over. Life is not over for a very long time. You're always in it. And there are multiple goals in life, not just one.

Dan was all for my racing and I started training the next day. Warm-up, mobility drills, weights, and stretching. I trained at home while Emma was napping. We asked Aurelia, our housekeeper and sometime babysitter, to come for more time so I could extend my workouts.

We had our first team meeting in the conference room at Oxton, Rath, and Flynn. The office was centrally located and Natasha, for one, would already be there. The conference room had six leather and steel chairs around a polished wood table, exactly enough room for all of us.

Wendy Whitlock, our cross-country skier, appeared to be a gem. Serious but friendly in a reserved sort of way. The kind of person who stays on track and quietly does whatever she's made up her mind to do. She had always raced as an individual. This would be her first time in the Pole Pedal Paddle and the first time to compete on a team.

The student that Grace had recruited from Oregon State for the downhill skiing was late. She looked strong enough and she'd competed in high school. But she was barely twenty and the rest of us were in our twenties and thirties. I wondered if she'd stick with the project. No coach. No organized practice. The hassles of getting up to the ski slope. And the first part of the downhill leg of this particular race required sprinting uphill two hundred yards in your ski boots before you even got to your skis. That took quadriceps of steel, developed over weeks of painful squats. Would she do all that work without anyone pushing her?

Good women but not a close-knit group. Too independent. I was used to competing on a team. On my college crew team we had to row in sync and we were highly dependent on each other. Natasha had been on her cross-country team but the others were not experienced team players. Still, I thought, and Grace agreed, we could develop a bond, a team spirit. We'd have to trust that the teammates we didn't train with every day were working as hard as we were.

The college girl, our downhill racer, questioned the name Grace had picked for our team. She said "The Pickup Team" sounded misogynistic. The rest of us, mostly older and married, decided we liked it. It described how our team came together. It sounded a little racy. It even implied that we all drove pickups and came from Central Oregon's farming heritage, which none of us did. Wendy Whitlock was the only one who actually had a pickup. Her husband was in the landscaping business. Grace won the girl over by reading the ridiculous names of the previous year's all-women teams—CIA (Crazy Insane Athletes), She Wolves, Wondergirls, Bamtastic, Miles to Martinis, Faster Than Dialup, The Lame Ducks. The girl had to admit that The Pickup Team was a vastly superior choice.

I couldn't train in the winter by actually paddling a kayak on the river. I worked on dryland exercises at home to build strength—planks for my core, bent-over rows for strength, and kettlebell swings. For aerobics I rode our exercise bike and swam at the town's Juniper Fitness Center. While Emma was sleeping and Aurelia was watching her I ran out to the National Forest west of town and continued on the trails when they weren't filled up with snow. Sunny or not, cold or not, not even freezing rain could stop me.

Even though my days were full and I was tired in the evenings, Dan said I was jollier. More exercise, better diet, and a challenging sense of purpose.

Wendy had her own gym with a Nordic Track machine. I went out there twice to train with her in early January. Her seriousness motivated me. She worked hard. But the barn she trained in had steel walls and no heat. She was on the far side of town, actually outside the city limits. So I told her I enjoyed training with her but I'd stick to training at home and Juniper and running out to the National Forest.

The team members reported their training to each other by text.

Reassuringly, encouragingly, even a little boastfully. We reminded each other to be careful. We repeated that injury was the greatest risk to our success. It didn't occur to us, green and easy as we were, that one of us would die.

Chapter 5

# Sarah Chatham

I tried to reach Wendy Whitlock by email a few times after we met and got no answer. I first ascribed this to the Christmas and New Year's holidays. I took ten days off myself. Maybe Wendy was on vacation or traveling to some cross-country skiing competition. I had refreshed my understanding of the law on embezzlement and needed to get Wendy's agreement to a plan for restitution to Sisemore. In January, a week after I left her a voicemail and she didn't respond to that either, I decided to call her on a Monday at work, though I would be cautious about it. I wouldn't leave a message and I'd be careful what I said over the phone.

My house on Mirror Pond faces east over my deck, a small lawn and then the pond itself. The pond is really a widening of the Deschutes River where it backs up behind a 1910 power dam. The morning sun floods the living room where Bud and I eat our breakfast in the winter. I sit where I can't see the four-story building where my office is. It isn't that I don't like my office or don't enjoy being Oxton's only partner east of the Cascades. But I like to partition my life between my job and my life at home.

The day I tried to reach Wendy Whitlock at work started off well. The snow on the footbridge over the pond had melted and I walked the sunny but cold half mile to work, over the pond and up through Drake Park into town.

Our office was humming. Dan Martinez was bending his six-foot-four frame over a document on his desk, not a typical pose. He was usually on the phone or out of the office altogether, deep in conversation with a client or a potential client. Most of the business we had in our little branch office had come through Dan. He seemed to know everyone. Lou Hanley, a junior associate moved over from the Portland office, was editing something on his PC. He was smart enough but he didn't capture people's trust and friendship the way Dan did. I calculated Lou would do good work for us for about five years before joining the staff of some local company. He was dedicated to Bend now, owned a house, and was happy to be bringing up his kids here.

Natasha Korel, our newest junior associate, was on the phone, hopefully talking with another lawyer or someone at the courthouse. She wasn't quite ready to be spending time with clients on her own. She had the poise and the reassuring tone of voice she needed. But she was still learning our clients' businesses and she wasn't experienced enough to quickly and clearly frame legal alternatives for a client in the back and forth of conversation.

I hung my coat on the back of my office door and put my boots in a Rubbermaid tub by the wall. I hadn't walked in any snow or mud on the way to work but the tub was where the boots routinely went. If I had a client in my office, I'd slide the tub and the boots under my desk. I put on a pair of low heels that I took out of my bottom desk drawer.

No voicemails and no emails that couldn't wait. I picked up the phone and called Sisemore Orthopedics. When a young woman answered, I asked for Wendy Whitlock.

"Can I ask what this is regarding?"

"Mrs. Whitlock hired me to do some work for her and I need to ask her a few questions."

"Mrs. Whitlock no longer works here," said the woman. "I can take a message and have someone call you back if you'll tell me what this is about."

That was a surprise. Had the doctors terminated Wendy before the negotiations had even begun?

"It's a personal matter," I said. "Can you tell me how best to reach her?"

"She died," said the woman. "I'm afraid we're not allowed to give out any more information than that."

Well, that jolted me upright. "I'm so sorry to hear that. How did she die?"

"I can take a message for the new administrator to call you as soon as we hire her. Or him."

"Can you ask Dr. Dee to call me instead? Please tell him I am Mrs. Whitlock's attorney and the executor of her estate." I gave the woman my number.

What on earth had happened? Wendy had seemed as strong and healthy as a ponderosa pine. If death had come for Wendy Whitlock, it came as a thief in the night. Some day, not soon I hoped, it would come for me.

I had expected to work with Wendy on the Sisemore negotiation for at least a month. I thought modifying her will would take an hour, starting with removing me as its executor. Now I was locked into a responsibility I hadn't sought, like getting a Christmas present you didn't like but which required you to write a thank you letter and find something to do with it. I could renounce my responsibilities but the court would appoint someone who had never met Wendy and might not be diligent in tracking down the money she had tried to hide. Further it would be more efficient to have one person, myself, handle both the estate and the negotiation with Sisemore. Finally, I was intrigued by Wendy, a seemingly stable woman with a happy and orderly life who had gone off the deep end into criminal behavior and then died, I didn't yet know how. I had the time and resources to follow my curiosity, whether Oxton or I were ever fully paid for them.

The good news about Wendy's death, if I were searching for good news, was that she would never stand trial and never go to jail. Only lawyers think this way. The other good news, in a heartless way, was that Wendy's estate was in a stronger position than Wendy herself had ever been to negotiate a settlement with her employer. Sisemore Orthopedics couldn't threaten to have the district attorney press criminal charges.

I was on slippery ground myself, like climbing up a field of mossy boulders on the side of a mountain. The press would love this story and some sharp-minded person, probably an attorney, might file any kind of ridiculous suit to gum up the negotiation and get a share of the settlement.

Wendy's husband, Warren, was not my client but Wendy wanted their son, Ethan, to get the money. I decided, barring unforeseen circumstances, that Wendy's interests, my interests in representing her, and Mr. Whitlock's interests were closely aligned. I'd keep an eye on that assumption as the case proceeded.

I found Warren's company and called the number.

"Whitlock," said the man who answered. He sounded tense, even angry. At least he didn't sound depressed.

"My name is Sarah Chatham," I said. "I'm an attorney with Oxton, Rath, and Flynn in Bend. I understand from Sisemore Orthopedics that Mrs. Whitlock died. I am sad to hear it and sorry for your loss. She hired me recently and appointed me the executor of her will. I need to talk with you as soon as possible."

"Is this some kind of scam?"

"I promise you this is not a scam. Oxton, Rath, and Flynn is a highly reputable firm and I am a partner. I will fax you a copy of the will Mrs. Whitlock gave me and then we should talk."

"Wendy didn't need a will. The only assets we have are the house and my business, held as joint tenants. She has a separate checking account but your fees will probably eat that up in this phone call."

"Your wife told me her estate was substantial and I believe it is."

"You're going to tell me she won the lottery? Funny she didn't mention that."

"She didn't win the lottery. It's more complicated and we should discuss this in person."

"This is all baloney. Wendy doesn't have a will as far as I know and why would she name you as the executor instead of me?"

"I think she wanted to protect you. I'll explain when we meet."

"First let me see this will you're talking about. You know she was murdered, don't you? I want to know everyone who might benefit, in any way, from Wendy's death."

"Fair enough. I'm sure we'll talk soon." He managed a decent "goodbye" and we hung up. I didn't ask him how Wendy was murdered, if he was even right about that, and as far as her will and her estate went, it didn't matter how she died. But the sudden death of a healthy and rational person suggested either an accident or murder. If it were murder I expected Wendy's embezzlement might have something to do with it.

My next call was to Carl Breuninger, detective with the Deschutes County Sheriff. If he were investigating a murder I wanted to tell him at least part of what I knew about Wendy. I had worked with Carl before and I knew he would take me seriously.

"Hung from a rafter in the barn behind her house," said Carl. "Broke her neck. We're calling the cause of death undetermined for now to keep it out of the media. It looks like suicide but the husband says it has to be murder and he might be right. Why are you calling?"

"Wendy came to my office last week to make sure her will was valid. She didn't tell me she'd made me her executor but unfortunately she had. Her son is the sole beneficiary. I can fax you a copy since it has to go to probate anyway. She didn't seem to be contemplating an imminent death, suicidal or otherwise. Competent. In control. As upbeat as anyone working on their last will and testament could be."

"That's relevant," said Carl. "Anything else?"

"Yes," I said, "and that's the tricky part. Wendy told me she committed a non-violent crime and she wanted me to negotiate restitution with the injured party. But I need to negotiate the settlement before I tell you what I know."

"Come on, Sarah," Carl shot back at me. "If you know something that bears on this case you have to tell me now."

"No, I don't," I said. "My client still has the protection of attorney-client privilege. And furthermore, you don't know yet whether she was murdered."

Silence from Carl. He was trying to do his job and I was preventing him.

"I'll give you two weeks," he said. "After that I'm going to get a subpoena for everything you have on Wendy Whitlock."

"The court won't give you a subpoena," I said, ninety percent sure I was right. "But I'll see if I can wrap up the negotiations in two weeks and then tell you what I know. Please see it as my doing some of the legwork for you. A favor for a friend and for the sheriff's department." Carl wouldn't see it quite that way but he might come around, even appreciate it.

Negotiating with Dr. Dee at Sisemore Orthopedics would be strange. The bottom-line issue was how much money Wendy's estate would restore to Sisemore to replace the money she had embezzled. How much she had actually taken was secondary. If she'd been getting away with it for years then Sisemore wouldn't know the amount.

For my own part I'd have to find where Wendy had put the money and how much the estate could get its hands on to pay to Sisemore. Any records Wendy kept of that money were probably at her house and I'd need to search through whatever I could find. Warren Whitlock had gotten my fax and called to set a time for me to come to the house the next day. I counted on him to assume I was documenting Wendy's estate and I didn't tell him about the embezzlement or the negotiation with Sisemore. I didn't want to drag him into it until it was necessary.

"You'll have to work in the same room with me because that's where both desks are. I'll be home all day doing paperwork. You won't be on the phone, will you?" I assured him I wouldn't.

It still bothered me that Wendy claimed an investment in The Conclave in her will. It seemed an odd place for Wendy to put her money—a risky investment, hard to sell, and no payoff for years. I couldn't imagine that The Conclave would even want her investment. A big resort development like that wouldn't want tiny investments from the general population until the resort was ready to sell them lots.

Dan was handling The Conclave's local issues while Oxton's

Portland office handled corporate issues and financing. Dan helped them change the zoning from "agricultural" to "resort/residential." He said either zoning sounded like a joke if you cast your eyes over the 600 acres of sagebrush and juniper trees, totally useless without a big investment in improvements. Our firm was getting them utility easements. We were negotiating whether the jackrabbits on the land were a sub-species that required protection or only a variation that did not. It would cost money to move the rabbits or configure the golf course to save space for a breeding population. An archeologist had found evidence of ancient Indian camps but, fortunately for The Conclave, no camps substantial enough to require preserving. All that remained were a few arrowheads and rock chips. The Conclave donated the findings to the High Desert Museum.

Dan Martinez brought The Conclave to Oxton, as he brought in most of our local clients. Dan had a very wealthy high school friend named Sean Wray whose brewpub was Oxton's first client in the local office. In spite of his exceptional wealth, Sean kept his job as a manager at the Facebook data center in Prineville. He said he liked being around that humongous computing power, the way an Indianapolis race car driver would thrill at the roar of an engine. Sean had a friend at the real estate firm that invested in The Conclave and Sean recommended our firm to them and other investors. Sean himself had an investment in The Conclave through a special arrangement with his friend's company.

It was high time I knew more about The Conclave and also high time I took our client to lunch. I called Sean and asked him to join me. We met, inevitably, at the brewpub Sean owned, the Vandevert Brewing Company on Bond Street. Sean wasn't born rich and he understood his good fortune very well, laughed about it, and enjoyed it. He got into the beer business because he liked beer. That the beer pub barely broke even for its first two years hadn't bothered him at all. He said if the beer he brewed was as good as he and his brewmaster could make it the brewery would succeed. Sean could afford to be wrong but he was right in the long run. He invested more into the brewpub itself than was probably prudent—imported old wooden bars from two brewpubs in England and spent a fortune on lighting. The walls held rugby paraphernalia—balls, jerseys, shoes, trophies—and photographs of Bend rugby teams, men and women, with brass plaques enumerating the trophies they had won. You'd think the players were national heroes but they were regular people with regular jobs. After a rugby tournament the pub got raucous but most weekdays it was a civilized place to have lunch.

The brewpub was a good client for Oxton. Sean rarely questioned our bills or our opinions. He paid attention to what we said and mostly did what we advised him to do. When he went a different way he told us why clearly and rationally and we supported him as well as we could. When he brought us in on The Conclave we hired Natasha as a junior associate to take the load off Dan.

"I am executing the will of a woman named Wendy Whitlock," I told Sean. "Have you ever heard of her or do you know why she would list a holding in The Conclave as an asset in her will?"

"No idea," said Sean. "Maybe she hoped to buy a lot there when they became available. The Conclave is going to be a very special place."

"Super high tech?" I asked.

"Absolutely the opposite," said Sean, beaming at the surprised look on my face.

"Did you know that many of the top executives in Silicon Valley are sending their kids to schools that have no computers at all? The parents say the kids will have more than enough exposure to computers. What the kids need more is the ability to deal with people and a broader range of knowledge and experience than computers can give them. I think they're right. At The Conclave we're going to minimize the interaction with computers and technology. No cell phones, tablets, iPads, or laptops in the common areas. There's no Wi-Fi. If you want to book a tee time you call the golf shop and talk to a live person who writes it down on paper. You can have an electric cart but it won't have a screen to tell you what hole you are on or how far it is to the green. We'll have a ball machine for the tennis courts but it won't be programmable. It's all analog. Do you know how hard it is to find a machine like that these days?

"The residents can have internet access in their houses if they want but the idea is they will minimize their use of it. They'll want streaming on their TVs but one guy who's already contacted us about buying a lot says he won't even have a remote. If he wants to change the channel or the volume, he's going to have walk over to the TV to change it. And we had to make some compromises on the vehicles. We wanted to use old cars and trucks for maintenance and landscaping and the greenskeepers. It would be neat to see an old Dodge pickup taking sod out to the fairway. But those old vehicles pollute too much. So we said let's use electric vehicles and cover up most of the dashboard. It's the employees that will be using them, not the residents. And they're quiet."

"Sounds like you're trying to go back to the 1950's," I said.

"There is some of that, and the nostalgia appeals to people, but our emphasis is going to be interacting with the real world instead of cyberspace. We're going to have a good long nature walk around the outside of the golf course with signs explaining the plants, rocks, animals and the mountains and hills in the distance. We might have a guidebook for it but nothing online. If you want to learn about it you have to go out and walk."

"Air conditioning?" I asked.

Sean's head drew back. Was I mocking his vision or simply being stupid?

"Yes," he said. "We're not going retro for the sake of retro. But the thermostats will have analog dials instead of LCD displays. And we'll have great sports facilities, outdoors and indoors. We'll be the only resort in Central Oregon with a field we can use for baseball, soccer, or rugby. We could even do football but we don't see our homeowners doing that. It will be a great place for kids to spend time. We'll have a four lane twenty-five-meter pool that we can tent in the winter for year-round swimming."

"So you're going after families with children in school?"

"Prime prospects. But we'll have some things for adults like a spa with a sauna. We're going to feature sensory deprivation tanks for relaxation. You float in warm salty water in the dark and don't hear or see anything. It's terrific for relaxing your muscles and helping you sleep better. It decreases pain and anxiety. People say it makes you more creative."

"The whole setup sounds expensive," I said.

"It's high end, start to finish. Some owners will come in their own planes. It won't be far from the Redmond airport."

"Well," I said, "it's quite a vision." It would tickle the imagination but I wondered how many people would want to live there for any length of time. Very rich people with strong beliefs about how their children should grow up. I didn't think many Mennonites were that rich.

"Aiming for Silicon Valley people?" I asked.

"Right. And Silicon Forest people near Portland. Microsoft and Amazon people from Seattle."

"How many people have said they want to buy a lot?"

"It's too early for that. We're still working out how many lots and how big they will be. We don't know where the clubhouse and the golf course will go. We haven't spent a dime on marketing so far. We don't even have anyone who has time to keep track of possible buyers."

"None of them Wendy Whitlock," I said.

"As I said, we're not even keeping track of who calls right now. There are only six employees and they're all involved in either planning or lining up contractors."

"How about the investors? Could Wendy have a share in one of them?"

"I doubt it very much. Even with a multi-million-dollar investment I could only do it through a real estate company and I only got in because a friend of mine is a big cheese at the company. The frontline investors, all four of them, are big financial companies. The Conclave is small potatoes to them. Two of them are publicly traded but if this woman owns shares in one of them, she'd have no direct stake in The Conclave and the value of her stock would depend on a lot of other things." Sean paused for three beats and gazed absently at the front door of the pub. "One of the investors, not a public company, we haven't had much contact with. We've decided it's better not to ask. It's called Far Away Resorts and they're out of the Cayman Islands. We've only dealt with their bank and we don't know who actually owns it. We think it may be drug money or Russian oligarchs."

Sean's turn to ask questions. "What's this woman's background?"

"She works for a doctor's office and her husband owns a landscaping business. She doesn't appear to be a high roller or financially sophisticated."

"Like I said, it sounds like she hoped to build a house at The Conclave and wrote that into her will so she wouldn't have to change it when she bought a lot."

"Could be," I said, though actually I had my doubts. I didn't think Wendy would want a big expensive house in a golf resort next to people who had their own planes.

Sean was only slightly bothered that he had no answer to my Wendy question. We'd had a nice lunch and he had gotten to tell me about The Conclave. But I was still at a loss to know why Wendy put The Conclave in her will. And if the two million she said she'd embezzled was not in The Conclave where was it? Did it even exist or had she played some kind of game with me?

Chapter 6

# Sheriff's Detective Carl Breuninger

Three days after Wendy Whitlock's death I went over the photos Susan McCarthy took of the barn. They arrived on my computer, carefully labeled, and I spent two hours examining every one of them. There could easily be something I didn't see or didn't appreciate the relevance of when I was there. In some photos the tall aluminum ladder was standing below the cut rope where Susan first saw it and Ethan said he placed it to climb up and cut down his mother. In others the ladder was lying on the floor where Susan placed it to recreate the scene as Ethan said he found it. The saddest photos were of Wendy Whitlock lying on the workbench where Ethan had placed her.

Close-ups of the rope showed it wasn't knotted around the beam. Wendy could not have reached the beam and even a tallish man would have trouble reaching it. Someone had tied a loop in the upper end of the rope and thrown it over the beam, then run the hangman's noose end of the rope through the loop and pulled it to get the rope snug on the beam. Whoever did this knew their knots. Maybe they knew a thing or two about hanging as well. To generate enough force to break a neck a lighter person needs to fall further than a heavy person. Kristen's report said Wendy weighed 161 lbs. When states used to hang people the official calculation, which I checked, was that a 161 lb. person would need a six foot two-and-a-half inch drop, barely enough if Wendy's head were above the top of the ladder before she fell or jumped. If the rope had been too short she would have strangled to death instead of breaking her neck. If the rope were too long her feet would have hit the floor and she wouldn't have died at all.

In the next group of photos I didn't know what I was seeing. They showed a wide band of gray across the middle with a lighter but out-of-focus background behind the band. Susan's notes said they were photos of the top of the beam. She'd held the camera up there on a pole, like a long selfie stick, and snapped photos of what she couldn't see with her own eye. The first photos showed the rope still looped around the beam. Then came photos with the rope removed and bare metal where the rope had swept the dust away. There were photos of the length of the beam in both directions. About four feet away, a little past the center of the beam, there was an identical bare spot. Had Wendy changed her mind about where she wanted to hang? What would make her, or someone else, change the location of the rope? Neither rope location was in the exact center of the beam. If Wendy had a reason to move the rope I had trouble imagining what the reason was. It didn't appear that she slid it along the beam. The dust was undisturbed along the edges of the beam where dragging a rope would have wiped the dust away. I called Susan to ask what she made of it.

"You know we can't assume the marks were made by the same rope on the same day. Maybe she set herself up a week earlier and changed her mind. When she went for a second try she didn't care about putting the rope in the same place. The two rope marks on that beam could have been put there a few minutes apart or a few weeks apart. Same person or different people. Do you want me to go back up there again?"

"Yes," I said. "I want to know what the hell was going on with that beam. And I don't want any loose ends that some defense attorney can take advantage of down the road. Did you get any prints off the ladder you took?"

"Lots. As far as I can tell the most recent are Ethan Whitlock's, the son who says he climbed the ladder to bring his mother down. The next most recent belong to the victim. I don't want to jump to a conclusion here but it looks like she climbed that ladder under her own power."

Well, I thought, that's a three pointer for the suicide theory. I wasn't convinced, though, and I owed it to the Whitlocks to keep assuming murder. I called Warren and arranged to meet him at a jobsite. I wanted to show him Susan's pictures to see if he noticed anything he hadn't noticed before.

I found the man and his crew installing trees in a new business park on the north end of Bend. The pines and firs were about six feet tall, some planted and some sitting next to holes with their roots wrapped in burlap. The deciduous trees—Warren said they were ash, maple, and pear—were tall, skinny, and leafless. On this wintry day, it was hard to imagine that sticking these bare branches in the ground would ever make the parking lot anything but barren. We sat on the tailgate of Whitlock's pickup and went through the photos on my tablet. The only pictures I left out were the pictures of the body on the workbench.

"Look carefully," I said. "You're not checking that these are pictures of your barn. We all know that. We want anything that is unusual or out of place." We had a hundred photos to go through. Whitlock stared at most of them for about five seconds each and paused over others, especially the shelves at the back of the barn, for more time. I had to bite my tongue when he paused over a photo. He went through every single photo before he said anything. I was about to admit we'd found nothing and thank him for his time.

"The ladder's in the wrong place," he said. "I mean the second ladder, the one leaning against the back wall. It should be in front of the rear pedestrian door and the photos show it in front of the cabinets."

"Would Wendy have moved it?"

"I don't know why. The two ladders are the same. You want a ladder, you take the one on top."

"Isn't a bad idea to put ladders in front of an exit? If there's a fire, you want to be able to get out that door in a hurry."

"We don't store fuel or fertilizer inside. There isn't much to burn. If we ever needed to get out the back fast it would only take a second or two to tip the ladders away."

Warren's logic was sound but my instinct would not have let me put those ladders in front of a door. "You didn't notice the ladder had moved when you first went in?" I asked.

Warren gave me a look that suggested I wasn't using my head. "I had other priorities," he said. "I was focused on Wendy. And the second time I went in the barn, your photographer had used that ladder to get the top of the rope. Not the ladder lying on the floor, which she took away, but the ladder that's in the picture."

"Anything else out of place?" I asked.

"That's it," he said. 'Well, the rope wasn't mine. I don't know where that came from. It's white braided polypropylene and I always use yellow. There's a spool in the shelves on the left. It's still there."

"So either Wendy or her killer brought the rope with them," I said. I didn't like to speculate in front of civilians but I wanted to see what more I could pull out of Whitlock.

"That shows murder, doesn't it?" said Warren. "Wendy must have seen my yellow spool of rope on the shelf every time she came in here. She wouldn't have gone out and bought more rope."

I wasn't convinced. Wendy might never have noticed the rope on the shelf. Or some quirk of honesty kept her from taking the rope out of the business. Or the way she pictured her suicide, a yellow rope wouldn't do. She or her killer knew something about rope though. Or they were lucky. A nylon rope would have stretched and she would have broken her ankles instead of her neck. Why not a good old-fashioned manila rope? That could stretch as well, though not as much. Too scratchy maybe. I remembered a movie character once said, more or less, "If you're going to die, you might as well be comfortable."

I told Warren that yes, there were multiple signs pointing to murder and I would continue to investigate his wife's death as a murder, not a suicide. I asked him again whether he and Ethan had found her cell phone. They hadn't and he said they had searched everywhere. I myself had asked a doctor where Wendy worked to have the staff listen for her cell phone while I called the number. No one heard it ringing. They had already searched every drawer in Wendy's desk and hadn't found it.

My estimation of Wendy Whitlock, coming more into focus, told me she was the kind of organized, responsible woman who would keep her cell phone with her and have it turned on. If it were missing her killer took it. He or she would want to turn that phone off and get rid of it as quickly as possible. If I were fleeing a murder scene and wanted to ditch a phone, where and how would I do it? If I were driving back toward Bend the first likely place I would come to was a small irrigation canal that crossed under the road. I drove out there with my fishing waders and my polarized fishing glasses. Farmers didn't need water in the winter and the flow was a cold shallow rivulet. I put on the waders and sloshed along the muddy middle of the canal downstream of the bridge, scanning methodically from bank to bank as I walked. I found the phone, or a phone, resting flat on the bottom, the water purling around it as though it were simply one more rock.

The phone had a case on it decorated with a drawing of a woman in a vintage ski outfit jumping over a mogul with the caption, "And She Lived Happily Ever After." I was ninety-nine percent certain this was Wendy's phone. I took pictures of the phone, front and back, and would check them with Warren and Ethan.

The warrant to paw through Wendy's phone was sitting on my desk, signed by a judge, when I got back to headquarters. I put my parka back on and walked the phone over to the State Police Crime Lab that served the regional sheriff's departments and city police departments. I logged the phone in with their computer tech and gave him the PIN I'd gotten from Ethan. He said he'd have to surround it with desiccant for two days before he could try accessing it.

"In the meantime, see if you can get her iCloud username and password. You'll get almost all the data you'd get from the phone itself."

I called the Whitlock home in the evening and texted my photos of the phone to Warren's cell. He said the case with the picture matched his wife's phone. Neither Warren nor Ethan knew what Wendy's password for iCloud was. I was surprised when Ethan called me half an hour later.

"Forget password. I don't even know what her Apple ID is. You know, like a username. It's not my mom's email address. And Apple can't figure out her Apple ID when I enter her name. She must have used a name she made up. The only way to convince Apple it's my mother making a legitimate request is to have them call or text the phone."

"Catch-22," I said.

The tech called me two days later. "The phone is unrecoverable. It's been in the water too long. If the victim backed up her phone to iCloud, we could file a request with Apple to access the cloud. But if you don't know her Apple ID that may not work even if she did back up her phone."

"How long will it take to file a request with Apple and get an answer?"

"Months."

## Chapter 7 -

# Amy Martinez

How did I, mother of a six-month-old, have time to get in shape for a race in the first place? My husband and I had a terrific nanny named Aurelia, and Dan, my husband, helped out a lot when Aurelia wasn't around. Aurelia was learning English from tapes she listened to and with help from Dan and me. Dan spoke Spanish and we could fall back on him if we needed to.

A lot of the training I could do at home. Since Aurelia didn't live with us we'd turned one of the bedrooms into a gym. We had a Bowflex and free weights for strength training, bands and mats for stretching, and a wobble board for balance. I did planks for core strength. They didn't require any equipment at all. I simply propped my body up on my elbows and kept my back straight until I verged on collapsing. I did bent-over rows for arm and back strength, squats and presses with dumbbells, and kettlebell swings to get more power from my big muscles working together and to get my heart rate up. For aerobics I ran through the neighborhood and over to Shevlin Park.

I went to Wendy Whitlock's twice to train with her, partly to build team spirit and partly because she had pull ropes on her wall with weights on them to strengthen my arms for kayaking. I didn't have them and we didn't want to make holes in our walls to put them in. I'd trained hard for triathlons in the past and I could see Wendy trained very hard for her cross-country skiing. She worked half days and her only child was a teenager. She had more strength and endurance than I had, at least at that stage of my training. Wendy was friendly enough but being social was secondary to other things in her life, cross-country skiing and I guess her family and her job. Whatever she did, she did it with serious intent. No frivolity.

I was getting fitter and happier. In January my parents treated us to a long weekend in San Diego and I kayaked for hours in Mission Bay. Dan brought his laptop, of course, and kept up with work while keeping an eye on Emma. We took Emma to the beach for her introduction to the ocean. She loved being lifted over the waves. We rented a sailboat for an afternoon on the bay. We got Emma to grasp a rope while I held it tight. Dan told me it wasn't called a rope on a boat. It was called a line. I told him "rope" was good enough for me. He said I was mutinous and he would find an island to strand me on.

I got two calls from Grace while Dan and I were away. Our Pole Pedal Paddle team was falling apart. The first call was to say my friend the bicyclist was brushed by a car and hurt her knee crashing into the pavement. She couldn't train and her doctor told her not to plan on racing. Then Wendy, our strongest and most critical member, died. Her husband called Grace to tell her. When Grace asked him how she died he said goodbye and hung up. Grace was afraid to call him back and ask the same question again. She hinted I should call him to express my sympathy and ask him again how she died. It was a mystery to both of us. Wendy had seemed the healthiest and fittest member of the team.

"I've never met Warren Whitlock," I told Grace. "He's going to know I'm calling more out of curiosity than sympathy. He clearly doesn't want to tell us and I don't want to bother him. I'll write him a letter."

On top of losing Grace and our bicycle rider, our downhill skier, the Oregon State student, was getting flaky—not replying to texts or emails and not keeping us up-to-date on her training. She seemed to be skiing when she felt like it and not really training at all. It wasn't the kind of responsibility and enthusiasm we needed to keep the team going.

That left a core team of Grace, Natasha, and me. We beat the bushes half-heartedly for replacements but we were discouraged with the setbacks. It was hard to stay motivated when we weren't sure we'd have a team to race with. The three of us decided we had better skip the race altogether.

My training had not entirely gone to waste, however. I was in the best shape I'd been since before I got pregnant. I'd stay at that level but, without targeting the PPP, I'd dial back my workouts and start campaigning for a new job. It wouldn't be too hard. I had a bachelor's in biology and there were companies in Bend that could use my knowledge. Still, Dan could tell I was sorry to give up on the race. We talked about it while washing dishes together in our brightly lighted kitchen. It was a good time of day to have a real conversation. We'd had a simple dinner seated at the counter. We put Emma down and Dan was done with work for the day. We weren't quite ready to watch the news and go to bed.

"Why don't you and Natasha compete as a pair team?" he said. "You could do the downhill, the bicycle, and the kayak. She could do the cross-country ski and the run. Play to your strengths. You'd be a strong team."

"What about Grace?" was my first reaction.

"She'll understand. And the only way she could compete at all is if you have six people. She'll have a whole year to put together a new team."

"I could tell her nicely and remind her that she was the one who got me started, Natasha too."

But my second reaction, unspoken, to being half of a pair team with Natasha was simply "No." I didn't want to do that. I'd made up my mind not to bear Natasha any ill will, to accept her into the wider circle of people I knew, to be cordial to her, even friendly when we met. But I would not seek her out. We would not become true friends. Dan knew this but he had ignored it. He was wrestling with the problem of how to get me in the race and a Natasha partnership was a practical solution.

"Besides," I said, "they won't let a pair team use the same person for the cross-country and the run. Those would be Natasha's strongest events."

"I'd forgotten that."

"Well then, I'll have to run the race by myself," I said.

Chapter 8

# Sheriff's Detective Carl Breuninger

I knew Dr. Samuel Dee at Sisemore Orthopedics, where Wendy Whitlock worked. I'd spent five whole days fishing with him two years earlier and I expected he would want to be helpful whether he could shed any light on her death or not.

I'd seen Sam Dee at Cultus Lake and at the Orvis Fly Shop—back when Orvis had a store in the Old Mill. But I didn't meet Sam until Sean Wray introduced us. Sean I met fishing on the Crooked River. I liked to fish the Crooked because it was in Crook County, not Deschutes County, and it felt like a vacation. I was totally off-duty. And down in the canyon, below Bowman Dam, not even a cell phone call could reach me. There were rattlesnakes but if you moved slow and made some noise, you'd never see them. I left my pistol in my truck. On a fishy overcast Saturday in October, I was fishing the edge of a current where I'd found trout before. I was having a pretty good day—released three small fish and a modest thirteen-incher. There was a younger man upstream from me, fishing nymphs like me but not having much luck. I put off leaving the river to visit the toilet as long as I could because I figured he'd take my spot as soon as I left it. But when I came back from my visit to the willows he was standing on the bank waiting for me.

"Hi," he said. "I was wondering what you were doing that I wasn't doing. You are sure catching more fish." I showed him the fly I was using, a #12 midge imitation, and he was using a bigger midge, a #16 with a little lighter color. I didn't think the color would make much difference but he said he would go smaller and darker.

I could have made a suggestion or two about his technique but I'd said enough already. I didn't want to give him a lesson and he probably didn't want to hear it. He thanked me and went upstream to retie his line and get back to fishing. He caught two fish in the next hour and I caught one that ran for the weeds and I lost.

The canyon got suddenly darker when thick black rain clouds streamed over the edge. I'd been hearing thunder in the distance for half an hour and been ignoring it. Now I heard the sharp crack of thunder less than three seconds after a lightning flash. A few heavy drops of rain swelled into a downpour. I reeled my line quickly and sprinted uphill to the road. The young man was right behind me.

"Get in my truck," I yelled. We put our rods in the truck bed and I unlocked the truck remotely. He leapt in the passenger side and I ran around to the driver's side. I started the engine and turned on the heat. The rain had been cold and we were already wet.

The man's fishing clothes were high-end but not new, a mix of Simms, Orvis, and Patagonia. He rested his wet baseball cap that said "Vandevert Brewing" on his knee and swept the moisture out of brown hair that was overdue for a haircut.

"You a local?" he asked.

"Bend," I said. I didn't ask where he was from. Interviewing people was half my job. Usually probing for their weaknesses, their mistakes, their secrets. I didn't want to ask this man a single question. But he wanted to talk. So we talked, ignoring the crashing and banging and lightning flashes around us.

"Where'd you learn to fish?" he asked.

"Around here," I said. "Cascade Lakes, Fall River, Metolius, and the stonefly on the Lower Deschutes."

"Yeah," he said. "I've learned in those same spots, first from my father, more from my friends, and then from a few guides here and there. It's a good area." He waited for me to say more and I didn't. "I grew up here," he said, "in Bend. I work in Prineville at the Facebook Data Center. In the summer, I come here to fish late sometimes after work."

The storm passed quickly, our conversation wasn't going anywhere, and we agreed it was time to get back to fishing.

"I'm going to get my rain jacket," he said, "in case we get another downpour." He took off down the road toward a blue sedan. It was a Tesla Model X. This man, Sean Wray, I knew his name by then, did more than sweep the floors at Facebook. Who goes fishing in a Tesla Model X? Lots of rocks and dirt out here and no charging stations, not even in Prineville.

We moved upriver in the afternoon, still keeping each other in sight. It was chilly in our wet clothes until they dried in the sun. The juniper trees, the willows, and the yellow grass around us were as dry as they had been in the morning, as though they hadn't seen rain in weeks. About three o'clock we got a caddis hatch—millions of bugs coming out of the water, filling the canyon with random but furiously motivated insects hovering and swooping. If they didn't find a mate their lives would be pointless. The fish rose to the surface to gobble bugs as they stopped to dry their wings before taking flight. Rings rippled out in a circle whenever a fish broke the water to swallow an insect. Sean and I switched to dry flies. Floating on top of the water, our flies would have been ignored without the hatch but now the caddis were whetting the fish's appetite. It was a testament to hundreds of years of human fishing experience that our little flies, totally artificial, were more attractive to the fish than thousands of real insects they had to choose from. Sean fished a classic elk hair caddis and I fished a little creation of my own with a good caddis silhouette. We each caught and released five fish in the space of an hour.

We fished together two more times that fall, once on the Metolius and once again on the Crooked. I judged my ability to read the water and cast to the perfect spot was a little better than Sean's and I taught him a thing or two. He was eager to learn. He caught more fish than

I did but I resisted what he tried to tell me. His approach was more analytical than mine. He watched the temperature of the air and of the water, how many cubic feet per second the river was flowing. He had a glass tube with a rubber bladder on it, like a small turkey baster, that could suck the stomach contents out of a fish so Sean could see what the fish had been eating and pick a fly to match it. I fished more by instinct, sharpened by experience. I'd find a likely ripple of water and imagine where the bottom of the river and the currents were pushing the trout and how the bugs in the water looked to the fish. We said our different approaches made sense for what we were, he being an engineer and me a detective.

"You see fish as little people with their own little motivations," he said, "and I see them as meat and bone machines with a smattering of intelligence."

The next April Sean called me with a proposition. He wanted a team from Bend to compete in a three-day fishing tournament in Jackson, Wyoming. It was called the One-Fly because every team member started each day with the fly of his choice and had to fish that same fly all day. If it wasn't catching fish he couldn't switch. If he lost the fly to a fish or to a willow on the bank he couldn't replace it.

"All expenses paid," said Sean, "the flight, the hotel, the guides, the entry fee. All meals and drinks. We'll have some good dinners in Jackson. Any equipment or clothes you need too. Everything included." I knew Sean had money but this was extravagant. My public servant instinct kicked in and I wondered if I were being subtly offered a favor for something Sean expected in the future. He might not even see his offer in that light but it might seem that way later on to the news media or some overzealous attorney. I told him my concern.

"God no," he said, "furthest thing from my mind. I've never thought for an instant that our paths would cross officially. We're fishing friends. And I hope teammates."

"Are you paying for the other guys too?" I asked, trying not to sound suspicious.

"Yup, everything," said Sean. "And they aren't complaining. They are indulging me and you would be too. I want everybody to enjoy this."

"Wives coming?" I asked.

"Not the plan," he said. "They'd be bored. We're going to fish all day and talk fishing the rest of the time. I know your wife fishes but the One Fly is going to take over the whole river. All the boats. All the guides." So this would be fishing from a boat, something I'd only done once.

"The other guys are good fisherman too. You'll like them. Dan Martinez is a friend of mine from high school. Sam Dee is a doctor, an orthopedist and a real great guy. He's the doctor of record for the Pole Pedal Paddle and some other races around Bend. A popular man." I didn't know the doctor at that point but I did know Dan Martinez. He didn't like me because I'd once investigated him for a murder. And I still resented his not sharing information with me that would have helped me crack the case. Not a bad guy, really, but we had a history.

"Does Martinez know about me being on the team?" I asked.

"He's all for it," said Sean. Maybe Dan no longer bore a grudge. And Bend still was, in a way, like a small town. You kept bumping into the same people. It didn't help to be at odds with too many of them. I told Sean I'd talk over his invitation with Estelle.

"You'll have fun," she said when I got home. "You should go. You love fishing. You'll see some new territory. And you like Sean."

"I feel bad that he's paying for all of it," I said.

"Is he paying for the doctor too?" Estelle asked.

"Yes, everything for everybody."

"I'm sure the doctor could pay for it himself and he isn't. So don't worry about it. Go have a shot at the high life."

"So I'm going with a doctor, an engineer, and a lawyer. They're all more educated than me."

"Think about it. They won't talk Socrates and astrophysics. They'll talk about fishing and maybe sports. You know at least as much as they do."

I told Sean "yes" the next day. "But," I asked, "You're not expecting me to perform any kind of security function are you? Not even informally? I'm not going to bring a gun and my badge isn't worth two cents in Wyoming."

"Nothing like that," said Sean. "You're a member of the team. That's all. And Jackson is one of the safest places in the country."

So the first time I met Dr. Sam Dee was when we got on the plane at the Bend Municipal Airport for our flight to Wyoming. It wasn't United or Delta. It was a charter for the four of us, direct to Jackson. If Sean had that kind of money, I didn't have to worry about how much the hotels, restaurants, and fishing guides in Jackson were going to cost.

Sam was a very fit man about the same age as me, in his fifties. He eyed me suspiciously, even fearfully it seemed, for about five seconds and then broke into a big welcoming smile, shot out his hand, and spoke an enthusiastic, "Hello, how do you do?" That was what I needed, though I didn't show it. I gripped his hand firmly and gave him as much of a smile as I could muster. When I was a deputy my priority when I met people was demanding their respect. When I became a detective I learned to be more caring and sympathetic, or at least seem that way, while still claiming superior access to power. I had no special status with this group. Though Sean tried to instill a team spirit and camaraderie of equals, three of us were, in a sense, hired hands to help Sean compete in this tournament. Like the others I tried to shift my outlook to the team view of things and took the fishing cap he gave me with a smile. "Cascadians," it said on the front. Every team had a name and that was the one Sean picked for us.

The plane was a Cessna C525 Citation with four seats, not that I knew the pedigree of small planes. It could have been a DeSoto. The doctor and I had the seats facing forward and the younger men sat facing us. We talked about fishing, naturally enough, with Dan and Sam being the biggest talkers and Sean listening attentively. I half listened and half gazed out the window, the landscape getting less and less familiar the further east we got. I spotted the lower Snake River, Boise, and Idaho Falls.

Sam talked about trout fishing in New Zealand and Argentina

and fishing for bonefish on saltwater flats in the Caribbean. Dan and Sean asked good questions. I listened when I wasn't watching out the window. I doubted I'd ever see a bonefish.

I shared a room with Sam, Dr. Dee, in a three-story hotel in downtown Jackson, a city much smaller than Bend that was flooded with tourists and fishermen in town for the One Fly. Every afternoon the town staged an old western shootout on the main street.

I've never seen a man with so many creams and pills as Sam Dee. He took some of them with him in his fishing vest. All I had was suntan lotion and some Advil. He stretched and did pushups when we got up in the morning and he did more stretching and exercises before we went to bed. He looked as fit and healthy with his shirt off as he did with it on. Not many men in their fifties could say that. He didn't hog the bathroom and he told me to wake him up if he snored. He was considerate.

Over the three-day tournament we got points for the fish we caught—more points for bigger fish and fewer points for smaller ones. We fished in different boats on different stretches of the river on different days. Each boat had two fishermen from different teams and a guide who was supposed to see that his passengers had equal chances to catch good fish. The first day, a Friday, I shared my boat with an elderly woman that the guide had to help get into the boat. I was afraid she would get tired and we'd have to cut our day short. But that lady was determined. She never did get tired. She couldn't hear very well or move very well but she could cast like a bolt of lightning if the casts weren't too long. And the guide knew where the fish were. We both had a good day. The guide pointed me to fish that needed longer casts but they were there and I caught them. At the end of the first day my boatmate had more points than any other woman on the river, and some of those women were guides themselves.

The Cascadians were in sixth place after the first day. We barely held our place on the second day because Sam lost over an hour of fishing. His boat came across a man who had been fishing from the land, a man who wasn't in the tournament. The man had slid down a rocky bank and had broken his arm and gashed his leg. Sam stopped to help, disinfected and bandaged the leg, and tied a stick of wood to the arm for a splint. The disinfectant and the bandages came from a sling bag that Sam used a doctor's kit. The bag was teardrop shaped, blue, with a single shoulder strap designed to go over one shoulder while skiing. Sam told us he used the sling bag because people who saw an old-fashioned doctor's bag assumed there were drugs in it.

The guide called the park service from his cell phone to come help the injured guy get to a hospital. The guide and Sam's boatmate wanted to leave the man there and get back to fishing. But Sam said no. Then he told the injured man to jump on his back. The man wasn't too big but he was not a small boy either. Sam carried him piggyback up the steep bank, about a hundred feet high, and sat the man down in the sagebrush. The man carried his rod up the bank while Sam carried him. Then they both waited most of an hour for the park rangers to show up before Sam came back down to start fishing again.

Sam was the talk of the tournament that evening and he made the local paper the next day. He was a hero to the public. Dan muttered to Sean that the doctor was a show-off. The injured man would have been fine sitting on the bank by himself for an hour. We weren't there to be heroes, we told each other. We were there, on Sean's dime, to fish and to compete. Sean was too diplomatic to say anything. The other fisherman in Sam's boat filed a formal complaint with the race committee. Not only had both men lost more than an hour of fishing, all the other boats on that same stretch of river had gotten ahead of them and stripped out most of the good fish for miles.

That night we went to the premier spot in town for dinner, a large rustic restaurant with half logs lining the walls, like the inside of a National Park lodge. The ceiling lights were modeled on Indian drums. Two five-foot-high timber walls fenced our table in against the wall. It was like eating on a white tablecloth in a horse stall. As word got out that Sam was at our table people stopped by to talk with him. He had called the hospital and he gave updates to our visitors on the man's progress. If they asked whether Sam was a doctor he said he was only a good Samaritan. Then he reminded us, with a wink, that he wasn't licensed to practice medicine in Wyoming.

The constant interruptions and Sam Dee's celebrity status threw us off and we didn't have the friendly group dinner we had hoped for. But we were still coming together as a team, at least as a temporary team. I knew the sense of it from my time in the marines and my first months with the sheriff's department. I remembered it from high school football, though that was a long time ago. We were cheerful on the walk back to our hotel, though the air was cold and we hadn't dressed for it.

"They'll be a hatch tomorrow," said Sean.

We stayed in what Sean said was one of the nicest hotels in town. The two-room suite I shared with Sam Dee had one room with a king size bed and another room with a double that pulled out from a sofa. The rooms shared a bathroom and a narrow hallway that connected the two rooms together. Sam and I flipped a coin for the king bed and I won. We weren't going to spend much time in our rooms except for sleeping so it didn't make much difference. The living room Sam was in was large enough for all four of us to pile all our fishing gear and our bulky bad weather clothes into it.

We were on our way downstairs to breakfast the last day when we passed two housekeepers in the hall carrying towels and blankets. Sam stopped to talk to one of them, a short plumpish Latina in her forties or fifties. I noticed she was holding the towels very low under her left arm, pressed between her forearm and her hip, and she had a suffering look on her face. I couldn't understand Sam's conversation but Dan translated it for me later. Sam began it.

"¿La duelen el hombro?"

"Sí, señor," said the woman. "Hace dos semanas."

"Soy doctor, puedo ayudarla, claro, total confianza," said Sam. The woman's face relaxed and her eyes turned hopeful.

"Venga conmigo," said Sam. Sam carried her sheets and towels as she followed him back into our suite.

"What was that?" I asked Dan.

"Sam asked the woman if her shoulder hurt her and she said yes. He said he was a doctor and he could help her."

Breakfast was a buffet in the lobby—juice, milk, coffee, fruit, cold cereal, oatmeal in a cooker, bread and butter with a toaster handy if you wanted it. It would be enough for us, no complaints, and the guides always brought good lunches. The three of us dug in without waiting for Sam.

We discovered that Sean was going to fish a stretch of river that Dan had fished the day before and I had fished the day before that. Dan went upstairs to get paper and a pen from the pile of equipment in the suite. We were going to show Sean where our boats had caught fish. The fish might be long gone by now but it would be fun to talk about it and think we were helping Sean have a successful day.

Dan came back to the table without the paper but with a dazed expression on his face. He leaned over his chair and spoke softly so they rest of the room wouldn't hear him.

"You're not going to believe this," he said. "They're fucking." Sean's jaw dropped open and mine did too.

"Who?" said Sean.

"Sam and the housekeeper," said Dan. "Going at it."

"Did he force her?" I asked, getting ready to charge upstairs. Even with no responsibility to enforce the law in Wyoming, this was wrong and I was going to stop it.

"I wouldn't say so," said Dan. "Sounds like she's having a wonderful time."

I remained standing. Sam was a charmer. Not the type to force a woman to do something. Not the type to risk arrest for assault or rape either. And Dan had heard what he heard.

"Did you see them?" I asked him.

"I didn't want to look."

"God almighty," said Sean.

Dan sat down and I took a swig of coffee. I didn't like this one bit. When you've spent your career in law enforcement it's important to remember there are decent, law-abiding, virtuous, generous, fundamentally good people in the world. I considered Sam one of those people, far better than many. Now he'd seduced some poor woman with his status as a doctor. No matter what her life history was or how open-eyed she was about what she was doing, Sam was taking advantage of her and abandoning his commitment to his wife. He was gratifying his appetite for sex, or power, or adventure, or I don't know what. Maybe to prove once again how attractive he was.

We made no more comments about Sam. None of us knew what to say. Dan spread out a paper napkin and sketched out a section of the river at the top of a back eddy below a steep bank on the left shore. It was the corner where Dan had caught his biggest fish.

"We fished in that exact spot," I said. "I know where you were. We didn't see a thing." That was fishing for you, especially in a tournament like the One Fly. Maybe a dozen pretty good fisherman had fished to that spot both days. That fish had probably been caught and released two or three times, fighting for its life over and over. It was exhausted and intimidated. If it hadn't died, it was skulking in the deepest part of the river, afraid to eat anything. Its courage wouldn't return for days, driven only by its primal urge to eat and grow bigger. Sean would probably never get near that fish but he might get a different one, a smaller one, that had come in to take over his shaken comrade's feeding ground.

Sam quickstepped down the stairs, gave us a wave, and hastily filled his plate at the buffet.

"Did you fix her shoulder?" Dan asked when the good doctor came to the table.

"Yes," said Sam. "Simple A.R.T.—Active Release Technique. They don't teach it in medical school and you don't need a license to do it. It simply takes some training to do it right. It's a shame that some people have suffered for years from pain that could be fixed in five minutes." The doctor sat down and we went back to Dan's hand-drawn map. Sam concentrated on his breakfast. Fruit, oatmeal, and tea. A healthy diet. As for me, I do love hot buttered toast with a heap of jam on it. And coffee, lots of coffee.

We made a quick stop in our rooms before setting off.

"Did you use my bed?" I asked Sam.

"On top of the covers," he said. "I put a towel down." There was a wadded-up towel on the floor in the bathroom that I wished I hadn't seen.

The last day was overcast and cold. It looked like rain in the afternoon. I chose a black foam ant with a white polypro wing for my fly. It would float high and be easy for me to see. And I figured the fish would need something really attention-getting after seeing fly after fly for two days.

We couldn't change flies in the middle of the day but we could trim the flies we had. Sean had a fly he'd made he called the hairy monster. It was big and brown with long black rubber legs sticking out of it. If they wouldn't come to his fly on the surface he planned to shorten the legs and fish it wet, under the surface of the water.

We had a good day that last day and our team came in fourth overall. Sean stopped trimming his fly at something that resembled a spider and my ant did well all day in spite of not matching the hatch when the hatch did come. I won more points for our team than any of the other three and I was proud of that. We had done well and Sean was delighted.

Sam Dee's encounter with the hotel maid continued to bother me. I had no idea what kind of thinking or what kind of situation in life would lead her to spontaneous sex with a man she had never met before. Sam apparently grasped her agenda, or her possible agenda, the second he saw her. God knew he had people skills I didn't have and couldn't even fathom. Not always ones I'd be entirely proud of.

Sean and I fished together locally twice the next year and I met Dan's wife when she witnessed a shooting up in the Cascade Lakes. But I didn't see Sam Dee again until I interviewed him about Wendy Whitlock's work at Sisemore Orthopedics. I expected he would be helpful. But helpful in a way that, if possible, made him appear essential to the investigation and, because of his helpfulness and his relationship with me, more privy to the progress of the case than other people. That was the deal he would want. He would answer every question I asked if it allowed him to polish his image when we were done. I would interview him at Sisemore's offices and, with a wink as I left the building, tell him something the press wouldn't know for another week or two.

## Chapter 9

# Sarah Chatham

After our last conversation I didn't expect Wendy's husband, Warren, to reach out to me but he did.

"The clinic called me," he said, "to ask if I'd found any paperwork that Wendy might have at home—invoices, cancelled checks, bank statements or registers, stuff like that. Said they'd like to come by and pick them up. And, if I didn't mind, could they scan through Wendy's office for other things they might need. I didn't like the sound of it."

"Do you know why Sisemore wanted Wendy's files from home?"

"I told them Wendy didn't bring her work home and there was nothing here that belonged to them. Wendy told me that for years. And I've never seen anything in this house that said Sisemore on it. Their problem is they don't understand the records they've got and they think there's some magical document here that will make it all clear."

Warren didn't know why Sisemore was so eager to paw through Wendy's papers but I did. They wanted to know how much Wendy had embezzled from them and where the money was now.

"I told them I'd call them back," said Warren. "I don't know what they want in Wendy's records but I get the sense there's more going on here than I understand. Wendy was doing things I didn't know about. I need your help to unravel it all. I want whatever might be coming to me and Ethan. And I don't want to get us in trouble for something Wendy might have done."

"Who called?" I asked.

"Marguerite. She works at the front desk and makes appointments."

"Did she say who asked her to call?"

"No, and I didn't ask," said Warren. "My first reaction was this was one more damn thing to take care of and I would do it. I only thought of calling you later."

"I think that was a good decision. Can I come by and see if there is anything I can find? As executor of her will it's really my responsibility to do so."

"Anytime today," he said. "It's too cold and wet for landscaping. I'm home losing money and doing paperwork to prove it."

I said I'd stop by around 4:00. When I was a fulltime partner in Portland I would have had a paralegal search through Wendy's things. But we didn't have a paralegal in the Bend office and if I went to the Whitlock place myself I might find something that seemed irrelevant at first but would put the pieces together. What did Sisemore Orthopedics know about the extent of Wendy's theft? What might I find in her records that Sisemore would like to know but didn't know and would give me an advantage in negotiating with them? Most critically, where had she stashed the two million if it actually was two million? And, finally, if she actually had a stake in The Conclave, what was the connection?

Warren met me at his front door and handed me a box that originally held a thousand business-size envelopes. There were about two hundred envelopes left and there was a stack of papers that filled up the rest of the box three-quarters high.

"Do you mind if I sit down and search through this?" I asked.

"By my guest," said Warren, pleasantly but not enthusiastically and he waved me toward a stuffed chair in the living room. A kitchen table would have been better but I sat where Warren pointed me. Ethan came downstairs and both of them sat in the room, lost in thought and half asleep while I went through the box. They were hoping I'd find some explanation for Wendy's death. It might at least give them some solace to see someone working on it.

The envelopes were blank, no return address printed on them.

Most of the papers were bills for normal household expenses going back two years. Utilities, the house phone, a plumber and an electrician, garbage service. A complete set of Mastercard statements in Wendy's name also went back two years. Nothing remarkable popped out but I might go through them again later on. Two years of checking account statements didn't show any large checks. There was one paragraph-long newspaper clipping about the purchase of land for an unnamed resort development in Powell Butte that I presumed was later named The Conclave.

"Is there anything else?" I asked. "Any place she might have put things she didn't want people to find too easily?"

"I don't know," said Warren, blowing out his cheeks. "I didn't think she had any secrets but I guess maybe she did."

"Can I search through the drawers where she kept her clothes?" Warren pressed his lips together as though he'd been sucking on a lemon. "I'll make sure everything goes back where it was." He said okay and took me upstairs to the master bedroom. The room was neat and the bed was made. Warren was keeping a grip on things. There was a double set of drawers under a mirror on the side wall.

"Wendy's drawers are the ones on the left. I haven't looked in them since." He sat in the one chair in the room while I started with the top drawer and worked down to the bottom. I moved slowly, partly to make sure I didn't miss anything and partly to assure Warren I was being respectful. I reached into each open drawer and felt above it for envelopes taped up out of sight. I even lifted each drawer out, felt the back of it, and examined the inside of the bureau behind the drawer. Nothing. But under the sports bras, underwear, and athletic socks in the bottom drawer were two square envelopes. To my surprise one of them had my name on it. I showed it to Warren before I opened it. He was as surprised to see my name there as I was. I opened the envelope to find a Christmas card with a sleigh full of toys on the front. The message inside was crossed out and only two words were written above it. "Ask Ethan." I showed this to Warren as well and he called out Ethan's name.

"Come over here. We've found something."

"Ask me what?" said Ethan when I showed him the card. We'd gotten his hopes up only to hit him with a problem he had no idea how to solve. "Ask Ethan" was an important message from his mother and he couldn't begin to understand it. He was letting her down, letting his father down, letting himself down. I'd seen that look in my own son's face—the look of "How can the adult world hand me a problem that is so impossible to solve and expect me to solve it?"

"The other envelope is for you," I said. "I'd like you to let me read it but understand you don't have to." Ethan opened it to find an identical Christmas card that he eagerly unfolded. The expression on his face turned to disappointment and exasperation. He held the card down by his pantleg then picked it up again and stared at it, as though this time it might say something different.

"What does it say?" asked Warren.

Ethan held it up to him. "It says 'Twelfth birthday party.' What the heck is that supposed to mean?"

"Put the note down," I suggested. "Take a minute to think about your twelfth birthday party. What happened?"

Ethan stood still a minute, like a wrestler sizing up his opponent before the whistle blew, holding the dangling the card loose in his hand. A glimmer came into his eyes and he stood up taller.

"We had a treasure hunt. Mom wrote these clues all over the house and we each had to follow the clues to where there was a present for each of us."

"What was your present?" asked Warren.

"That's not the point," said Ethan, triumphantly. "She wrote the clues in invisible ink and we had to use ultraviolet flashlights to read them."

"Do you still have one of those flashlights?"

"Sure. Might need a battery." Ethan shot out of the room and we could hear a scramble of objects being pushed aside in a drawer or some sort of wooden box. He returned with a small flashlight that gave off a weak bluish light. But when we shined it on my card, we found exactly the kind of information I'd been hoping to find—bank accounts and how to access them.

**The Bank of Boise**
124103677 0214597345
PW = Cultus1859

**The Bank of Cayman Brac**
069753681495
PW = Hosmer1904

The Bank of Boise was in Idaho. The Bank of Cayman Brac had to be in the Cayman Islands, a tiny nation in the Caribbean that was famous for offshore banking. People put their money in Cayman Islands banks when they owed someone, or expected to owe someone, a lot of money they didn't want to pay. With a United States bank, like the Bank of Boise, a court could order the bank to pay out your money. But a Cayman Island Bank would tell a U.S. court that the court had no jurisdiction in the Cayman Islands and would they please go away and stop bothering them. Furthermore, a United States Bank might have to turn over your bank records to law enforcement or someone who sued to get them. That would be next to impossible at a Cayman Islands bank. If you wanted to hide money, a bank in the Cayman Islands was a good place to do it.

I turned away as Ethan pointed the flashlight at his own card.

"Don't show that to me, Ethan. It's better if I don't even know what it looks like." I turned to Warren. "You probably don't want to look at it either."

"Why is that?" asked Warren.

It was time for me to tell her loving family the truth, as painful as it might be. Their wife and mother was a crook. Of course I didn't say it that way. I told them Wendy had embezzled money from her employer, Sisemore Orthopedics, and that she meant that money to go to Ethan. Warren and Ethan both gaped at me with their eyes wide as searchlights, like father like son. Wendy had kept her secrets well.

I said Sisemore had found out about the embezzlement and Wendy had hired me to negotiate a settlement with them. But neither Sisemore nor I knew how much she had taken or where she put it. Today, thanks to Wendy's note, I might have partial answers to those questions, answers which Sisemore would not have and could not get.

With the account numbers and passwords Wendy had given me I could find out what money was in the accounts and how much had come in and gone out. As executor of Wendy's will I could transfer money out of the accounts to pay restitution to Sisemore and give whatever was left to Ethan.

"Here's the deal," I said. "Sisemore will probably settle for much less than Wendy actually took and much less than is in these accounts." I held up the copy of Wendy's note to me to indicate which accounts I meant.

"Embezzlement is a crime but, given that Wendy is deceased, that you two had no knowledge of the crime, and that Sisemore will probably want to put this whole thing behind them, the district attorney will do absolutely nothing and, even if he did, you'd have a so-called 'innocent spouse' defense, not to mention an 'innocent child' defense. Ironclad, I think."

"I sure as shootin' didn't know anything about any embezzling or any of this money you're talking about," said Warren.

"I believe you and I'm sure a judge and jury would believe you too. It probably won't come to that anyway. But you do have to be very careful about the note that Wendy left for Ethan. It may tell him how to find money that is not in the accounts in the note that Wendy left for me. I'm speculating. I don't know and I don't want to know.

"And you don't want anybody, including me, to know anything about it. Don't touch that money. Don't move it around or spend a nickel of it. Someday you can get another lawyer, not me or my firm, to figure out what to do with it. In the meantime, don't mention it to anyone."

I was risking my law license and even my freedom trying to serve Wendy and her estate. I was helping the Whitlock family hide assets, or at least I wasn't helping Sisemore or law enforcement find them. I hoped I'd protected all of us, including myself, well enough to stay out of court.

## Chapter 10

# Dan Martinez

Sean Wray asked me to meet him for lunch.

"Are we going to discuss business?" I asked. Sean and I had known each other since high school. Amy and I were good friends of Sean and Grace. We could have spent three or four lunches not talking about business. But Sean was also a client, one of the first clients I ever signed up for the Oxton's new Bend office.

"I guess this is a business meeting," he said. "I have something to tell you."

"Well then," I said, "I'm paying. It's a client lunch." We both knew this was slightly ridiculous. We'd inevitably have lunch at a rugby-themed brewpub near our office named Vandevert Brewing Company. Sean owned it. Furthermore, Sean could have bought me lunch in Paris without breaking a sweat, first class airfare included.

"So let me get this straight," he said. "You're buying me lunch out of the fees I'm paying your firm."

"That's right," I said, "partially subsidized by the IRS. Part of the lunch, at least, will be tax deductible."

"Then we can have dessert," said Sean.

"Sky's the limit," I said, though after the obligatory pint of beer I didn't expect to have a hankering for dessert.

Sean usually got a table in the center of things where he could watch other people enjoying their lunch. This time he chose a booth in the back, quieter and more private. He'd already ordered a small glass of beer for me to try and a waitress brought it as soon as we sat down. She was dressed in a rugby uniform, blue and white stripes on a short-sleeved shirt and baggy blue shorts.

"Do you play rugby?" I asked her.

"Hah," she said. "I don't even know the rules. All I know is what I pick up from the TVs in the pub." There was a big screen over the bar and two more on other walls. They showed rugby games when games were broadcast, often from England, Australia, or South Africa, and condescended to show American football when there was no rugby available. We ordered a pulled pork sandwich for each of us.

"She played some team sport," Sean said. "It's a requirement for working here. I don't get involved in hiring but it's one rule I insist upon. It makes for employees that cooperate with each other and a better work environment. At least I think it does."

"Seems to work," I said.

"Here," said Sean, pushing the glass we already had toward me. "I want you to try this. The brewmaster thinks we can make it a hit this summer." The beer Sean wanted me to try was light-colored and didn't smell like beer. I took a sip of it and made a face. Sean didn't seem surprised.

"What is that?" I asked.

"It's called a shandy. It's a mix of beer and lemonade. You're supposed to find it refreshing. It was popular in the nineteenth century."

"Sorry, Sean," I said. "I'd say we've made progress since then. I expect beer to taste like beer."

"We think it might catch on with the younger set."

I used to think I was the younger set. Sean and I, now both thirty-three, didn't qualify any more.

"Do you like it?" I asked.

"Not really," he said. He waved the waitress over and ordered two of the pub's Bear Hunter beers. They came before the sandwiches and we took life-affirming swallows. We'd taken our outdoor jackets off and hung them on hooks next to our booth.

"So what's up?" I asked. "If this is a business lunch we better not forget to do some business."

"Well," said Sean, "it's about The Conclave." Sean was an investor in the development, pooling his money with a real estate investment company where he had a friend. He'd had a hand in The Conclave's hiring Oxton, Rath, and Flynn to be their attorneys. To date he hadn't gotten involved with the project's legal work.

"I'm a dilettante," Sean said. "I dip into the interesting parts of the project and avoid any real responsibility for anything. The management tolerates me. And I'm an engineer. So I get the daily reports on everything, even the well logs for the wells we're drilling on the property. It's a geeky thing to read, just to see what's down there, what kind of rock there is and figure out when and how it got there. Do you know The Conclave is in the Crooked River Caldera?"

"I did not know that," I said, getting ready to tell Sean, if necessary, that the topic was not business related and perhaps, not as interesting as he thought it was.

"You do know that Yellowstone Park is a supervolcano? It's over a hot spot deep in the earth. It last erupted over 600,000 years ago."

"So before you and I were born," I said. Sean ignored this.

"And of course you also know the whole North American plate has been moving west for millions of years."

I looked down critically at the floor. "Never noticed it," I said.

"Well, thirty million years ago that same hotspot was right under where The Conclave is today."

"That must have sunk the price of land," I said. "We should have bought."

Sean's mouth flickered in amusement but he was intent on telling me what he wanted to tell me. "So I keep up with the well logs to see the different kinds of rock at different depths. Do you know what a well log is? When you drill a well you need to keep a report of what kind of rock you're finding at what depth and what kind of water—how fast it's seeping into the well and what minerals it has in it. You do know why we're drilling wells, don't you?"

"Because you couldn't get irrigation water from the Deschutes."

"That's right," said Sean. "Water rights were sold to farmers over a hundred years ago and the farmer's heirs won't sell them. No water. No farm. We had a chance to buy what are called junior rights. The problem with junior rights is that if there isn't enough water, like in a drought, the people with senior rights get water first and the junior rights holders get what's leftover. In some years, that means no water for junior rights holders at all. Wait for water next year and hope you don't go bankrupt in the meantime. The Conclave can't risk having no water when we have a golf course and multi-million-dollar homes with landscaping.

"So the answer," Sean continued, "was to dig wells. Deep wells. A thousand feet deep, a hundred thousand dollars each. And there are aquifers everywhere in Central Oregon. The land is dry up top but you go deep enough and there's water all over the place."

"Except under The Conclave?" I asked, guessing where Sean was going.

"That's not the problem," he said. "There's water down there. But it's terrible water—chloride, sodium, sulfate, calcium, even selenium. You can't drink it and you can't irrigate a golf course with it. It's worthless. That's not supposed to happen in Oregon. The aquifers have always had good clean water." Sean paused to let the enormity of what he was saying sink in.

"Go deeper," I said.

"They tried that. Same result."

"And you need a lawyer to help you solve this problem?" I asked.

"Not the water problem. The Conclave has another problem and I have a problem." Our sandwiches arrived and we paused while the waitress set them down and asked if there was anything else we needed. Our glasses were still mostly full. We had silverware, napkins, salt and pepper, ketchup, mustard, and all kinds of hot sauce and steak sauce.

"Thanks," I told her, "I think we're set." Sean started speaking as soon as the waitress turned away.

"The bottom line is, or will be, we can't build the development. The management doesn't know that yet, or they don't understand it. We've bought the land, drawn the plans, gotten permits, and started grading. We'll have to stop work, sell the land for less than we paid for it, and try to return as much money as possible to the investors. It's going to be a bust."

"And your own problem?"

"My problem, or you might call it an opportunity, is that the other investors don't know about the water yet. Neither the big ones—Baybridge Partners, Rockwood Lodging, the Skene Trust—nor the little ones like Far Away Resorts. If I could quickly sell my shares to one of them, even at a discount, I'd get a lot more money out of this than if I wait around to get clobbered."

"Don't even think about it," I said.

"It's not fraud," said Sean. "They have the same information I have about the wells. Or at least they have access to it. They just haven't looked at it. Or they don't understand it yet. That's not my fault."

"It would be dishonest," I said.

"These investors are much bigger than I am," said Sean, "and I've been dealing with them for years. They would feed me to the sharks in a minute if they could make an extra dime."

"And what they'll do, if they buy your shares before they realize the shares are junk, is tie you up in court and threaten to take your entire investment and more besides, until they extract as much money from you as they can. Better to take your lumps, share and share alike with the other investors, and move on. That's my advice anyway, as a friend. You could pay a lawyer a lot of money to fight a losing case for you if you wanted to."

Sean sat and thought about this. He absentmindedly picked up his sandwich and began to eat.

"Sean," I said, "you're a thoroughly honest and decent guy. My best advice is don't get caught up in clever ways to make a quick buck. Keep your integrity and your sanity. You'll be a lot happier." Sean swallowed and thought about this for a moment.

"How much of your net worth do you have tied up in this project?" I asked. I'd never asked Sean how much he and Grace were worth and I didn't really want to know.

He swallowed the bite he was chewing and took a sip of beer.

"Eight percent, give or take."

"You'll probably get some of it back," I said. "It won't be a total loss. And you'll make up some of it in other investments." Sean held his sandwich over his plate and stared down at the table.

"There has to be a way," he said. Sean built software systems, computer networks, enormous banks of high-speed servers. He worked on problems until he found a solution. It was hard to tell him there was no solution.

"As far as The Conclave's problem," I said, "you've issued me an early warning and I appreciate it. But my official contact at The Conclave hasn't told me about it and hasn't asked me to do anything about it. I'll think about what steps we should take when he does tell me. Oxton will have a lot of work unraveling the investment, paying off commitments, selling off assets, and returning whatever is possible to the investors." This always ticked off entrepreneurs. When a business failed the accountants and lawyers made a lot of money.

"I'm sorry, Sean," I went on. "I know The Conclave wasn't simply money to you. You poured a lot of yourself into it. Maybe you'll find another project."

"What should I tell the other investors about the water?" Sean asked.

"Tell the board of directors, at least someone who's on the board of directors. Tell them what you told me. Then it's their responsibility to tell the investors."

"Well, thanks," said Sean. We ate in silence for a few minutes.

"Have you told anybody else about the water?"

"I mentioned it to Sam Dee. He's a big fan of The Conclave, even though he's not an investor, and he's been talking it up all around town. He loves the low tech/no tech idea. He's been out to the site with me a couple of times. Says he can't wait to see plans for the golf course. I told him about the water because I don't want him to be embarrassed still gabbing about The Conclave when the news gets out that The Conclave is kaput."

"All the more reason for you to alert the board of directors before news about the water does get out. Do it this afternoon and document that you did it. Text or email that you need to talk with them and then follow up with phone calls. Write down what time you called them and the highlights of what you said."

"Will do." He pulled an iPhone out of his pants pocket and sent texts while I finished my hamburger and slowly drained my beer. Frank, the assistant brewmaster, was at the bar serving beer samples in small glasses to two overweight but neatly dressed men. They sipped each glass and scribbled notes. I guessed they were beer distributors deciding which of Frank's new concoctions the public would like and which taverns would want to give them a try. Sean put down his phone and took another bite out of his burger.

"I'm sorry Grace's team for the Pole Pedal Paddle fell apart. But Grace sure got Amy working out hard for it," I said. "I'm starting to feel flabby and weak by comparison."

"Grace is okay about it. She'll start earlier next year and have some backups if people on her team start to drop out. And we're all rooting for Amy."

Chapter 11

# Sarah Chatham

I took the time to search for the Maybach Property Company, the name that was on the Bank of Boise account. Google couldn't find an exact match but it did come back with a very interesting result. While the Maybach Property "Company" might not exist, the Maybach Property "Corporation" did exist and it happened to be in Bend, on Franklin Street. I searched Deschutes County tax records for Sisemore's address and learned, as I expected, that the building belonged to the Maybach Property Corporation. The corporation was Sisemore's landlord. I began to see how Wendy might have embezzled a fortune out of Sisemore without detection. She could have written two checks every month, one to the corporation in Bend to pay the lease and another to the company in Boise for other expenses. She might have simply entered "Maybach" in the ledger so it looked like the checks were going to the same place. I was considering this, and going through my email, when I got the call from Sam Dee.

"You'll be glad to know my knee is doing fine," I said, "but I'm calling you about Wendy Whitlock."

"Yes, I know," he said, as confident and sunny as usual, his resonant fatherly voice coming through perfectly—a voice that said there was no problem in the world that couldn't be solved. "Our admin tells me you are representing Wendy Whitlock's estate. I'm so glad it's someone I know. How are you in the midst of this tragedy?"

"Life is good. I got married to a wonderful man and we're very happy."

"Still 'semi-retired,' as you called it?"

"Working hard when I work but not burning the midnight oil. I'm calling because Wendy retained me to help negotiate a sum of money to be paid to Sisemore Orthopedics. I'm also the executor of her will so I'm calling you on behalf of her estate. Wendy said Sisemore appointed you to represent them."

"Right, right," said Dee. "The doctors are very disappointed in Wendy but they are pleased to finally know why profits weren't meeting expectations and even relieved that Wendy, and you as her representative, have come forward to make things right. But I think we should not discuss this here in our offices. Some people here know more about it than others and I'd like to keep our negotiations entrenous for now. Could you meet me at my house this evening right after dinner, say seven-thirty?"

I was prepared. The critical amount was not how much Wendy had stolen but how much her estate could pay back. I'd logged into the accounts Wendy listed in her note to me. The Bank of Boise account had three hundred thousand in it. The account at the Cayman Island Bank held twenty thousand. But over the past five years, over two million dollars had passed through these two accounts. The statements listed the transactions but they didn't show where the money had come from or where the money went when it left. Two million went into the Bank of Boise over time, was transferred to the Bank of Cayman Brac. Only very recently, shortly before Wendy died, was money transferred back the other way. A three hundred thousand transfer out of the Cayman bank matched a three hundred thousand transfer into the Boise bank. Why would Wendy do that?

Even more interesting were the names on the accounts. The Bank of Boise account belonged to the Maybach Property Company. The Cayman account was in Wendy's name. What the hell was going on? The address for both accounts was on South Route 97 in Bend and I recognized it. It was a private mailbox company for people who wanted an address separate from their home or business. It shared a parking lot with the Freddy Meyer store.

I handwrote a table of the two accounts, rounding off the numbers, to help me make sense of what I'd learned.

| Bank | Bank of Boise Account | Bank of Cayman Brac |
|---|---|---|
| Name on Account | Maybach Property Company | Wendy Whitlock |
| Five Year Cash In | $2 million + $300,000 | $2 million |
| Where the Cash Came From | Unknown. (Embezzled from Sisemore Orthopedics?) $300,000 recently received from Bank of Cayman Brac. (Date and amount of transfer match) | Maybach Account at Bank of Boise? (Dates and amounts of transfers match) |
| Five Year Cash Out | $2 million | $1.68 million + $300,000 |
| Where the Cash Went | Bank of Cayman Brac. (Dates and amounts of transfers match) | $300,000 to Maybach at Bank of Boise $1.68 million transferred to unknown accounts |
| Current Balance | $300,000 | $20,000 |

The table answered one important question for me: What was the maximum Wendy's estate could pay in restitution to Sisemore? The answer was $320,000. That would be my absolute negotiating limit with Dr. Samuel Dee.

The big question I still didn't have an answer to was where did all the money go after it left the account in the Caymans? If Wendy wanted that money to go to Ethan, as the will she left behing implied, why didn't she tell me, her executor, where it was? The Bank of Cayman Brac statements didn't show where the money went, only the amounts and dates of the transfers. But they did give the name and phone number of Wendy's representative at the bank, a Mr. Nigel Buckhampton. I reached him on the phone as easily as if he were next door. He had a pleasant voice and a relaxed tone, as though he had been looking forward to my call and had all the time in the world to help me with whatever I needed. His accent was English with a Harry Belafonte lilt.

"The bank is here to serve its clients and honor their wishes, Ms. Chatham, but our client's privacy is paramount. The bank could transfer the twenty thousand now in the account if you provide all the proper documentation to us by mail or facsimile. But we cannot reveal where the funds transferred out of the account went unless you are actually in our office with a passport showing you are who you say you are. I'm sure you understand."

I said I did understand, though I regretted the bank's limitations. I thanked him for his time and said I would be in touch.

It took more phone calls, faxes, and emails to work through multiple managers at the Bank of Boise but, once I had established my credentials it was straightforward getting all the records I wanted. Cash came into the account monthly by wire transfers from Sisemore Orthopedics. The amounts varied but hovered around twelve thousand dollars. All the cash went out to the same place, the account at the Bank of Cayman Brac. There was an abrupt break in the pattern, in early January, shortly before Wendy died, when three hundred thousand came back into the account from the Bank of Cayman Brac. Wendy had been getting ready to settle with Sisemore. Now that responsibility had fallen to me.

Negotiating with Sam Dee was going to be a game of skill and chance, like poker. Neither of us knew what cards the other player held. I didn't know whether Dee knew how much Wendy had embezzled and he didn't know her estate had three hundred twenty thousand available to pay Sisemore back, no more and no less—unless I could find out where the other money went when it left the Bank of Cayman Brac.

Sam Dee and his wife lived in a community where I had to check in at the gatehouse to be let in. The community was called Broken Top because it had good views of the fractured volcano to the west. The mountain wasn't as high as the Three Sisters or Mt. Bachelor but it was closer to Bend and it dominated the view from the golf course. Dee's house had that same view, over the fourteenth fairway to acres of sagebrush still clawing back to life almost thirty years after a fire had burned it to the ground. I couldn't see Sam's view at night in the winter but I knew it was there. I'd seen the doctor's house twice from the golf course while playing there as a guest.

Sam met me at the door and introduced me to Charlotte. It was the first time I'd met her. She was a short brunette with a warm but subdued smile. Stand-offish, I thought, in contrast to the bubbly manner of the doctor. She left us right after Sam hung my coat on a wooden peg in the front hall.

"Let's sit in the living room." He led the way from the front hall to the room beyond it. "Can I offer you a drink?"

"No, thanks," I said with a friendly, grateful smile. "It's evening but this is still a business meeting."

"Gotcha," he said. "Shall we sit at a table? I didn't bring any papers but sitting at a table seems right for a business discussion." He led me to a polished wooden game table with a checkerboard painted on the top of it. We sat in leather chairs turned halfway toward the table and halfway toward the room. Sam crossed his legs.

"Well, Sarah, I've spoken to the other doctors and we're planning to hire a forensic accountant to determine how much Wendy took from us, and then go to court to get what's due."

"That will cost your doctors a lot of money with no guarantee that they will prevail. Even if my client did take the money, do you know where it all is? I don't." That was true for virtually all the money, excepting the three hundred thousand now at the Bank of Boise and the twenty thousand at the Bank of Cayman Brac. I turned my ignorance to my advantage. "No matter what number the accountants come up with you may not be able to get it back."

"That's a good opening statement, Sarah," he said. "But I was hoping we could skip all the tough talk and simply name an amount. I knew Wendy pretty well and I've never seen any sign she was spending more than her salary. No expensive cars, no fancy clothes, no vacations in far off places. So I think the money is still there somewhere. The deal that Sisemore would like to see is we get the money back, or most of it, and we agree not to pursue the matter any further. We don't go to the police and we don't say anything about it to the media."

That was music to my ears. "How much do you expect Wendy's estate to pay you?"

"We think she owes us about five hundred thousand," said Dee. It was a much better number than I was afraid I would hear, much lower than the two million Wendy said she had taken. But it was still higher than the cash available.

"I don't think the estate can manage five hundred thousand," I said. "I think two hundred fifty thousand would be a fairer figure." Sam gave me a sharp glance before gazing into the room to ponder the number. "You'd avoid a lot of hassle and risk," I added.

"Four hundred thousand," he said. "That's as low as we can go. Not a penny less. But we've been talking theoretically here. Up in the air, unattached to the earth below. How much cash does the estate have and do you have the power to deliver it?"

"I am the executor of Mrs. Whitlock's estate. I can pay her debts and I can pay the amount we settle on. But there isn't that much. The estate can do two hundred fifty thousand."

Sam gave me an even sharper look than before. Incredulity mixed with anger. He scowled at the room before he turned back to me, uncrossed his legs, sat square across the table, and glowered at me with barely controlled fury. "It's four hundred thousand or forget it," he said. "I will make your life a holy hell and Sisemore will wind up with at least that much." He was a good actor, was Sam Dee. He could recount this entire conversation to his partners and they would be convinced it was genuine. Perhaps he was even recording it.

I was not affected by Sam's anger, real or feigned. This was not my first negotiation.

"The most I can possibly do," I said, "with no money left for Wendy's estate to pay taxes or legal fees is three hundred thousand. Can we agree on that and consider the matter closed with the promise of no further legal action by Sisemore?"

Sam's face was still angry but he paused to consider my offer. "All right, we can agree to that if you're sure you can deliver it," said Sam, his scowl gradually giving way to an expression of relief, perhaps on its way back to the jolly confidence he had projected every time I'd seen him before. I'd brought two copies of an agreement with the amount of restitution blank. I filled in three hundred thousand and signed both copies as executor of Wendy's estate. If Sam and the managing partner of his clinic would sign the document I would wire the money to Sisemore.

"You know you'll want to talk with your tax accountant," I said, "about how Sisemore is going to describe this sudden influx of cash."

"We'll think of something. Maybe imaginary patients from out of the country who paid cash. No insurance to wrangle with." That was a shifty idea and not what I expected. For all his charm and self-assurance I had thought Sam would steer closer to the law and the truth. I was glad I wasn't his lawyer.

It was cold outside when Sam opened the front door.

"Why don't you start your car and come back inside while it warms up?" he said, still gracious, poised, and considerate, a doctor, a gentleman, and a generous human being.

"That's okay," I said. "I have my coat and the car has heated seats." I wasn't an old lady yet and I wasn't going to act like one. Nonetheless he gripped my arm firmly above the elbow and walked with me down the steps. He was a strong man. That was the point. He wanted me to know that. His one obvious flaw, as visible as his virtues, was that he was vain. Kernels of snow crunched under my feet.

I drove home in empty streets. No pedestrians braving the cold. No one hunched over while stepping briskly between their car and a bar. My negotiation with Sam had been a success. Wendy's estate would not find itself in court and Ethan Whitlock might get some money if I could ever find out where it went. Wendy's legacy, ill-gotten as it might be, would not go down the drain in attorney fees. Warren would not be charged with complicity in Wendy's crime and Wendy's name and reputation would stay pristine. I could tell Bud, waiting at home for me, that I'd had a small victory, even if I couldn't tell him much about the case.

Chapter 12

# Sheriff's Detective Carl Breuninger

I didn't summon Sam to the sheriff's office, I invited him. Our interview about Wendy Whitlock's death would be an excuse for a friendly visit to my place of work. I would introduce Sam to the Sheriff and show him around the department before we sat down to talk about Wendy. I needed Sam to round out my picture of Wendy's life. I still had to decide whether her death was a murder we needed to investigate further or simply the suicide it first appeared to be.

My motives in making this visit interesting for Sam, and hopefully pleasant, were twofold. First, he was a friend and we had fished together in Wyoming. I thought he would like to get an insider's tour of the sheriff's office and meet the sheriff. But my second motive, which I had in almost every interview I had, was to get the interviewee to relax, to feel safe, and to trust me with whatever he might have qualms about revealing. I hoped Sam would even enjoy telling me about his practice and Wendy Whitlock's role in it.

Sheriff Knapp, Walter, helped me out. He got a little community relations out of it. He and Sam both knew members of the City Council and the board of St. Charles Hospital. Walt and Sam chatted away as though they had all day but they actually spent less than two minutes together. I showed Sam around the department and we walked over to the forensic lab in a separate building. We couldn't go into the lab itself or inside the county jail but Sam enjoyed the tour nonetheless. Back in the sheriff's break room I offered him a cup of coffee. He didn't want coffee because he was operating the next day and needed his hands to be steady. As steady as a rock at the bottom of a river, he said. He took a paper cup of tap water and we moved to the interview room. I told him our conversation would be recorded but he wasn't under oath and if there was a question he didn't want to answer he could pass on it. He said he didn't mind the recording and he wanted to be as helpful as possible.

Wendy was hired as a bookkeeper in 2005 and became the office manager for Sisemore in 2008. She handled personnel, finances, and buying whatever equipment and supplies the practice needed. She was a trusted employee.

"As I think you know, Carl, doctors can be very high and mighty with anyone who isn't a doctor. But if one of us didn't have his act together on billing or trying to buy something for the practice, Wendy would demand we do it right. We obeyed because she always had the facts on her side and the board, the doctors who oversaw the practice, would back her up. If you had a disagreement with Wendy you knew you would eventually lose and the other doctors would wince at your prima donna act. She was friendly enough, though, as long as you stayed on the straight and narrow."

"Any problems with anyone, inside or outside of the clinic?" I asked.

"None, really. From what I knew she had a good marriage and her son Ethan wasn't getting into trouble. Happy home life as far as I know. I don't know why she would commit suicide but people have strange reasons."

"Can you think of any reason anyone else would want to kill her?"

Sam stared at the corner of the ceiling while he thought about his answer. But he didn't stare long. "I've been asking myself that and I can't come up with anything. I hate to think of Wendy committing suicide and that doesn't seem like something she would do. But I can't think of anyone who had any reason to kill her. And given who she was it's hard to imagine that anyone would want to. Could it have been some random guy who picked her out somewhere and followed her home?"

"Could be," I said. Professionally non-committal.

"There is something you should know and I ought to tell you for the record," said Sam. "It doesn't reflect well on Wendy but it's over and done with. The clinic and Wendy's attorney agreed to put it behind us and forget it ever happened." He eyed me so I would realize he was telling me something that he and his fellow doctors would rather keep hidden, possibly something I would never find out except through him. He was playing the hero again, the key man who would tell me, based on our friendship, what no one else would.

"There's no nice way to say this," said Sam. "Wendy took money from the clinic. She embezzled. This was a few years ago. It wasn't obvious at all. It was just that some of us had this gnawing feeling that the clinic should be making more money. Dr. McGrath did a back of the envelope analysis. Well, he did it in an Excel spreadsheet but it didn't include every last detail, only approximations. He looked at what we were charging, what our expenses were, and what we paid out to the doctors. It simply didn't seem to square with the reports we were getting from Wendy. The doctors appointed me to look into it.

"I hated asking Wendy about it. We'd worked together for years and I knew she had more facts at her fingertips than I would ever have. But I went in her little office, closed the door, and told her how things looked. She admitted it right away. Surprised the hell out of me. She said she'd been taking money for years. She'd been hiding it. Neither her husband nor anyone else knew about it. She said she wished she'd never started it and absolutely did not want to go to jail."

"Do you think any of the doctors could be angry enough to kill her or even threaten her?"

"I can't imagine it," said Sam. "Doctors aren't only in it for the money, you know. Most of us truly want to help people. It's why we became doctors. Besides, the doctors here could afford to lose the money. They barely suspected it was missing."

"So how did you leave it with Wendy when you talked with her?"

"Wendy said she knew she would be found out someday and she would be having the conversation that she and I were having right there in her office. She was glad it was me and not the police or some of the other doctors. Then she said she was ready with a proposition. What if she gave the money back? All of it. All she wanted in return was a promise the clinic wouldn't get the law involved and wouldn't press charges. And she wanted to keep her job. She'd learned her lesson, she said. She'd been in hell over this and she never wanted to go through that again. She would be so scrupulous we'd never have dime missing anywhere. I said she should give the money back if she felt so bad about it. Then we'd see what the legal situation was."

"'The clinic is not getting this money without an agreement not to prosecute,' she said. 'It's the only leverage I have to stay out of jail and I'm going to use it.'"

"And when did all this happen?"

"My conversation with Wendy?" asked Sam. "About a month ago. And then she died. The attorney representing Wendy's estate, Sarah Chatham, brought us an agreement and we signed it. Three hundred thousand in restitution. We got the money last Friday. We have a committee to work out how to distribute it to the doctors."

"Embezzling is a crime," I said. "Does the district attorney's office know about this?"

"We haven't contacted them. Now Wendy's dead there doesn't seem any point."

"You should write a letter to the DA anyway," I said. "If he hears about it later and Sisemore hasn't told him about it, he may give you a hard time."

"I've told you about it," said Sam laughing, "and I think that's enough." Sam was a friend but he could be an asshole. He was making more work for me and putting me in an awkward position. I was going to have to tell the DA's office about the embezzlement, probably write a report they'd have to read, and at the same time explain why I didn't think they should pay any attention to it.

"How did the embezzlement work?" I asked. "How did Wendy

get the money out of the company?"

"I don't know," said Sam. "None of us know. We simply felt we weren't making as much money as we should. But we didn't know where the leak was. We debated for a long time about getting a thorough audit of our books. As I told you, when I finally talked to Wendy about it she came forward with the truth and made us an offer. She felt terrible about it, she said, but once she got started, she said, it was hard to stop. She said she had hardly spent any of it and she would give back virtually all of it."

"And how did you arrive at the three-hundred-thousand-dollar figure?"

"That was the figure we negotiated with Sarah Chatham, Wendy's attorney. We think it is close to the amount Wendy took and, in any case, according to Sarah, the amount that the estate had available to pay. Sarah negotiated pretty hard."

"I get the picture. But I'm still calculating why Wendy Whitlock was murdered. Did Wendy get into debt thinking she had all that money?"

"I don't know but I doubt it. She was too smart and too disciplined for that. I saw no signs of big spending. No fancy clothes, no expensive cars, no trips to Vegas."

"Drug problems?"

"I'm a doctor. I think I would have spotted any. And she didn't seem the type."

"You're a doctor, Sam," I said, "and I'm a cop. A lot of druggies don't seem the type."

"I bet you're right," he said. "She didn't seem the type to embezzle either." Sam cocked his head at me and squinted a little. "I think she did it because she could. She wanted to exercise her brain. She calculated the odds and she liked them, like holding twenty in blackjack and the dealer is showing a six. She wasn't greedy. She just liked to win."

"Do you know any reason why she might decide to commit suicide?"

"Your guess is as good as mine," said Sam. "Remorse over

embezzling? Fear of getting caught? Something in her home life that none of us knew anything about? She didn't seem stressed or depressed. Have you checked whether she had cancer or early Alzheimer's?"

"The autopsy will find whatever diseases she might have had. Nobody, including you, has mentioned any sign of mental breakdown."

I was done with the interview. I wanted to step out of our roles in this investigation and reaffirm our relationship as friends, or at least as fishing buddies. An indulgence on my part, I guess. Sam may have been thinking the same thing. He turned the tables on me and I was glad to have him do it.

"What do you think, Carl? Will we ever know what happened? In my field, for all the training a doctor gets, and all the advances in medical science, we can't figure out what's wrong with some people. They have terrible pain, or they haven't got the energy to get out of bed. We can't figure out what's wrong. We can't help them. I suppose that happens in police work too."

"More often than I'd like," I said. "But it's often a question of time and resources. Somebody knows what happened even if it's only the perp. If we can dig hard enough and long enough we'll find the person." I went into a story to show Sam what I meant. A little insight into law enforcement, a little friendship maintenance.

"We had a case where we had rash of burglaries at Upriver Ranch, down south of Lava Butte. No fingerprints. The burglars wore gloves. They robbed empty vacation homes at night. Nobody saw them. All we knew was a neighbor saw a dirty white pickup near one of the robberies—no make or model or license number. We got DNA but so many people had been in and out of those houses it was impossible to analyze it all. Then a rich guy who lived in the neighborhood, hadn't even been robbed himself, decided to hire a detective agency to track the criminals down. We gave his detective a list of what had been stolen and some of it was big stuff, like a snowplow attachment for a truck and an air compressor on a trailer. The detective hired two men to drive around the area where the robberies were, in wider and wider circles, searching for the stolen equipment and the white pickup. It took days and they repeated the circuit to make sure they didn't miss anything. They found fifteen houses with white pickups parked in the front or on the street and some piece of construction equipment in the truck or on the driveway or lawn. They ranked the houses from most likely to least likely. Then the detective went and talked to the people next door to the houses. No warrants, no police presence. Just a guy knocking on the door. People told him they hadn't seen anything suspicious or they simply told the detective to get lost. But he found one old lady who was tired of her neighbors coming and going at all hours of the night, playing loud music and smelling up the air with marijuana smoke. She said she'd seen them unloading their pickup truck late at night. Things she'd seen, mostly big-screen TVs, matched up with goods reported stolen. She could only remember two dates when she'd seen the late night unloading but they matched up with the dates of two burglaries. So the rich guy and his detective came to us with everything they knew and pictures and the license plate number of the truck. It was enough for us to get a search warrant.

"The district attorney said he could prosecute the guys in the house for possession of stolen goods but unless they turned on each other he couldn't convict them of actually stealing the stuff. So we needed the old lady to testify who'd she seen unloading the truck. She was afraid to do that because they could have broken her door down and beaten her to death without breaking a sweat.

"She was renting her house and living hand to mouth off Social Security. The rich guy told his detective to offer her a brand new house and car in Arizona along with thirty thousand dollars if she would testify. She took it. The guy probably spent more money than the value of what the burglars took in the first place. He never got his name in the press and no one knew what he did, not even his friends who had been burglarized."

"Why did he do it, the rich guy?" asked Sam.

"He said he wanted to keep the area a good place to live and that meant keeping it safe."

"Justice is different for the rich, I guess." A slightly odd comment from a guy who was pretty wealthy himself.

"Well," I said, "he got those bozos off the street and protected a lot of taxpayers at no expense to them. It's better than spending his money on a chateau in France. But my point is that justice costs time and money. Catching criminals depends on the resources you want to put into it."

Chapter 13

# Sarah Chatham

Natasha Korel, the junior associate in our office, had been on a team to compete in the Pole Pedal Paddle. But the team fell apart when Wendy Whitlock died. Natasha said she had decided to run the entire race on her own. She'd moved to Bend from our Portland office expressly for the area's outdoor sports and the race brought five of them together in one event. No golf, mountain biking, or snowmobiling but just about everything else. I allowed her to adjust her work schedule to fit in her training. She was mostly reading and writing documents anyway, not meeting with clients, so the adjusted times would hardly interfere with her work at all.

She could do some training at night—lifting weights and running on a treadmill—but skiing and bicycling she had to do when it was light out. Twice a week she'd leave at lunchtime and come back at six, a little pooped but flushed and tanned from her exercise. Dan's wife, Amy, was training for the race as well. I seemed to be surrounded by racers.

My two children, Kurt and Kate, with their spouses, stayed with Bud and me during ski week in February. Kurt, the oldest and taller than any of his forbearers, drove over from Portland with Gwen, his wife. Kurt had met Gwen in Alaska where he was scratching out a living as a wildlife photographer and she was an administrator for the Indian health service. She was an Alaska native from Fairbanks who graduated from the University of Alaska. Kurt was a movie producer for documentaries now, more of a businessman than an artist as he put it, and Gwen was an assistant dean for alumni at Lewis and Clark College.

Kate and her husband came all the way from Hawaii. She was the reservations manager for a resort hotel on the beach but they lived in a pretty little town up in the hills away from the tourists. Her husband was an astronomer at an observatory at the top of Mauna Kea.

The two guest rooms in my house had photos of Kurt and Kate's childhood on the wall, including a portrait photo of their father who had died before I met Bud and married him. I still missed Ray but I shared my life with Bud now. I thanked God he had come along. Every once in a while I went into a guest room to study Ray's picture. I didn't have any other pictures of him hanging in the house. I was sure he would understand.

My children and their spouses had hatched a plan among them and sprung it on Bud and me over a special Norwegian dinner we had at home. My parents were both of Norwegian descent, as many Bend residents were when I was a child, and I'd had mutton and cabbage throughout my childhood. My children had grown up with it too. It wasn't elegant but it was a hearty dish that should suit them well after a long day of skiing.

"This is terrific," said Kate's husband, knowing how to warm the heart of his mother-in-law. Lars actually was Norwegian. He'd grown up there and I was sure he'd had this dish many times before.

It was Kate who broached the idea. "We want to come back in May to do the PPP as a family team. Is it acceptable for us to invite ourselves?"

"Delighted," I said. Bud said that would be wonderful.

"We still have to sort out who is going to do which event but it will be fun."

"And something we can train for without all being in the same place," said Kurt.

"We want you and Bud to be on the team," said Kate, "if you're willing."

"Your mother would be perfect for the bicycling," said Bud. "It's all downhill." My children, and their spouses even more, didn't know whether to take this suggestion seriously or not. I knew Bud was joking. At least I hoped he was.

"Are you racing for time or for a countryside outing?" I asked. "Because I'm not going to speed down that road on a bicycle risking life and limb. My reactions aren't as quick as they were and my bones take longer to heal."

"Oh, we're racing," said Kate. "We're not training for a picnic."

"I'm out," I said.

"I think you should do the sprint at the end," said Kurt. "It will take you less than ten minutes and you get all the glory of crossing the finish line for the team." Well, I could at least jog a mile even if I was almost seventy. Not in ten minutes, perhaps, but all my essential parts were working, including the knee that Samuel Dee had so expertly replaced.

We decided Lars would do the cross-country because he'd grown up doing it in Norway.

"I won't be able to practice much in Hawaii but when it does snow at the top of the mountain I'll go out and shuffle around."

Kurt would do the bike and Kate would do the run. Gwen would do the kayak. She could practice on the Willamette River and the Columbia Slough.

Long before the race Bud and I made a point of keeping ourselves fit so we could hike, ski, and play golf. But I would have to work at it if I were going to run. The good news was I could probably improve a lot in the three months before the race. The bad news, I suppose, was I'd have to be a little more cautious skiing for the rest of the season. I couldn't afford to lose my place on the team by straining a muscle. Actually, if I couldn't do the mile then Kate or Gwen could step in and do it. But I dearly wanted to be part of the team, to do my part. It surprised me how much I cared.

We had apple cake and ice cream for dessert and toasted the Chatham family team with brandy. A happy time for a happy family. Kate would order t-shirts for our team and we all had dreams of glory in the race. Bud said he and I would do the dishes so the next generation could get up early for skiing the next day. We waved them all upstairs to bed.

The only thing that could make me happier about my family, though I didn't push it, was the prospect of grandchildren. No news so far.

"When they are teenagers we don't want them to have sex," said Bud. He had children of his own that we also loved. "When they are adults we wish they would."

Chapter 14

# Sheriff's Detective Carl Breuninger

I knew Sarah Chatham from an earlier case and I thought she might tell me a lot about Wendy Whitlock, at least her finances, that I didn't understand yet. Like any attorney, Sarah would use the law in the interests of her client, even if her client were dead. But Sarah wasn't cynical about the law, as many lawyers were, and she believed in justice. In her sixties, she'd run a car into a flagpole, risking her own life, to stop a fugitive from fleeing the country. Her response to my call was not a surprise.

"Carl, do I really have to come into your office for this?" she asked. "I will tell you anything that doesn't compromise my client's interest. There is a line between what I can tell you and what I can't and that line is not going to move one scintilla if I'm sitting in a bare bones interview room. Can you ask your questions over the phone?"

My habit and my instinct would be to get Sarah into the office and control the interview as much as possible. But she wouldn't be intimidated and she wouldn't be thrown off-balance. She would only get annoyed and that wouldn't help. I might need more of her cooperation in the future. Even now, if she were relaxed and willing to help, she might come up with some useful ideas.

"Okay," I said, "let's start over the phone and see where it gets us.

How about now?"

"I have twenty minutes," she said, "and we can continue later if necessary. I don't think I have that much to tell you."

"Am I right that you represent Wendy Whitlock's estate and that the estate agreed to pay Sisemore Orthopedics three hundred thousand dollars in restitution for Wendy's embezzlement from them?"

"The agreement says nothing about embezzlement or restitution. The estate agreed to pay a certain sum to Sisemore if they promised not to make any further claims or press any charges against the estate or any member of Mrs. Whitlock's family."

"And what is the value of the estate?"

"Attorney client privilege," said Sarah.

"Come on, Sarah," I said in an amicable tone. "I already have the copy of the will you faxed me."

"That tells you where she wants her estate to go," said Sarah, "but it doesn't tell you how much the estate is worth."

"So answer me this. Why did Mrs. Whitlock hire you?"

"Three reasons: She wanted me to help her in negotiating with Sisemore. She wanted me to verify that her last will and testament was valid. And she wanted me to be the executor of her will. I've done the first two and I'm still executing the will and arranging to file a tax return."

"Okay," I said, "so when did Mrs. Whitlock hire you?"

"Two weeks before she died."

"Did she say anything to suggest she thought her death was imminent?"

"Nothing," said Sarah.

"Did she seem fearful or depressed?" I asked.

"Not in the least. She was a businesslike woman taking care of business. Everyone should have a will. She made a will with a form she downloaded and she wanted to check that it was valid."

"And why did she want to make you the executor?"

"She never said. The first I knew I was the executor was when I read her will. I want to be helpful, Carl, but I have to protect my client and, frankly, there are things I don't know or understand myself. It seemed to me when I met with her that this was the first time she had hired an attorney for herself and, now that she had one, she thought she might as well ask that attorney to be her executor. That's the way it seemed at the time. But if she was thinking she might die soon, and I repeat she gave no sign of it, the Sisemore negotiation would likely take place after she died and it would make sense to have one attorney handle both the negotiation and the will."

"Sarah," I said, in a hard-pressed tone, "I'm trying to determine whether the woman committed suicide or was killed by someone else. Can you shed some light on this? Do you have any ideas? Got a clue either way?"

"She was in trouble with this Sisemore thing but she was handling it, at least working on handling it. No other issues I know about. She seemed a woman who had her act together, a sense of purpose, a sense of connection to the world—her family and her work. From what I know I can't picture Wendy Whitlock killing herself. But I have no idea who might have wanted to kill her. Aside from Sisemore I think she was square with the world."

"What is your impression of Warren Whitlock, the husband? He's not a suspect but Wendy's family might be the key to whatever is going on."

"Mr. Whitlock wasn't happy when I met him but he wasn't falling apart either. And I have no insight into what might have been going on between him and Wendy. As far as a financial incentive to kill her, it doesn't seem worth the risk. Her estate goes to their son, not to him. He gets her half ownership in the house and the landscaping business, plus odds and ends in bank accounts and fifty thousand dollars in life insurance that Wendy had through Sisemore."

"Anything else?" I asked.

"Well, there's one thing," said Sarah. "It's more a funny feeling than a fact. Lawyers like facts and don't like funny feelings. But you may want to hear this. Negotiating the settlement with Dee was almost too easy."

"He took your first offer?" I asked.

"No," said Sarah. "It was more as though he knew how much

money the estate could get its hands on. It almost seemed that Dee and Wendy had already decided on the settlement and Wendy sent me in to make it look like an arm's length negotiation."

"They were in cahoots," I said.

"Maybe," said Sarah. "It's an idea."

## Chapter 15

# Amy Martinez

On race day Dan would help me with the later transitions in the race, from the bike to the run to the kayaking to the final sprint. Sean would help me with the transitions up at Mt. Bachelor, from the downhill ski to the cross-country ski and then to the bike. Sean drove me, my skis and boots, and my duffel bag up the mountain in his Hummer, as glossy white as a washing machine. I'd never been in his Hummer before. The ceiling was low and the windshield was short, top to bottom, as though we were in a moveable dugout. It was spacious side-to-side, with a high hump between the seats for an elaborate gear shift and a cavernous storage compartment. I relaxed and we didn't talk much. I was going to thank Sean several times today and I didn't want to overdo it, as though I were reciting by rote.

Sean dropped me and my skis at the base of the slope and parked. He would reappear two hours later to help me in the transitions from the downhill to the cross-country and from the cross-country to the bicycle. I walked to the bottom of the lift up to Pine Marten Lodge. I thought racers should get the lift to themselves but we had to wait in line with people who had come to ski for the day and had nothing to do with the race. I rode up with three people who didn't even realize there was a race.

I'd gotten there early to have a practice run on the downhill course set on a ski trail called LeeWay. Then I'd take the chairlift up a second time, leave my skis at the top of the run, and walk two hundred feet downhill in my ski boots to the race's start point with an uphill run.

The racers started the race in waves, the elites in the first wave with individuals and teams of all ages and genders in the following waves. I was in Wave Three for women competing as individuals. I'd run up the two hundred feet on my own a few times to get my bearings. I'd heard of a woman in a past year doing the cross-country leg on a relay team whose trainer took her to the wrong starting place. When she realized the mistake she had to run a thousand feet up the hill to get to the official start. She was in such good shape, though, that she made the climb in her cross-country skis and still had the energy to pass people on the course. She was exhausted at the end but she was the legend of the entire race. I wanted to make absolutely certain I was in the right place at the right time.

The uphill run was designed to spread us out so we didn't all start off on our skis at the same time. We'd burn a lot of energy and get our hearts pumping right before we even started skiing. The air smelled like we were baking cookies rather than getting ready for a race. We were spraying the bottoms of our boots with PAM so we wouldn't have to scrape snow off the boots to fit them into our ski bindings. Not a lot of chatter. Each woman was in her own world. I wished "good luck" to Natasha in a strong voice that probably sounded as much like a challenge as it did encouragement. She wished me a short "good luck" with an abbreviated wave. If I could keep my head, the thought of beating Natasha, even the concept of losing to her, could spur me on to my best effort.

The surprise in the group was the girl from Oregon State who had joined Grace's pick-up team and then lost interest. I resented her being there. She was irresponsible and self-indulgent. She probably hadn't trained hard for this race, at least not in any disciplined way. Yet here she was, on equal footing with the rest of us. She didn't acknowledge Natasha or me or even seem to recognize us.

"Don't get rattled," I told myself. "Concentrate. Think. Do what you practiced. Keep up the pace."

I beat most of the women in the uphill run to where our skis were waiting. I slammed my skis down, snapped into the bindings, grabbed my poles, and started off, first aiming not to collide with anyone and then picking up speed as I flew down the slalom. The downhill was a short portion of the overall race. This was not where it would be won or lost. But I was in my element and it gave me confidence. I passed five women on the way down. Only two women passed me and one of them ran off the course right after she did. The other was the OSU student. She was fast and she was brave.

I didn't see Natasha in the transition to the cross-country skiing. Sean positioned my cross-country skis and put a mat down in the snow where I could shuck my downhill boots and put on my cross-country boots. New poles, a quick "thanks" to Sean, and I took off.

The cross-country would take a strenuous thirty minutes. I pushed hard with every step but paced myself, breathing deeply but steadily in the thin mountain air. After twenty minutes, Natasha passed me. My legs were strong but Natasha's stride was longer, more graceful, more efficient. We didn't acknowledge each other, both focused on getting the most out of every second. She had already left on her bike when I got to the next transfer.

I changed from my Nordic boots to the running shoes that would fit into the toe clips on my bike pedals. Sean laced up my shoes while I gulped down a bottle of Gatorade and sucked down a Gu for nourishment. There were plastic water bottles on the handlebars when I needed to hydrate more. I took off straining to accelerate across the enormous flat ski area parking lot. The twenty-six miles down to Bend and the river would be a good leg for me. I felt at home on a bike no matter what surface I was riding over. Most of the ride would be downhill. I would need confidence more than power to ride fast. Confidence in my bike, my skills, and my ability to dodge other riders who got in trouble or behaved erratically.

I listened carefully for cars coming from behind me, especially for the first four miles. After that almost all the downhill traffic had to take the road to Sunriver instead of staying on the road to Bend with the bicyclists. That was to keep the bicyclists safe. The few cars that were allowed to continue downhill to Bend were carrying one member of a two-person pair team, the member who wasn't doing the bicycle leg. Hardly any cars would pass me in my direction after the Sunriver turnoff, maybe none, because the pair teams hadn't started until thirty minutes after I did. Cars did pass me going uphill, in the opposite direction, on the other side of the road. The road was open all day in the uphill direction so that skiers coming to the mountain simply to ski, nothing to do with the race, could still get there.

One car that passed me from behind, swinging way over to the other side of the road to give me a wide berth, was Sean Wray's white Hummer with my skis and poles in top of it. Sean had found a way to drive directly to Bend on the same road as the bicyclists. Sean was an exception to the Sunriver turnoff rule because his passenger would be Dr. Dee, the Surgeon of Record for the race. Dr. Dee told Sean he needed to be where most of the racers were and that meant the ski area in the beginning and the end. Dee's role, Sean said, was as much honorary as functional. There was a medical tent at the finish line and there were ambulances with EMT's along the course. But Dee was a big cheese and could take the direct route. Sean beeped hello after he passed me. I nodded back in acknowledgment though I doubted he could see my abbreviated nod in his mirror.

Over the next mile and a half, after the Sunriver turnoff, the road climbed two hundred feet in the bike leg's one uphill stretch. It was critical to my race plan to power through that stretch and pick up some time. I passed four women and one man going up that hill. Three men passed me but it didn't matter. They weren't my competition.

At the peak of the road where it began to go downhill a car sped out of a gravel road on my right and almost hit me. I hadn't allowed for anything like that and a flash of panic shot through me. I gripped my brakes as hard as I could, almost falling over my handlebars. My front wheel was inches from a small gray sedan and I could see the driver plainly. He was a thin-faced man roughly forty years old wearing a heavy lined hat with ear flaps folded down, a hat like the Forest Service wears in the winter. He looked anxious and he didn't scan for traffic when he pulled out onto the road and turned left toward the mountain.

I stepped hard on my pedals and cursed at the seconds I'd lost stopping for that idiot. I was so focused I didn't think until later the car could have killed or injured me. In mountain biking I had to slow down, dodge obstacles, and speed up all the time. I told myself I probably handled this near accident better, both physically and mentally, than most of my competitors would have. I was already back in the race.

I wore my ski gloves the whole bike ride so the air rushing past wouldn't chill my hands. The road was dry but there was a gusty wind from the southeast that threatened my balance. I stayed far away from the road's painted lines because they were slicker than the asphalt. I rode as fast as I dared.

Doubts crept in as I knew they could in a long race. It was painful to exert myself this much. It was risky to be going this fast. What was I doing? I didn't need to do this. I was not fleeing the advance of an army or racing for a million-dollar prize. I was racing for vanity, really, and that was foolish. I should slow down, meet Dan at the next transition, and tell him I was done with it. We should go home and be happy to be there.

Dan would not criticize me. He would understand. But he would be disappointed. And pretty soon, I knew, I'd be even more bitterly disappointed. I imagined how much work it would take to try this race again. How foolish I'd feel starting training again when here I was almost fully trained and halfway through the race already. I might not even get the chance to run this race again. This could be it for all time. I remembered all the work I'd put in and how disappointed my past self would be to find out I'd quit. I decided, with renewed conviction, that this day was my day and I steeled myself to make the absolute best of it.

On the straightaways I could see Natasha ahead of me, in the distance at first and then closer as we came further down the hill. I was catching up and I felt the urge to overtake her rise up inside me. I knew I had to make a judgment. Was it worth expending more energy now to get ahead or should I conserve my energy for the run and the kayak? I experimented with pedaling five to ten percent faster, not a lot. I found I could sustain the pace without feeling overtaxed. Natasha was no slouch and if she knew I were catching up it might spur her to pick up the pace. Thirty feet behind her I slowed my pace to match hers and save some energy. Five minutes later I passed her at a faster pace but one I could sustain until we were done with the bikes. I thought she might try to speed up but she didn't. From here to the transition point I could see Natasha behind me. I could only hope the gap between us was widening.

Only one person passed me the whole way downhill, a man on a top-of-the-line aero bike.

When I got to the transition I threw my gloves on the ground with my jacket and my bike helmet on top of them. Dan took my bike while I grabbed a bottle and took two gulps of water.

"Eighty-nine thirty-one, you're doing great," Dan yelled at me, calling me by the number on my racer's bib. My target was to get to this transition in under ninety minutes and I had made it. Dan was the most important adult in the world to me, and I'd barely nodded to him—less attention than I'd give a ticket taker. He would understand.

Most of the running trail was level but I had to keep an eye out for rocks and roots sticking up out of the dirt. There was one place where the trail climbed up and over a short hill of boulders. I'd made this run many times in practice and knew exactly where I wanted to place my feet going up and going down. But after the skiing and the bike ride my legs did not have the spring in them I was used to. I had to find a new path with new steps and be more careful coming down the far side.

"On your left," I heard as I approached the footbridge over the Deschutes, roughly the halfway mark in the run. Natasha passed me and I kept up with her for the next two hundred yards but it was too much. I wasn't keeping a rhythm my body could handle. I went back to the speed I knew. Damn.

Running down the west side of the river I passed the girl I'd forgotten about, the OSU student who had once been our downhill skier on Grace's team. She was a good athlete, obviously, but she hadn't paced herself. She'd overdone it in the cross-country skiing and the bike. She was getting tired and slowing down. Her head and shoulders were beginning to hang forward. She would never catch up. She might not even finish the race.

I knew where Dan and I had left the kayak yesterday evening but there were hundreds more people obscuring my view when I got to Riverbend Park. On a long bamboo pole we'd made a flag out my old blue and gold UC Santa Barbara t-shirt and I spotted Dan waving it high above the crowd.

Dan dropped the flag and handed me the life jacket I was required to wear. I would carefully avoid falling in the water, life jacket or no. The water temperature was fifty-one degrees and, with only the t-shirt I'd worn for the run, I'd lose critical time recovering the kayak, the paddle, and my equilibrium. The course started upriver, turned a long leg downriver, went around an island and then turned upriver again to the starting point. I should need a little under thirty minutes to complete the 2.4-mile course. I passed Natasha on the final upstream leg and we smiled at each other. Our competitive juices were running full flood but we were having fun, competing full throttle. Spectators had been dispassionate observers on the earlier legs and there hadn't been very many of them. Here lines of people on the shores cheered us on. Dan steadied my kayak as I climbed out of it. The rules wouldn't let him give me a hand up onto the shore.

I ran the one-mile sprint in chaotic desperation. My muscles were weak and I didn't have the energy I'd had before. People passed me and I passed people who were struggling more than I was. I knew Natasha was behind me, almost certainly running faster than I was, but I couldn't turn around to see where she was. I ran as fast as I dared, fearing my body would quit, ignoring the commands and pleas from my brain. My legs felt heavier and heavier, as though they were long buckets filling up with water. Thoughts of glory and pride were fading. The finish line called to me, less as proof of my accomplishment and more as a chance to finally stop, to rest, to be done with this torture for good and never race again in my life.

I ran through the final gate, jogged for ten steps, and slowed to a walk, hands on hips and breathing heavily. The clock for Wave Six read two hours, thirty-eight minutes, and sixteen seconds. I figured I'd crossed the finish line about ten seconds before that. I'd beaten my target by two minutes, give or take. Natasha came through the gate looking stronger than I felt. But she hadn't caught up. I congratulated her on finishing the race. I was gracious. She was gracious. We were brief.

The racers spilled into a grassy area with water, porta potties, the medical tent, and dozens of tired, dazed, but glowing racers milling around, basking in satisfaction. We happy few met each other's eyes, seeing in each other all the work, the worry, and the mental toughness that had gotten us through. Having others know, from their own experience, all I had accomplished was heady for a while. I hesitated to give up my transponder and leave this very special club.

But I wanted to see Dan, wanted to join the party in the amphitheater where the city held big concerts in the summertime. And I very much wanted to sit down. My legs felt in need of a federal infrastructure project, like bridge towers riddled with rust and likely to collapse without notice.

Mt. Bachelor shone white in the noonday sun and I took a secret moment to admire how far I had come. I'd run from winter to summer. Or at least spring about to become summer.

Dan had a beer in his hand for me and we managed to embrace without spilling beer all over us. Not that it mattered. The sweat in my t-shirt and shorts was sopping and I told Dan I was a mess already.

"A happy, glowing mess. How was the race?" he asked.

"Great," I said, "no problems. A little windy on the bike ride." Then I added in a whisper, "And I beat Natasha." Dan gave me a conspiratorial smile. My gloating was unbecoming, I knew, but I took real satisfaction in my narrow victory and Dan was happy for me. "Where's Sean?" I asked.

"Haven't seen him," said Dan. "Maybe Sam had some emergency he had to go to. Are you ready to go home?"

"Shower. Advil. Food. Nap. Yes I am."

Chapter 16

# Sarah Chatham

Bud picked up the racer packets for our team two days before the race. It had course maps, instructions, bibs for each of us with our team number on them, and the team's transponder, like a little electronic baton on an elastic band, that our racers needed to pass along to the next team member. All six of us got up early for breakfast though only the "mountain squad" had to leave at 7:00 to get to Mt. Bachelor in plenty of time to allow Kurt to get his bike checked in and Bud to get in one practice run on the downhill. The race started at 9:15 and the racers went off in twenty-four waves of about forty-five people. The Chatham Family Team, bib number 3407, was in the fourteenth wave, along with other Family Teams whose average age was forty-five to forty-nine, similar to ours at forty-six. In our group we might have a chance to do well. If we finished first, second, or third we would get a mug that signified our achievement. "Getting a mug" was the goal for all the contestants in all the various groups. Bud would start his mad dash uphill to his skis at 10:30.

We put the team's kayak at the launch point the night before so the three of us in the "flat country squad"—Kate, Gwen, and me—could all be at the Bend Athletic Club about 11:30 to meet Kurt finishing up the bicycle leg. Our squad had a leisurely breakfast and did the dishes. We sat around the living room, Kate and Gwen monitoring their phones while I tried to read. We were too keyed up to sit still very long and we left early, even if it meant hanging around in a parking lot.

I got a call from Bud as we backed out of the driveway. He had fallen at the end of the downhill but he hadn't gotten hurt and it cost only a few seconds in the race. Kurt and Lars, waiting for him at the bottom of run, had tried to wave Bud away from an icy spot where many skiers had fallen before him. Bud hadn't understood and he fell exactly where all the others had. He had to shuffle into the transition zone with only one ski on. But he had transferred the transponder to Lars and Lars had gone off on the cross-country skiing leg.

"We think a bicyclist must have gotten hurt," said Bud. "While Lars and Kurt were waiting for me at the bottom of the slope an ambulance and a sheriff's car took off down the road with sirens and lights going. I wanted you to know, if you hear about it, that everyone on our team is fine. Kurt was nowhere near the bicycle leg when the ambulance left."

Most years the race had no injuries at all, except for sore muscles, but the damage from falling off a bicycle at thirty-five miles an hour could be serious. I thought of Natasha and Amy, possibly on the bicycle leg race when the ambulance was called out. I hoped that the ambulance had nothing to do with either of them. Probably not. There were over a thousand people riding bicycles down the hill that day.

Bud went on to sheepishly confess that he and Kurt had been idiots. Once Lars took off on the cross-country, they decided they had time to get a cup of coffee. Kurt was cold and Bud needed to recover his breath. But Lars was faster than they thought and he skied his heart out. When Kurt and Bud put down their coffee and sashayed over to the ski-to-bike transition, they met Lars madly dashing to come and get them. Lars, the always composed astronomer, may have been angry but he didn't say so. Kurt took the transponder from him and ran the rest of the way to his bike. Our team had lost a good five minutes. We didn't have our hearts set on winning but still it was a disappointment. We'd all trained hard to do our best.

When the flat land team reached the Athletic Club parking lot,

Kate got out of the car to warm up for her five-mile run. We watched bicycle after bicycle come in, the riders transferring their transponders to teammates and wheeling their bikes away. We finally spotted Kurt and Gwen pushed forward to pull the transponder off his ankle. Kate leaned on Gwen while she slipped the transponder on. We shouted good luck as Kate took off but her mind was already on the run. I didn't think she heard us.

"Sorry I didn't start on time," said Kurt. "I didn't think Lars would be so fast."

"Never mind," said Gwen. "How was the ride?"

"I passed five people and two people passed me. I guess that's good. The road was dry but it was windy in places. It took me by surprise a couple of times. The bike held up but my legs are tired. I need to stretch them and then sit down."

"Did you see any accidents?" I asked.

"None at all," said Kurt. "If there was one the ambulance must have come and gone before I got there." He got a bottle of water and a banana from the aid station. We were comfortable standing in the sun, calm while others rushed around us.

"We need to get down the kayak launch and get ready," I said. "Kate will be there in forty minutes." We chained the bike to a tree because I didn't have a bike rack on my sedan.

The drive to Riverbend Park was only a mile and a half. But hundreds of other racers and support teams were driving the same route and trying to find parking at the end of it. We arrived with time to spare and waited next to the kayak we'd borrowed for Gwen, all three of us watching up the bank of the river for Kate to finish her run. We were in a crowd of other support teams and other kayakers waiting for their runners, all of us excited, none of us bored, and yet actually doing nothing at all until one small clot of people after another suddenly sprung into action to grab the transponder and get their kayaker in the water.

Kurt spotted Kate first and guided her to the transfer point. She sprinted as well as she could the last few yards.

I felt a little badly that we were more eager to get our hands on the transponder than to welcome Kate and congratulate her. My daughter, breathing hard the whole time, rested her hand on her brother's shoulder and lifted her foot while I got the transponder off her ankle and handed it to Gwen. Gwen, shorter than Kate, had to reach up higher to lean on Kurt and put the transponder on herself. Kurt carried the kayak down to the shore and held it steady in the water while Gwen climbed in. She'd been wearing her life vest and helmet since we left the car.

My two children and I retreated to higher ground to wait for Gwen's return.

"Do you want to wait in the car, Mom?" asked Kurt. "Gwen won't be back for at least half an hour." I said no, it was exciting to watch the runners and kayakers rush in and out, everyone focused, anxious, but in a happy kind of way. As fast as everyone was trying to go, no one cut anyone off, or jostled a competitor, or shot out an angry word—everyone competing but, at the same time, full of a common mission to do our best and to celebrate this day, this race, this place. Flags waved madly in the breeze across the river.

A young man came up to a group next to us, cell phone in hand. Apparently the group knew him.

"Someone's been shot," he said. "Up at Mt. Bachelor." I could tell by the expressions on their faces that his group didn't want to hear about it. Their minds were on the race. The young man spoke into the phone, listened a few seconds, and spoke to the group again. "It was along the bike route somewhere."

"We'll read about it in the paper tomorrow," said another young man. The news was a distraction, like a commercial on television or rumors of a coup in a third world country that he could not have found on a map. The man with the phone said, "Thanks" into it and put the phone in his pocket.

I had already handed my cell phone to Kurt to hold while I ran the last mile. I asked for it back and called Bud. I wanted to make sure that he and Lars were uninjured, that neither of them had by some wild twist of fate been the person who was shot. But I said I was calling to say our team was still very much in the race and we'd had no mishaps. Bud and Lars had driven past Sunriver long ago and were finding a parking place in the shopping center so they could walk across the river and join us. They didn't know anything about the shooting.

We spotted Gwen lashing up the river to the transition zone. Kurt and I met her as the kayak's bow touched the shore. She was too exhausted to get herself out of the kayak. Kurt dragged her up to her feet while I steadied the kayak and she stepped out into the water. With one arm wrapped around her legs, Kurt bent down and lifted her foot to get the transponder off her foot. I dragged the boat a few more feet onto the shore so it wouldn't float away. We lost some of the seconds that Gwen's supreme effort had gained us but the kayak next to us was having a worse time. The paddler had taken his transponder off before he beached the kayak and had dropped it in the river. Three of them were crawling in the water now, feeling along the muddy bottom for the transponder.

Kurt slipped the transponder up over my raised foot and yelled, "Go!" I took off, dodging my way through the mix of people on the shore then reaching the paved path that took me upriver, over a pedestrian bridge, down the other side, along a blocked-off path through part of the shopping center, and back over another pedestrian bridge to the finish line. I'd run this route ten times in training but it was totally different now. I'd run it on cold wet mornings and in a beautiful evening light. I shared the path with a few other runners and walkers and, here and there in the shopping center, people walking to and from shops, restaurants, and the movie theater. Today, in bright midday sun, there were more runners than ever, all going the same direction, and the course was lined with spectators, more and more cheering us on the farther along we got.

"Way to go!"

"Go for it!"

"You're doing great!"

They called out my bib number and told me to keep charging. I hoped none of my clients saw me straining in my Chatham family t-shirt, or maybe I hoped they would. I wasn't graceful or fast. I passed one old man but five other runners passed me. I was proud of myself nonetheless. Proud, motivated, and ecstatic to think I was the finisher for my family team.

The last bridge was jam-packed with people on either side of the narrow path that led right down the middle. The spectators yelled and clapped as though I were the one contestant they had been waiting for all along. It was a heady moment until I heard the same cheers for the runner behind me. I ran past the inflatable gate signifying the finish line and stopped on the asphalt where I rested my hands on my knees. Not for long. I needed to breathe deep and I had to stand up straight to get the maximum air my lungs could absorb. There was juice and Gatorade on a table and I leaned on the table to take my transponder off so I could turn it in. Bud met me and led me further into the grassy area to join the rest of the team, all of us smiling and feeling exultant. Even better, I realized later, than Christmas morning.

"Three hours, thirteen minutes," said Kate. "We did well whether we get a mug or not."

I put on the sweatshirt that Bud brought for me. We agreed we shouldn't care how we placed. But there was funny thing about racing. Once we were in it, we wanted to win.

Bud and Lars went to pick up the kayak and drive it home on the top of Bud's SUV. Kate drove the rest of us home in my Mercedes. Our team hadn't finished in our group's top three and we didn't get a mug.

"Next year!" said Gwen with a fist pump. I looked forward to it.

Chapter 17

# Sheriff's Detective Carl Breuninger

I was at the ski area the day of the race. I wore my uniform with a department parka and a gray fur hat with ear flaps tied together over the top, badge on the parka and gun on my belt. I would have to take my gloves off and open my coat to get the gun. I wasn't planning on using it.

I told the sheriff I would take this duty because I wanted to watch the race. It was a deputy's duty and I didn't have to do this sort of thing anymore. It was forty degrees and windy. There was a deputy in the ski area and another at the turn off to Sunriver on the road to Bend. He was there to back up the volunteers directing cars to Sunriver instead of allowing them to take the direct road to Bend where the bicyclists were riding. Only those cars with special placards showing they were ferrying racers in a two-person pair team could use that road.

The deputy and I were in the parking lot mostly to remind people that law enforcement was there. I'd driven up in a marked sheriff's department sedan to reinforce the department's visible presence. We parked a sheriff's patrol car, an SUV, at the exit and left the dash cam on. We'd have a time-stamped video of every racer and every car that left the parking lot.

We didn't expect any trouble. If some racer broke the rules the race officials would handle it. If somebody got into a fight we'd take our time breaking it up unless it started getting out of hand. If someone had their skis stolen we'd take a report. With thousands of people and thousands of pairs of skis around we'd probably never find the skis again or the person who took them. But virtually all the people there were good law-abiding citizens out for an event that didn't involve drinking or drugs. Virtually all of them would be within sight of other racers and spectators all the time. Not a good place to commit a crime or even start acting belligerent.

The race started on time and skiers began coming down the hill. Twenty minutes later, after they'd done the cross-country leg, the first racers started off on their bicycles. Forty minutes later dispatch called me on the radio.

"There's been a shooting at the highway department sand station east of Vista Butte. Caller says one dead, one injured. No one else around. We're sending an ambulance."

"I'll be there in ten minutes. Tell the caller to wait." The sand station, where the highway department stored finely crushed red lava that they used instead of sand to spread on icy roads in the winter, was only five miles away. I got to my car and followed the ambulance that had been stationed at the ski area for the racers. Both of us, with lights flashing and siren wailing, tried to stay wide of the bike racers.

Well into the sand station, in back of a three-story pile of crushed rock, I came up behind three vehicles all facing away from me—first a blue Subaru SUV and then the ambulance parked next to a white Hummer that I recognized as Sean Wray's. I parked behind the Subaru and walked past it toward the other vehicles. The double doors at the back of the ambulance were open and two EMTs, a man and a woman, were hovering over two men lying flat on their backs beside the Hummer, one near the front, one near the back.

"This one's gone," said the man, kneeling by the man closest to me.

"This one's still with us," said the woman by the front of the SUV. The male EMT slid one end of a gurney out of the ambulance and the woman released the undercarriage and dropped the wheels to the ground. The man spun the gurney around like a shopping cart and wheeled it up beside the man at the front. Together they lowered the gurney to the ground and lifted the injured man onto it. When they slid the gurney back into the truck I confirmed what I had feared. The injured man was Sean Wray, his eyes closed, his body motionless.

"Sean," I yelled. "Who shot you?" No response from Sean and a flicker of a disdain from the woman's face. I was idiotic to expect a response but I refused to let go of the opportunity to ask. The man shut the back doors of the ambulance and hustled toward the driver's door.

"How's he doing?" I shouted.

"Breathing on his own. Could go bad fast if the bullet hit an organ." He climbed into the front, started his lights and sirens, and drove off.

I didn't step near the body on the ground but I checked him up and down to make sure. It was Sam Dee, parka unzipped and a hole in his Scandinavian style sweater. No hat. The blue sling bag he used for his doctor's kit lay beside him. He was dead, getting colder by the minute. I called dispatch for more resources—Susan to document the crime scene, a hearse to take Sam Dee's body to the morgue, and a deputy to protect the scene so I could leave.

I hoped Susan could use her technical wizardry to tell me more about what happened here. No snow or mud so no obvious footprints. If there were any footprints on the asphalt roadway or dirt next to it the EMTs had probably stepped all over them. I took cell phone pictures of Sam with his blue medical bag lying next to him. I photographed faint sprays of red on the Hummer but I'd leave it to Susan to determine how they got there. I didn't think the pictures would help much but something might change before Susan arrived.

I went back and tapped on the driver's window of the Subaru.

"You phoned it in?" I asked.

"Yes." The driver, alone in the car, was an overweight man in his twenties whose dark stubble showed he hadn't shaved in a week or so. On the passenger seat sat an expensive camera with a hand grip.

"How did you happen to be here?" I asked, as though we were going to have a casual conversation. But it was a serious question.

"I drove up from Bend to take photos of the bike race. I got a few photos along the way but I wanted to get photos of the uphill part where the bicyclists would be pushing harder. I came in here to park. When I saw the two bodies by the Hummer I called 911."

"Did you get out of your car?"

"After I called. I thought it would be safe because I didn't see anyone else around. I put my parka over the guy who was still breathing and told him I called an ambulance. I don't think he heard me. No sign of it. Then I got back in my car and turned the heat up. The ambulance guys took my parka when they took the man. Do you think I can get it back?"

"Did you take pictures?" The man hesitated a second.

"Yeah. I would have done more for the man who was breathing but I don't know first aid. I didn't know where to begin."

"I'll need to take those photos," I said, "the memory card from your camera."

"I'll text the photos to you," said the man.

"No," I said. "You'll give them to me now."

"I saw you taking photos of the exact same scene. You don't really need mine. I promise to send them to you. And my photos of the bikers are on that chip. They are my property."

"They'll be returned to you," I said.

"Don't you need a subpoena or something?" asked the man.

I knew a judge might decide the man was right but that was in the future. Right now I knew that if those photos showed something I wanted to present in court I needed to be stone cold certain that nothing had been deleted or tampered with. And I wanted to control what photos of the crime scene, if any, showed up in the media. Or, even worse, online.

"Direct evidence of a crime," I said. "I don't need a subpoena." I was bullshitting. The term "direct evidence" didn't apply to physical evidence or photographs in any way, shape, or form. But my unshaven friend didn't know that. He clicked the memory card out of his camera and gave it to me. I didn't have an evidence bag or even a Ziploc. I put the card in my pocket.

"Show me the date and time on your camera," I said. He pressed a few buttons and held the back of the camera up to me. I took a photo of the display with my phone. "I'm letting you keep the camera." The guy was being cooperative and I was being a hardass. But I had a job to do.

"And you didn't see anyone or any car around when you drove in here?"

"Nobody here and no cars except the Hummer."

When I asked him for his license and registration, he hitched his wallet out of his back trouser pocket and handed it to me. He lived in Bend.

"The registration is in the glove compartment," he said. "I'll get it." He kneeled on his seat and reached across the car. Out of habit I kept an eye on his hand as he rifled through maps and papers to pull out the single sheet of paper that showed the registration. I put both documents on the hood of his car and took pictures. Then I wrote down his name and address in case the pictures didn't come out.

"Thanks for your help," I said. "Either I or the district attorney may need to ask you more questions. Let me know if you plan to move."

"My plan is to be in Bend forever," he said.

"Give the scene a wide berth when you drive out. And be careful of the bicycles when you get out to the road. Remember you have to turn left."

"Will do," he said. He drove off slowly without shutting his window. There were two driveways into the sand station and he went out the downhill one.

I got back in my car and called Sheriff Knapp.

"Can we alert the wives?" I asked after I'd given my verbal report. "And give them some protection? This looks targeted and the shooter may have others on his hit list. We don't know who the shooter or shooters might be right now but the wives might." I had Sean and

Sam's home addresses and I gave them to Moore. "I don't think the shooter's on a random killing spree. He got the people he wanted. We don't have twenty bicycle riders dead on the road."

It was quiet, sitting in my car. Bicycles zipped past in my rearview mirror. I waited for the deputy, pulled from his duty at the ski area, to come secure the scene. Susan would get here after the deputy did. Then the hearse. There wasn't anything more I could do but ruminate on the shooting and how I could find Sam Dee's assassin.

Most killings I'd seen came from domestic disputes or one low-life individual killing another. Or a drug deal where somebody cheated. But I knew both the victims here, had seen Sam Dee only a few days before. Sean Wray in particular was a friend and I hoped to God he lived. I'd met Sean's wife, Grace, and I would talk with her, both as friend and as detective. I'd talk to Sam's wife too, searching for leads on who might want to kill either of them and why.

The deputy arrived and I left to find the killers, as futile as that effort first seemed. I didn't know what car they were driving, what they looked like, or which way they had gone. I could only pick a direction and cast around for anything that caught my eye, anything that didn't fit.

The killers had probably turned right toward Bend, the quickest way to thousands of destinations and hundreds of routes, many more than law enforcement could cover even if we knew what car they were driving. To the left, in the other direction, the ski area was a dead end until ODOT opened the Cascade Lakes Highway for the summer. It was the less likely direction for them to go but it was the direction I was most likely to spot them if they went that way. So that was where I went. I was like the man who lost his watch at night when a friend asked him why he wasn't looking where he lost it.

"The light's better here," the man said.

Along the road to the ski area I stopped to talk to the volunteers directing downhill traffic to the Sunriver turn-off. I asked them whether they'd seen a car come up from Bend about ten thirty a.m. and turn left toward Sunriver. A short and very bundled-up woman said no.

"No cars turned left here," she said. "They're all going to the ski area. If any wanted to turn left I'd remember. We'd have to stop them and make sure there were no bicyclists coming before we let them go. Besides, if anyone wanted to get from Bend to Sunriver this would be way out of their way." She was right about that.

I made a run through the ski area parking lot, careful to give the bicyclists a wide berth. The temperature had gotten up into the sixties and slush puddles dotted the parking area with more cars in the lot than when I left with the ambulance. Hundreds of cars, hundreds of people. People there to ski and people there for the race. People wearing tropical shirts and Bermuda shorts carrying skis. A bicyclist went by with her legs covered but wearing a bright pink tutu. The place did not lack for the unusual. The only car that stood out was a bright red Corvette with the top down. Not the car you'd choose to escape unnoticed from a crime scene. No one I saw looked at all like a person who had shot two people less than an hour ago.

If the killers were here the camera in the sheriff's SUV at the exit would have a video of their car even if, at this point, we had no idea which car it would be. The only way the killers could have left the area, if they came this way at all, would have been to head downhill and turn right at the Sunriver turnoff. That's the route I followed, doing my job diligently and ignoring the likelihood of finding absolutely nothing.

I was exploring. Right after the Sunriver turnoff there was a Sno-Park at Kapka Butte and I drove in to survey the place. The long Sno-Park parking lot could fit fifty or more vans, RVs, SUVs, trucks, and regular cars with trailers for snowmobiles. But even in the middle of winter the lot was rarely full because Dutchman Flat Sno-Park was closer to more trails. On this warm day in May the lot held only a lonely RV and, down at the far end, a dark gray Ford Focus with no trailer. I got out to check out the car. There was no one sitting inside but the hood was warm to the touch. I peered in the passenger side door without touching the car. The interior was covered with hair, as though someone had swept out a barbershop and dumped the contents all over the seats, the dashboard, and the floor. I knew what that meant. The killer would have a good reason to dump all that hair and there was a good chance I'd just found the killer's getaway car. Good news. On the minus side, though, we'd never find him through DNA he'd left behind, if he left any. Spread through the car was the DNA of dozens of people, maybe a hundred or more. The time and cost of sorting through all that hair and identifying all the owners would stop the lab investigation of DNA dead in its tracks. I could only hope that once I found a suspect through other means the lab might find his DNA among all the others. Even that was unlikely. If he'd gone to all this trouble with the hair he'd probably worn gloves and a tight cap on his head.

Why did the killer leave the car here? He knew someone might see him near the crime scene, maybe even gotten the license plate. He wanted to get as far from the car just as fast as he could. He'd probably gotten into another car, driven by an accomplice or parked here earlier. He'd gone down the Sunriver Road and turned north or south on US 97. He could be home in Bend watching TV or on his way to California by now.

I called dispatch to requisition a flatbed to take the Focus down to the lab. I needed a deputy to sit on this car until the flatbed got here. They said they would send the one who had been overseeing the traffic redirection as soon as the last racer had finished the bicycle leg. I'd have to stay where I was until then, making phone calls and thinking. To learn more about the Ford Focus, I called admin at the sheriff's department and asked them to look it up, then call me back with the owner's address, phone number, and any prior convictions.

I drove over to the RV and parked my sheriff's car where anyone inside could see it out their back window. It was too dark inside for me to see anyone but when I stepped out of my car I could hear a TV going. A man in his sixties or seventies, unshaven but in a clean winter bathrobe, came to the door when I knocked. He and his wife had parked there the night before and had the entire parking lot to themselves. They hadn't seen anyone come or go this morning but they hadn't been watching. And why did they choose to park here? The state was supposed to open the Cascade Lakes Highway tomorrow and they wanted to be among the first to drive it. I told him I was investigating a crime in the area and I might need to contact him again. He said okay but he didn't know what use he could be. I photographed his license and registration and wrote down his phone number.

I parked over by the Ford Focus again and made a call to St. Charles Hospital to find out about Sean. The police liaison said he was in surgery. They couldn't say yet how bad the damage was. If Sean survived he might regain consciousness by this evening and have the strength to talk for a minute. More likely I'd have to wait until tomorrow or later.

I wasn't ready to interview Sam's and Sean's wives and associates, particularly over the phone. I needed more facts first. Sam's partners at Sisemore wouldn't be back at work until Monday. His wife would need time to settle down after the news of his death. Grace Wray, Sean's wife, would be too worried about Sean to help me very much until he was, hopefully, on the road to recovery.

I sat by myself and went over the many questions and few conclusions I had so far. Call them suppositions. Probable facts. Working assumptions. Lines of inquiry.

First, the killers wanted to get away with their crime. They weren't suicidal or so wrought up they didn't care about getting away. They had lives they wanted to get on with.

Second, whether they were equally motivated or one of them was talked into it, the murder took two people. There was no way one person could get two cars up here by himself unless he walked all the way down to Bend to get the second car.

Third, this was a targeted killing, not the act of a crazy man who didn't care who he killed.

Fourth, the killer was an amateur or he was nervous. If he wanted to kill Sean, he should have made sure Sean was dead. If he didn't want to kill Sean and was willing to bet Sean's eyewitness account wouldn't lead to his arrest, then he shouldn't have shot Sean at all. Did the killer shoot Sean by mistake or was he so rattled, he left without checking whether Sean was dead or alive?

Staring across the almost empty parking lot, a pad of paper on my lap and a pen in my hand, I began to plan my investigation.

I couldn't concentrate. The victims were men I knew. Employed, responsible, respected men in the community. They were friends even if they moved in different circles than Estelle and I did. I was sad. I was angry. In law enforcement we have to be mentally strong. And we have to project an image of being even stronger than we are. I wasn't as tough as I was supposed to be now. That annoyed me. And scared me.

The guiding question was who would want to kill Sam or Sean or both? And why now and why here? I needed to know the sides of my friends' lives I hadn't known about before. I might find out things I didn't want to know. If Sean survived I'd start with him. The doctor would take more digging—his wife, his fellow doctors, his friends, his financial records, his patients. There had to be more to him than I had any idea about.

## Chapter 18

# Sarah Chatham

The day after the race, when the rest of my family was still asleep, Bud and I drove out to an Indian reservation I knew well from earlier visits. It was Bud's first visit. Edgar Manning, chief of the Fort Rock Indians, had invited us to a pow wow. I'd represented the tribe in court multiple times over the years.

Edgar said, "Come and dance, Sarah."

I immediately created reasons why I shouldn't. "I don't know how to dance like that," I said. The Indian dancing I'd seen did not resemble the Foxtrot.

"The basic step is very simple. You can learn more but if that's all you do you'll be fine."

"I have no group to dance with. I'd be on my own."

"That's fine. You can dance in the grand entry and the intertribal dance. It's everybody doing their own thing. You know that." Edgar was right and I knew I was making excuses. "I think I know the real reason," he said. "You don't feel you're entitled to dance."

"I'd feel like an imposter," I said.

"But you really are an Indian," said Edgar. "It's your right to dance. You should dance. Maybe it's even your duty."

I didn't know about "duty" but technically Edgar was correct. My paternal grandmother, who died soon after my father was born, was Cherokee. The grandmother I knew and loved was my grandfather's second wife. I didn't know I was part Indian until I was sixteen. I wasn't raised with any Indian culture or history beyond what every girl learned in school and saw on TV. It never occurred to people I met that I was part Indian, though I had black hair and high cheekbones. That changed when Oxton, Rath, and Flynn made me their specialist in Indian legal affairs. That didn't seem like a career enhancing assignment until Indian casinos took off and Indian legal work was a booming business. I worked with tribes all over the United States. I met a lot of Indians, saw a lot of powwows, heard a lot of Indian singing and drumming, and visited many casinos, replete with the definitely un-Indian sounds of slot machines—clanging coins and two persistent harmonica tones shifting back and forth with no recognizable pattern. Eventually I was adopted by the Cherokees as a full member of the tribe.

"It will bring you closer to us, to dance," said Edgar.

"I don't know what to wear," I said, feeling ridiculous, like some spoiled brat of a wife who has nothing better to worry about.

"You'll figure it out," said Edgar. If I sounded like a spoiled brat he wasn't going to indulge me. Better have me rise to the challenge, trivial as it was.

I found online what's called a Cherokee woman's tear dress. "Tear" sounds like "tare," as though you snagged your dress on something. The shape resembles a nineteenth century pioneer woman's dress with a high neck, a long skirt, long sleeves, and buttons down the front. The cotton cloth is mostly one color or pattern, including a cloth belt, but the dress has broad rectangular bands of a different pattern over the shoulders, around the sleeves, and around the skirt at about knee height. My dress was basically bright red and the bands were a light turquoise with yellow stars in them. I wore suede boots with beadwork on them and I circled my neck with a beaded necklace.

"You could pass for an Indian as far as I'm concerned," Bud said when I first tried everything on at home. I smiled a witching smile and did the little dance step I'd learned so far—bend the knees a little and bounce up and down. Put one foot forward and bring it back.

Then the other foot. "You could have fooled me."

"I'm not fooling anyone," I said with my chin raised. "I'm a Cherokee woman." In fact, when I stood in front the long mirror in the bedroom, I believed it myself. I would not indulge the fantasy that I had somehow awakened my genetic Indian heritage. That was ridiculous. But I had represented Indians for many years in court and visited them on many reservations, some reservations impoverished and others prospering with gambling or oil and gas.

Would my three-quarter Anglo face stand out at the powwow? I didn't think so. Many Indians had mixed blood. Half the owners of the outrageously profitable Foxwoods casino in Connecticut, the Mashantucket Pequots, looked to be African American. There would be tribes at the powwow from all over the western United States and Canada. Paiute, Cheyenne, Apache, Nootka, and I didn't know what else.

I still felt like an imposter. American Indians had suffered so much and I had suffered none of it, bore no scars of it. In a half-baked way, though, I was part of, or an offshoot of, an Indian resurgence. There might have been five million Indians living in what is now the United States when the first Europeans arrived. There were only about two hundred thousand left at the time of the Wounded Knee massacre in 1890. The population is back to five million today.

The Grand Entry of all the dancers began at eleven o'clock led, as tradition dictated, by veterans. I'd been impressed, time and time again, how much Indians honored their warriors. It surprised the heck out of me the first time a powwow emcee proudly recalled, in one minute, how Indian braves defeated the U.S. Army under Custer at the Battle of the Little Bighorn. Less than thirty seconds later, the emcee just as proudly recalled how courageously Indians had fought for the United States in World War II, Korea, Vietnam, and the Middle East.

I placed myself at the back of the dancers, surrounded by people in regalia more elaborate and more colorful than mine. I couldn't tell how closely the dancers adhered to their tribe's traditional dress. In the swirling feathers and beadwork there were more modern elements —DayGlo plastic strips and sequins. Cloth was often much brighter than I think traditional costumes would ever have been. In a fan of feathers hanging from a man's waist was the mirror-like side of a CD. We all had paper numbers pinned to our clothes. There would be dancing competitions later and prizes awarded. Even the Grand Entry would be judged. No smiling and greeting yet. For many this was serious competition.

Bud was one of several Anglo spectators who sat on folding chairs outside the circle reserved for dancers. He wore a long sleeve deep blue shirt with a geometric Indian pattern on it, a design that might have come from a Navajo blanket. He took pictures of the dancers but, as required by the rules I told him about, scrupulously avoided taking photos of anyone else. When the Grand Entry song and drumming was over Bud called me over with short but emphatic waves of his hand. I didn't really want to join him. I was hoping to strike up conversations with my fellow dancers. There was a man in a Cherokee ribbon shirt and a black bowler hat that I had my eye out for.

"You get the prize for best lawyer dancer," said Bud, "at least as far as I know." I appreciated his enthusiasm but was impatient to get back to the dancers. "You remember we heard about a shooting during the Pole Pedal Paddle yesterday? Dan Martinez just called me. You know the people. Sam Dee is dead and Sean Wray is in the hospital. Dan said you would want to know."

I did want to know, even though the news immediately put a wet blanket on my powwow day, like snuffing out a smoke signal fire.

"Who shot them?"

"Nobody knows. Nobody saw it happen and whoever shot them cut and ran."

Sean was a good man. Sam was an excellent doctor and a highly respected man. Whatever had brought this on, whoever had wanted to kill Sean or Sam or both of them, there had to have been a better way to fix their problem. A discussion, a mediation, an arbitration, even a trial. Reconciliation, compensation, restitution. Anything better than shooting good people. Or even quasi-good people.

And this whole thing I'd been working on—squaring things between Wendy Whitlock and Sisemore Orthopedics, tracking down the money Wendy squirreled away somewhere, trying to figure out whether Sam Dee knew more about the embezzlement than he let on—had taken on entirely new dimensions. Even if Sam had a hand in Wendy's embezzlement, who would go so far as to kill him for it? Warren Whitlock in some calculation that Sam Dee had led Wendy into the theft? A fellow doctor angry that Sam had siphoned money from the clinic? Neither of these theories seemed likely to me and I couldn't think of any other.

And Sean. Why would anybody want to shoot Sean? Maybe he was simply a bystander, a witness that had to be eliminated. What were he and Dee doing together in the first place? How did they even know each other? I dearly wanted to push this tragedy aside, or at least postpone dealing with it. I wanted to escape back into the dancing. My thoughts would not let me.

If the shooting took place up on Mt. Bachelor the crime was in the county, not the city, and Carl Breuninger would be investigating it. I owed it to him to volunteer as much as I could about Wendy's crime without compromising her interests, or the interests of her estate, any more than absolutely necessary.

One of the two drums, the North Drum, started up a new song for the Intertribal. Anyone in regalia could dance any dance they wanted. It was more social than the Grand Entry. Dancers admired each other's dress and dancing. We could stop and talk with each other. I pushed the shooting out of my mind but my steps lacked some of the lightness they had before. I talked with a Cheyenne woman dressed for competing in the jingle dance later on. Her regalia was hung with hundreds of little metal cones that jingled when she danced. She said some of her jingles were very old, made from the lids of chewing tobacco tins. And I met my fellow Cherokee, the man in the ribbon shirt. He'd grown up in Oklahoma but lived in Portland now. He had his own home security company. His wife was a Spokane Indian. She hadn't come with him.

"We don't think very much about being Indian in our daily lives," he said. "But every once in a while I like to stay in touch. We visit the res, hers and mine, to see family once a year."

Bud and I said our goodbyes to Edgar Manning and left halfway through the dance competitions in the afternoon. I never did see the jingle dance.

Still wearing my red dancing dress I didn't want to stop for anything along the way home. We'd had tacos made with fry bread for lunch at the powwow. My mind jumped back and forth between savoring the day, debating what I could tell Carl Breuninger about Dr. Dee, and worrying whether Sean Wray would live or die. Sean was our client and also a friend, a good-hearted man, easy to work with.

Bud started singing "Cherokee" to distract me or pull me out of my silence. "Sweet Indian maiden…".

"I am not sweet," I said.

"You're sweeter than you think you are," he said.

Chapter 19

# Sheriff's Detective Carl Breuninger

The Ford Focus that I thought Dr. Dee's killer used and left at Kapka Butte we traced to a guy who lived on Northeast Seventh Street in Bend. I knocked on his door the night of the murder. He was home watching a baseball game I could hear in the background as he stepped outside his front door. He was a young man with short hair in jeans and a t-shirt. A woman was gently encouraging a little girl to leave the front room to gather pine cones in the back yard. I told the man I was here because his car had been involved in a crime.

"It sure was," he said. "It was stolen. Did you find it? Is it drivable?"

"Where did you last see it," I asked.

"I dropped it off Thursday night for service at Robberson Ford," he said. "When I called them about picking it up on Friday they said they didn't have it. My appointment was on their schedule but they had never seen the car. I dropped the keys in the slot in their door and asked service if they had the keys. They said they didn't have them either. I reported it stolen on Saturday."

"Your car was used in a crime." I held off telling him the car was evidence and he wouldn't be getting it back for a while.

"Holy cow. What was the crime?"

"I can't say at this time."

The man stared at the short driveway in front of his house.

"I hope you don't think I had anything to do with this crime, whatever it was?"

"No," I said. "We have some criminals smart enough to use a car that couldn't be traced to them. We're picking up fingerprints and DNA from the car and it would help if we could have yours so can concentrate on what corresponds to the suspects. Could you come down to the sheriff's department with me and let us get that information from you?"

This time he locked his eyes on mine while he considered it.

"Tell me honestly," he said, "if I come down there you're not going to lock me up or hold me for some long interrogation are you?"

"You are not a suspect. It should take less than half an hour." I hoped he had enough trust in law enforcement to believe me. He thought some more.

"How about I come by Monday after work?" he asked. I could see he'd come up with a test of what I was saying. If I really considered him a suspect I would have insisted on today. I would not say come in tomorrow on your own.

"That will work," I said. "Be sure and call me if you're going to be late." I gave him my card and said goodbye.

With a wiped down steering wheel and all the hair and dirt in that car we'd never find our killer through his fingerprints or DNA. But I'd gotten a good lead on where I might find a picture of our criminal.

The morning after the murder I called the manager of Robberson Ford and asked to see security footage of the service drop-off area from Thursday night through early Friday morning. Even though the dealership wasn't a victim he was glad to help. He gave me a desk with a PC on it, started the video at closing time on Thursday and gave me instructions how to start, stop, and rewind.

"It's all on a disk now and it's backed up. You can't erase it or mess it up. You can stop it and print out a still picture whenever you want. Use the fast forward until you get to where you see something. But you have to watch carefully because it can go by quick."

I watched six people drop keys in the slot. The guy who owned the Focus dropped his keys in at 9:06 pm. Nothing much happened for a while. Some guy walked into the picture at 11:35, turned around, and walked out. Paid no attention to the key slot. When the video got to 1:00 am I paused it to visit the bathroom and get another cup of coffee. Then I watched a whole lot of nothing. I told myself it was like fishing with bait while sitting on the bank of a pond. You sit there a long time with no fish at all. Eventually you get a bite. You have to wait. At 4:13 in the morning a man walked up to the key slot and I sat up straight in my seat. At least I judged it was a man. He walked like a man. He must have known he was going to be caught by the surveillance camera. He wore a shapeless poncho and a big round hat that hid his entire head. He pushed something into the key slot that resembled one of those grabbers that people use to pick things up off the floor without bending over. He fiddled around with it a bit and then pulled a set of keys back out of the slot. He scanned one hundred and eighty degrees to see if anyone had seen him. Apparently not. He walked rapidly away from the building and out of the frame. Half a minute later I saw red lights reflected in the glass of the door. I supposed they were the taillights of the car the man had taken. I reversed the video and went through it again, printing stills along the way.

I skimmed through the video until a worker for the dealership unlocked the door in the morning and picked up the keys left overnight. I stepped out of the building and walked around to the key drop to examine it carefully. It was narrow, top to bottom, and in back of the slot for pushing in the keys was a cavity shaped like a cigar box with a hole in the bottom at the far end. The keys dropped about two feet to the floor. What puzzled me was how the man got the grabber to turn down. The grabbers I'd seen would have to go in straight and hit the back of the box that formed the mail slot. There was no way I could imagine it turning down to where the keys were. I measured the mail slot and the drop to the floor. I took pictures from the inside and the outside. Then I picked up a DVD of the whole night's video the general manager had put aside for me and left.

Watching the video had taken the whole morning. Too bad I couldn't have gotten a car serviced at the same time. I got lunch at the Pilot Butte Drive-In, one of the old-fashioned places where you park under a roof and somebody comes to your car to take your order and bring you your meal. Rumor was it was going to close and I wanted to pay a last visit. I had a hamburger, bigger and better than at a franchise. Also bigger than I should have eaten.

I wandered into the crime lab after lunch with my stills from the security video and the pictures of the key slot still on my phone. Somebody in that lab should be engineer enough to figure out how the guy in the big hat lifted the car keys up out of the two-foot drop.

"It looks like a grabber but it isn't," the woman I buttonholed told me. She was a prim, all-business kind of woman in a white coat. Not in a hurry but not about to waste time on introductions or comments about the weather. "A grabber has a rigid shaft. What you're seeing is a stent removal tool. A doctor can put a stent in your heart by going into a vein in your groin. If something goes wrong with the stent they have to pull it out and they go in the same way. The cable is flexible so it can follow the vein and it has tines on the end for grabbing the stent."

"Do you have to be a doctor to get one?"

"You have to be a doctor to use one," she said. "But it's a hunk of steel, not a drug. Anybody can buy one. A hundred and thirty dollars on the internet."

I walked down the road to my office, thinking I should keep Sam Dee's fellow doctors in consideration for his death. How likely were orthopedists to know what a stent removal tool was? Was one of them angry or scared enough to kill Dr. Dee? If Sam was on drugs while operating on patients he'd put the clinic at risk for a malpractice suit. But was that sufficient reason to kill him? I'd have to get more to go on than a misapplied surgical tool to justify interviewing any more doctors.

Perhaps I had more already. Two people at Sisemore Orthopedics had died in the last five months, Wendy Whitlock in January and Dr. Dee in May. I wasn't making much progress on Wendy Whitlock. I couldn't even say it was murder instead of suicide. But, at the cost of Sam's life I had a new angle on Wendy's death. I'd interview Sam's patients who weren't happy with their outcomes and especially those who weren't happy with the bills Wendy sent them.

## Chapter 20

# Sean Wray

I was in a bed but hadn't the will to open my eyes. So my brain hadn't powered off completely, only restarted. Restoring my conscious mind to where it had left off, I remembered lying on the ground in the sand depot parking lot, thinking I might be dying and not wanting to die, trying to think of a way to not die and not coming up with any ideas. Now at least I was still alive and in a warm place where people were taking care of me.

My eyes opened to a room with sound-absorbing ceiling tiles, plastic curtains, and electrical equipment on stands with wires coming out of it. I was thirsty. There was a woman wearing a mask gazing down on me.

"He's waking up," she said. "How are you feeling, Sean?"

My brain wouldn't engage with my mouth and my muscles didn't feel as though they could move. "Cold," I said. It took some computer time to get the word out. "Thirsty."

"We'll get you a blanket. Would you like some apple juice or some water?" Another woman put a soft blue blanket over me.

"Apple," I said. "Thanks." I wasn't anxious. The people around me were following a procedure here, like starting up a machine, and they knew their responsibilities. If they didn't get it right the first time, they'd work at it until they did. My role for now was dependent, passive. I would be patient and trusting. Quiet. I wouldn't be a bother.

Every once in a while I would say something to encourage them.

I must have dozed off because when I opened my eyes again I was in a different room, one with a window, a pillow under my head, and my wife standing beside the bed.

"They said I could wake you up," said Grace. "I think that was more for my sake than for yours. You were sleeping so peacefully but I wanted badly to talk with you, to make sure you're all right. How do you feel?"

"What happened?" I asked.

"That's what Detective Breuninger wants to ask you. He said I shouldn't tell you anything until he talks to you. He's waiting outside and he wanted to give me a minute with you first. How do you feel?"

"Sleepy," I said. "Lazy, like I don't want to move. But I guess I can." I raised my hands a little where I could see them and put them down on the bed again. "I'm wiggling my feet. Are they moving?"

"Yes. The doctors say your spine is okay and you'll get back to normal with physical therapy. I'm just glad you're alive. Do you know what day it is?"

"Last I knew it was Saturday but it might be Monday by now."

"That's right, and do you remember whose birthday is coming up?"

Grace was testing to make sure I was all there, whether I had lost some mental capacity temporarily or permanently. Whether I was still fully myself.

"Ben will be seven on May 27," I said. "We're having a party for his friends at our house."

Grace seemed relieved.

"And the cube root of 27 is five," I said with a proud smile on my face.

"Cut it out," she said.

"You're right," I said. "It's actually six."

She made a fist as though to poke me in the arm but thought better of it. "You behave yourself and get better," she said. "I'm going to tell Carl to come in now."

"I love you," I said.

"Remember that," she said, "and vice versa."

I wanted to see Carl. Whatever happened he would put things right. Or at least he would tell me what was going on. He came in and stood by my bed.

"Hi Carl," I said, "have a seat."

There was a metal chair with a brown padded bottom that Carl picked up with one hand and brought over to the bed. He pulled a pad and a pen out of his jacket pocket.

"Tell me the news of the world," I said.

"Before I tell you anything at all," said Carl, "I need you to describe everything you remember about your ride with Sam."

I told Carl how we'd left the ski area right after Amy got on her bike and we stowed her skis and stuff on and in my Hummer. We passed her just before the turnoff for Sunriver. The race officials let us stay on the racecourse because Sam had a placard that said he was a race official.

"There was a Forest Service ranger at the entrance to the ODOT sand depot and he waved for us to turn in. I asked Sam to wave his 'Race Official' placard at the man to let us through and I started to slow down so the guy could see it. Sam said we should ask the man if someone was hurt. So I turned in and rolled down my window and asked. I wondered how the man knew a doctor was in my car.

"'Other side of the sand pile' said the ranger. No more explanation than that. I figured someone needed Sam's help so I drove in. I did wonder how the ranger knew Sam was in my car, if he did. Or why he stopped us, or anybody, instead of radioing it in. But I guess I was caught up in the heat of the moment and I figured I'd find out soon enough. So we drove around the sand pile, went past a small gray sedan, and stopped in front of it. Not a Forest Service vehicle. There was a man sitting in the passenger seat.

"Sam told me to stay in the car while he found out what the problem was. He got out and started back toward the sedan. I wanted to know what was going on so I got out of car too and walked around the front so I could see over Sam's shoulder. The man in the other car got out and met Sam halfway between the cars. He was a stocky white guy. I didn't get a good look at him because I was coming around the front of my car and then Sam was between me and the man. The man was wearing a dark sweatshirt with the hood up. Then the man pulled a gun, a pistol, out of his pocket and pointed it at Sam. I heard a shot and felt a hard punch to my shoulder, like Mike Tyson had hit me. I remember examining the snow close up from ground level and wondering how I got there. After that I don't remember anything. I don't know how the guy could have missed Sam and hit me instead."

"We're still working on that," said Carl. "What did other guy look like, the guy in the ranger uniform?"

"I don't remember very well. Once I saw the uniform I guess I didn't look much at the man. Besides, I think he had sunglasses on and a Russian style hat with the earmuffs down over his ears. Medium height, I'd say, not fat, maybe forty or fifty. Kind of a narrow face."

"Any facial hair?"

"I don't think so. I don't remember any. But, as you know, I wasn't paying much attention."

"White guy?"

"I think so."

"What kind of gun?" Carl asked me.

I summoned up a mental picture of the gun but I was getting very sleepy. I answered with my eyes closed.

"Some kind of pistol. Straight sides. Not a revolver."

"Okay," said Carl. "Thanks. Take a nap."

"One more thing," I said, my eyes half closed. "Sam took something out of his medical bag and held it out to the man before the shot went off. Don't know what it was. Good night."

I made a deep dive into sleep, not expecting to die before I woke up but not worrying too much about the possibility.

# Chapter 21

# Sheriff's Detective Carl Breuninger

Sean fell asleep before I could ask him who might want to kill him. Or who might want to kill Sam Dee. Grace was waiting in the hallway when I stepped out of Sean's room.

"He's asleep," I said. "Can you and I talk for a minute? Do you want to check on him first?"

"I'll only be a second," she said.

I understood. The machines Sean was hooked up to would signal the nurse's station and start beeping like mad if Sean ran into trouble. And it was unlikely he would. His condition was stable. But Grace needed to reassure herself. She watched him breathe and we both scanned the monitors. Heart rate 65, blood pressure 130 over 72, temperature 98.8, oxygen 97%, respiration 13 breaths per minute. The heart rate probably wasn't as low as the Pole Pedal Paddle racers but still, he was a healthy young man peacefully sleeping. Grace wasn't a nurse but she was a biologist. She was satisfied with what she saw.

"Sleep well," she said.

We went to the cafeteria and picked a table off to one side.

"Would you like me to go tell your kids Sean is going to be good as new?" I asked. I'd met Sean's children. They'd recognize me. And the uniform would add authority and credibility to what I said.

"Thanks but no," said Grace. "A doctor spoke to them over the phone. And my sister is with them at our house. What I need to know is who shot Sean and will they try again?"

"We both need to know that," I said. "I'm going to be full time on this case and I'll have the help of the entire Sheriff's department. The FBI too if necessary. But I very much need your help too."

"Of course, I'll help," said Grace, "but I don't think I know anything. I can't think of any reason anyone would want to hurt Sean."

"Maybe nobody did. But somebody wanted very badly to kill Dr. Dee. Sean may have gotten in the way or been shot by accident. Or the killer shot him because he was a witness to Dee's shooting. We've posted a deputy here to protect Sean and another in your driveway to make sure you stay safe. The Bend police will help us out."

"Thanks, Carl."

"Did Sean mention anything he was worried about?"

"Well," said Grace, "I know The Conclave project isn't going well. Some of the big investors want to pull out. Sean and Sam were both kind of down about it. I think knowing The Conclave was not going to happen bothered Sean more than the money we lost on our investment. I have no idea how much it will be. Sam didn't have any money in it and Sean said maybe he was embarrassed because he'd talked it up so much with his friends. Sam wanted them to buy lots for houses but The Conclave wasn't selling lots yet so none of them had bought any."

"Anything else?"

"I can't think of anything. You really need to ask Sean when he's feeling better."

"Okay, thanks," I said. "If you think of anything, or if you think you need more protection, give me a call, night or day."

"Thanks, Carl."

My next stop was Sam's house to interview Charlotte. I knew her from the one time our fishing team had gotten together with our wives. That had been a potluck dinner at Sean's and Grace's house. Lots of conversation and we all said we had a good time. The wives got along well and the men were careful not to dominate the conversation over drinks and dinner. Everybody loved Estelle's King Ranch Chicken. Yet the party didn't gel the way we hoped it would. Estelle and I and Sam and Charlotte were twenty years older than Sean and Dan and their wives. We'd all gone to college but Sean had a graduate degree in engineering, Sam had an MD, and Dan a law degree. Sean and Grace were immensely richer than any of us, though they tried not to act like it. Sam was a well-off doctor and Dan, though he wasn't rich yet, was headed to a lot more money than I'd ever see.

And there was something about my being in law enforcement that separated Estelle and me from people who weren't. It was part of the price I paid for choosing this career.

Sam said he never would have gotten through med school without Charlotte. She'd been a nurse back then and they lived off her salary. And she kept him organized, made sure he studied the right thing for the right test at the right time. He was very smart, he said, as though it were not bragging, simply a fact of life—but he was forgetful and he lacked discipline. She was head-turning pretty and she'd been even more beautiful when she was younger and slimmer. Sam carried a wedding photo around with him in his wallet. She had a non-confrontational way of talking with you, made you want to tell her everything on your mind because you knew she would understand. If she were a detective, she'd be great at interviewing witnesses and suspects. If Sam made a practice of seducing hotel housekeepers and other women he met along the way, I'd have to bet Charlotte at least sensed it. I wondered how she made peace with the idea.

The Dees had a house on the golf course at Broken Top, pretty swell by Bend standards. A deputy, a woman, had gone to the Dee house to notify Charlotte about Sam's death. The deputy told me over the phone that Charlotte had handled the news better than many. She sighed a big sigh and slumped forward as though she'd been hit in the stomach. But she didn't burst into tears, or fall down, or shout out a denial, or slam the door, or collapse on the deputy's shoulders. The deputy told her where and when Sam was shot and where Charlotte could call about the body. The sheriff's department would investigate the shooting thoroughly and would keep Mrs. Dee informed all along the way. A detective would contact her.

Charlotte might take some comfort that the detective turned out to be me—someone she'd met and who knew Sam.

Her two kids were sad and confused. Charlotte introduced me and I got their names, Brent, about sixteen, and Waverly, about twelve, who looked like her mother. I told them about the death of their father and said that I knew him from our fishing trip and that he was a good man. The girl affirmed this with a faint smile and a quick nod of her head. The boy simply sulked.

"I need to talk with Mr. Breuninger outside," said Charlotte. "You should call your friends and tell them what happened and what you're thinking. Nobody knows what to say at a time like this so make allowances. You won't know what to say either but you need to talk with your friends anyway."

"Have you caught the man who shot him?" the boy asked me in a challenging tone.

"Not yet," I said, "but we're working on it."

Charlotte and I sat on the back deck of the house where the kids could see us but not hear us. They needed reassurance that their mother was still there for them and I needed her to speak freely.

"I've always been afraid this would happen," she said. "He led people to expect too much from him. He wanted people to believe he cared about them deeply and that he could move mountains for them. That he'd get them out of debt or fix their god-awful marriage or tell them how to get their impossible children back on track. He'd make them better, wiser, and stronger. Or he'd make them rich or something. He'd give them a golf tip and they'd expect their handicap to drop five points. Then it wouldn't happen. He'd encourage them for a while, tell them to keep the faith. Then he'd give up on them and they'd feel worse than they did before. I warned him that somebody, somewhere, would be mad enough to go after him. He brushed it off. And finally somebody killed him."

Charlotte shot a glance back through the glass slide door. The son was sitting in an upholstered chair staring off into space. The daughter was on the floor writing something or drawing something in a workbook. "I had a first-class security system installed. I got a gun and learned how to use it. I take the kids to school and pick them up almost every day. They don't like that and I really don't either. I'm sorry Sam is dead, and it is a shock to the kids. I don't know how they'll handle it. But in some ways, very frankly, I'm relieved. We can finally get our lives back and live like normal people."

"You sensed in advance he'd be killed?" I asked. Keep her talking. Don't ask hard questions just yet.

"That or something else," said Charlotte. "Someone once crippled him on purpose. Did you know that? Smashed his foot with a baseball bat. It hurt for months afterward. Couldn't go hiking or skiing until it healed. Couldn't stand up to do surgery for more than an hour at a time.

"The man who broke his foot was the husband of a patient who died on the operating table. The woman who died, the wife, couldn't wait to have the surgery. She worshipped Sam. Sam forgave the man who smashed his foot and didn't press charges. That was like him. The heroic gesture. It's classic tragedy. Hamartia, hubris, nemesis, and so on."

I didn't know what those words meant but I could see what was happening here. Mrs. Dee was dealing with her husband's death by retreating into something she knew.

"Hamartia?" I asked.

"Sorry," she said. "I majored in literature before I became a nurse. Hamartia is the hero's fatal flaw."

"And what was Sam's fatal flaw?" I asked.

"Like I said, he wanted people to think he was exceptional in every way—handsomer, smarter, braver, kinder and more generous than everybody else. It was like a Ponzi scheme but with people's good opinions instead of money. He couldn't keep it going forever." Now she gazed off her deck, toward Mt. Washington in the northwest.

"He really was an excellent surgeon, you know. But not every surgery is successful. He set high expectations and patients thought they'd been lied to when things didn't work out."

"What about The Conclave? Any problems there?"

"Oh, that damned thing," said Charlotte. "Sam talked it up night and day. Told his friends they could make a lot of money buying lots as soon as they came available. He couldn't believe it when the whole thing fell apart. We talked about it. He didn't know what he was going to tell his friends."

"Did he invest in it?"

"No. I kept the books. All his income from Sisemore was deposited in our joint bank account and I was the only one who wrote checks on it. Sam used a credit card for everything but I paid the credit card bill. He wasn't on a leash if that's what you're thinking. But I would have noticed any big or unusual expenditures."

"Any threatening phone calls or letters? Anyone lurking outside your house or following you or the children?"

"No. Nothing. And I would have seen it. I expected some lesser mortal who thought revenge was the only statement he could make. Some patient who expected a miracle. Or a relative of a patient. You'd have to go through the records at Sisemore. Some patients wind up worse off than before the operation. It happens. Some even die. Somebody decided it was Sam's fault and decided to kill him."

"How about his volunteer work, the races he worked on, Doctors without Borders?"

"Never heard of any problems," she said. "Sometimes Sam was more show than go. He wanted to be the hero. But he meant well. I guess you want to talk to all these people. I'll make you a list of the organizations I can think of."

She got up and walked back into the house. I didn't like letting her out of my sight. Bad procedure. But I live in the real world. She wasn't going to flee. She wasn't going to get a weapon and go after me. And she wasn't going to go kill herself. She was going to do exactly what she said. She came back with a pad of lined letter-sized paper, a thick ballpoint pen with an artistic design on it, and a leather-bound address book. Strange, I thought, that she doesn't keep names and addresses on her cell phone like most people these days. She opened the address book on the coffee table in front of her and started to write on the pad, no comments as she went along. Nothing for me to do but keep my mouth shut and wait. True to their name, coffee table books were stacked three deep on the low wood and glass table. There was a book about the Ganges River called River of Offerings. The cover showed the prow of a wooden boat carrying a hundred or so little bowls with a lit candle in the center and flower petals all around it. It was evening or night in the photo and lights from the shore were reflected in the water beyond the boat. I considered how much work it took to decorate all those bowls and light the candles. Work to no practical purpose. The work was the offering as much as were the bowls shining out over the water.

Charlotte handed me her list. The Red Cross, the High Desert Museum, the Humane Society, Oregon Adaptive Sports, and Doctors without Borders. Five or six races where Sam was the doctor of record. She had the name of a person and a phone number for most of them.

"Did he ever find time to practice medicine?" I asked.

"He spread himself thin." I knew what that meant. Not a lot of time for his wife and family. "I'm very sorry for the children. It's upsetting to lose a father and maybe worse to learn about his faults and weaknesses. I hope they can be spared some of that.

"And there was a girlfriend. You'll want to check on that. What can you do to keep the kids from finding out about her? Can you keep it out of the press?"

"Girlfriend?" I said. "I can try to keep this quiet but I can't prevent her from saying whatever she wants to the media or anybody she likes."

"Oh," said Charlotte, "no threat of that. She's dead." Charlotte said this with a certain satisfaction. "Her husband might talk if he even knows. God knows who else."

"Name?"

"Wendy Whitlock. She worked for Sisemore Orthopedics."

Damn! I said to myself. Did this investigation just get simpler or more complicated? Did I get a break in two cases I was working on or was I trapped by a coincidence that would waste my time and drive me crazy?

"Hung herself in her barn," said Charlotte. "Sam told me she'd been embezzling from the company and was about to be exposed. That part had nothing to do with him. Their relationship was purely physical, he said."

"So you discussed this with him? You were okay with the affair?"

"Absolutely not," said Charlotte, "and I told him so. But Sam could be like an untrained puppy. He was more of a child than my children. I'm embarrassed I put up with it. But that's the way life turned out. He did love his family and he needed me. He would never have left us. He was brilliant and he did a lot of good for people. It was a strange sort of balance, not the way I expected my life would be."

"Any other secrets tucked away in Sam's life?" I asked. "I thought I knew him after our fishing trip."

"I wish we could have the funeral, bury Sam, and be done with him," said Charlotte in a rush, as though she'd been holding back that idea since we sat down. "I mean I don't care who shot him or why. It'll be some sordid tale I won't want to hear. But," Charlotte hesitated, "and I don't want you to repeat this. I have to be frank with somebody. He was a big part of my life but a part of me, like a cancer, I'll be better off without. I'm already glad this masquerade is almost over. I hope it will fade away when he's not around to polish his image. I'm so tired of pretending that Sam is flawless and that we have a perfect life together. I'm tired of constantly watching over him to make sure he keeps his medical license, pays his taxes, doesn't invest in anything stupid, doesn't risk his life trying to save some desperate people on the other side of the world. Well I guess I've failed, finally, in some way, to save his sorry ass. At least I'm done. He got into something, it hardly matters what, he pushed somebody too far and they shot him. End of story."

"I understand, Charlotte, that you may not care who shot Sam but the law does care." I spoke more directly and clearly to Charlotte now, while still aiming for a friendly tone. Not angry or threatening. "I need your help. The sheriff and the district attorney are not going to leave either of us alone, you or me, until we've exhausted every reasonable avenue of investigation. So while we're here in your own house, having an unofficial conversation, not recorded, and we're not in a windowless interview room at the sheriff's office with the DA hanging over my shoulder, what other secrets was Sam keeping that would help me solve this case?"

"Pills," said Charlotte

"Pills?" I asked.

"Pills," she said. "He started taking them for pain. After the baseball bat to the foot. He kept taking them. When he tried to stop he got angry and he was miserable. He might have toughed it out but he wanted so badly to project the image that he was in control, confident, on top of the world. He couldn't stay away from work long enough to get clean. I couldn't get him to stop. He hid it from the kids but they've noticed his mood swings. They may have figured it out. The other doctors did. They were threatening to get his license suspended and kick him out of the practice. That would have devastated him." She paused to think about this for a minute.

"Listen," she said. "Can you take the drugs away, at least the ones where I know where they are? I want them out of the house."

"Yes, I'll take them," I said. "We'll keep them as evidence. And if you find any more we'll send a deputy around to pick them up. Where'd he get the drugs?"

"Easy. He wrote prescriptions for patients. I suppose some of them never existed. Then he kept the drugs himself."

"That's illegal," I said. "I presume you had no knowledge of this at the time." Actually I presumed the opposite. Much as she didn't like it, I was pretty damn sure she knew exactly what her husband was doing. She squinted in confusion for a moment and then she figured it out. I was helping her in return for her cooperation. If she denied any knowledge of her husband's illegal prescription writing she couldn't be charged as an accomplice. "Did you know about this before he died?"

"No," she said. She was lying, I was sure, but I let it pass.

"How was he financially? Did he owe money to anyone?"

"I kept the books, as I said, and I wrote all the checks. I've done it since Sam was in medical school and I was a nurse. After that Sam made good money and I managed it. We paid off the mortgage early and we have money in the bank for college. More than enough."

"Are you going to keep the house?"

"At least until the children leave. Maybe forever. I don't know. That's a long time from now. We have savings. Sam had life insurance. A lot of it."

"How about your kids? How are they taking their father's death?"

"Confused. Afraid. Angry. Waverly adored her father, even though he didn't always have enough time for her. She doesn't know what life will be like without him. But most of her life will go right on as before—school, sports, friends, and all her relatives. She'll still have summer camp, Christmas, and her birthday. I will always be here.

"I'm more worried about Brent, even though he's sixteen and Waverly is only eleven. Brent always had trouble with Sam. Everyone told him what a wonderful man his father was. But Brent saw how needy his father was and how self-obsessed. When Sam could have been spending time with Brent, teaching him something or doing something together, he was lifting weights or running to get in shape or out being a hero in the community. Now whatever chance Brent had to get close to his father is gone forever. I'll never make up the gap. I only hope he doesn't think he needs to be like his father."

"How did Sam pay for the drugs he took?"

"Pocket change," said Charlotte. "Oxycodone costs twenty dollars a pill if you get it illegally. You probably know about that. But it's only thirty-three cents if you're a doctor, and doctors get free samples all the time. It's like working in a candy store."

"How much was he taking?" I asked. The autopsy would tell me how much he had in his system and whether he was injecting it or not. But I wanted to know what Charlotte had seen and what she knew about it.

"I don't know," she said, lifting her hands in a subdued gesture of exasperation. "He never zonked out or blissed out or whatever you call it. He took it for the pain."

"I didn't know about the pain or the drugs," I said. "If he took pills during our fishing trip I'm sure I thought it was Advil."

"That's comical," said Charlotte. "We have a bottle of Advil in our medicine cabinet. Sam never touched it."

"Who can you think of that might give me a different perspective on Sam? People I should talk to?"

"The doctors at Sisemore Orthopedics obviously," said Charlotte, as though she doubted I had the brains to think of that. "And you could talk to his buddies down at the Athletic Club. He went there to play tennis and to rub shoulders with the movers and shakers. He liked that. His usual tennis partner is Revett Cook and I can give you his number."

"Thank you for your time, Charlotte," I said. "I'll keep you informed and I may be back to ask you more questions as the case develops."

"Listen, Detective. You may think I'm better off without Sam but that's not the way I see it. He did a lot of good for a lot of people. He was the best orthopedic surgeon in all of Eastern Oregon. I made that possible. I put him through med school and I organized his life so he could work. We were a popular couple, more due to Sam than to me. Now I'm a widow and not a young one. I have to rebuild half of who I am from scratch."

"I understand," I said. "It won't be easy. In the short run it will seem impossible. But you can do it. I've seen people far worse off rebuild their lives. People come out of prison, no college degree, no work experience, no friends, a shaky relationship with their family, and they've succeeded. They've gotten jobs and built a life—house, family, a place in the community. You'll have to figure it out for yourself. It will take time. But you can do it."

Charlotte would get by. She had time and money and people who needed her.

Chapter 22

# Dr. Boyd McGrath

The clinic paged me twice on the golf course and I ignored the pages. My partner put his ball in the water on seventeen and my drive rolled into a trap on eighteen. We lost our match. I sat in my cart by the Broken Top clubhouse to call the clinic.

"Dr. Dee was shot. Dead," said Melissa, "and a detective from the sheriff's department, Carl Breuninger, says he needs to talk with you urgently."

"Did it happen in the office?"

"Not here. And not today. Yesterday by Mt. Bachelor. Dr. Dee went there for the Pole Pedal Paddle. Nobody knows who shot him. I've called his appointments for the week and am trying to rearrange them with the other doctors. It will take longer to reschedule his surgeries."

"And this detective wants to talk to me?" I asked. "I don't have the faintest idea what happened. This is the first I've heard of it."

"He's very insistent. I told him you weren't answering and I didn't know where you were."

I draw a sharp line between the times I am on call and the times when I am not. In the clinic my patients get my full attention and all the knowledge I can bring. But I have little tolerance for patient emergencies when I am pursuing the private life I've worked so hard to earn. Sam's death, unfortunately, was an emergency I was going to have to deal with.

"Tell the detective I'll meet him at my house in ninety minutes. Give him the address." I hung up and turned my phone off.

On the way to and from the men's room I allowed my mind to fill up with Sam Dee, hopefully for the last time. People don't shoot doctors. You work like a draft horse through medical school and residency but then you build up a practice, you change people's lives, you make some money, and you become established. You live in a nice house in a nice area. You're protected, you're safe. You're in the top one percent of the population, or at least in the top five percent. We didn't have to live in the same world that other people did. But there's always risk, in spite of everything, that you can lose it all. You can be in a car accident. Or, like Sam Dee, somebody can come along and shoot you.

But I was not like Sam Dee, not like him at all. He was, frankly, a show-off. Whether in surgery or in golf he would take on the impossible. And he would succeed far more often than he deserved to. He'd do surgeries that had a one-in-ten chance of succeeding, on people who should never have walked a step again in their lives. A year later they'd be playing tennis and singing his praises. And he would stick with them after the surgery, make sure they did their rehab, even train with them sometimes. For free. He seemed to be, I admit, the model of what a doctor should be. When he succeeded. When his surgeries failed he'd be very sympathetic but he would praise those patients for being willing to take the chance, tell them they were the exception, and ask them not to broadcast their experience because it would discourage the people that he really could help. He talked about his work as a life-long mission rather than a job and career.

Frankly, I resented Sam Dee. His patient outcomes were, on average, no better than the rest of us at Sisemore. But he was in greater demand. We all had good practices, all the patients and fees we could ask for, but we had patients who demanded Sam, even patients who switched to him after their first appointment with one of the other doctors.

My golf partner and I owed the winners drinks, beer for everyone else, ginger beer for me. Even if we lost, though, we enjoyed talking over the game, the most challenging shots, the choices we'd made, the intervention of luck. If I'd hit my shot a little more left on eighteen, the match might have ended differently.

I sipped my drink and said nothing. My three companions, engaged in their animated conversation, didn't notice. We sat at one end of the long room, next to the large windows that ran down one side of the long dining room and looked out over a large pond with the first and tenth tees on the other side. I was facing the room's entrance and noted the entrance of a barrel-chested man compressed into a light brown shirt with a black down vest. The man surveyed the room and stopped a passing waiter with a commanding glare. The waiter, Coulter, clearly offended by the man, gave the man a short reply and led him, at a businesslike pace, directly to our table. The man had a badge on his vest.

"Robert McGrath?" the man asked me. As though he were about to make an arrest!

"Yes," I said with my best unperturbed calm. "I'm Dr. McGrath."

"Detective Carl Breuninger, Deschutes County Sheriff's Department. I need to have a word with you."

I could have shown my annoyance at the man's not waiting until I got home, and I could have established my own authority by replying, "Regarding?" Fully justified. But he and I both knew what it was about and a power struggle would devolve into something ridiculous in front of the other men. I overlooked the man's impertinence.

"By all means, detective," I said. "Happy to help you." I rose from the table and turned to my companions. "Excuse me, gentlemen. This may take a while. Thanks for the game. See you next time." They were surprised but they stood up and we shook hands goodbye. Coulter would know to bill my drink to my account.

The detective and I passed the entry hall and sat on a bench at the end of an indoor balcony over the pro-shop. I always resented the fact that this was wasted space, completing the aesthetic design but too narrow to serve any function in itself and not leading to anywhere else. Now it was finally useful.

"I don't want to waste your time or mine, doctor," said Breuninger.

"Let's skip the details of Dr. Dee's work life and his qualifications as a doctor. I need to know about problem areas in his life, including problems with other people. What can you tell me?"

"All right," I said. "You will promise me that nothing I say will get out to the media, especially not anything attributed to me. Is that right?"

"I won't report anything you say to anyone except the sheriff and the district attorney. The county always keeps information received from the public on criminal matters as confidential as possible. Now, so I don't have to come back again, what can you tell me about what was going on in the life of Dr. Sam Dee?"

I gave Breuninger a hard stare and decided to get this over with. I had nothing to hide and I was not responsible for Sam's reputation.

"What was going wrong was he was high on drugs. I don't know what drugs they were or where he got them. But I prescribe drugs for pain all the time, people recovering from surgery. I know what people on those drugs look and act like, including when they take more than prescribed or take them longer than prescribed.

"At the quarterly meeting of all the doctors in the clinic, this was in March, we told Sam he had to leave the clinic. He could lose his license and jeopardize the whole practice. It's not in the minutes but I agreed to review the partnership agreement with our attorney to see what it would take to force him out. We were going to have a formal vote at our June meeting. Now we'll have to settle up with his wife what he owed us and what we owe him. This would be a lot easier if we still had Mrs. Whitlock.

"Which brings me to another thing that was going wrong for Sam. We learned that Mrs. Whitlock had been embezzling from the firm. Right under our noses. She got away with it because we all trusted her so much, treated her like one of the family, relied on her. I am not a bookkeeper or an accountant. I didn't go through all the ins and outs of the business. But I had a sense we should have been making more money. Some of the other doctors did too. Sam said he would hire a special accountant, a forensic accountant, to check the ledgers. He took his time doing it but we were more right than we knew. Half a million dollars. Missing. Maybe more! And taken by Wendy Whitlock, a person we trusted and relied on for years."

"But you didn't notify the district attorney," Breuninger said. "Why was that?"

"We didn't want to prosecute her. We wanted our money back. We even let her keep her job while we worked with her on a way to get back what we could. Sam was in charge of it. He negotiated with her. After she died we got three hundred thousand back. Sam said we were lucky to get that much and the accountant backed him up. Couldn't find any more of it. Her husband says he never had a clue what she was doing and never saw any money beyond her salary. We could take the husband to court but he doesn't have any assets beside the house and some landscaping equipment. There's no evidence he saw any of the money Wendy took. Never knew about it. So Sam negotiated the restitution with Wendy and the rest of the doctors voted to approve it. Done deal."

"And this is trouble for Sam because…" Breuninger asked.

"Because he was dragging his heels in order to protect her. It turned out he and Wendy were having an affair! Sordid little thing. If people could simply behave themselves their lives would be a lot easier."

"And you were planning to expel Sam from the clinic?"

"Irrelevant now, isn't it?" I replied. "Let's not even talk about it. I don't want the firm to have any more to do with Sam than strictly necessary. We should send flowers to his funeral from the clinic, extend sincere sympathies to Charlotte and her children from each and every one of us, all say positive things about Sam, and, frankly, wash our hands of him. And guard Sisemore from anything and everything Sam may have done—malpractice or theft or drugs, or whatever else. We're done."

"Did he have a life insurance policy through the clinic?"

"I don't even know," I said. "Wendy would know all that. It's a disaster she's gone. She took care of everything so the rest of us could practice medicine. We don't even know how to hire her replacement."

"Speaking of Wendy Whitlock," said Breuninger, "any insights on what led to her death?"

"Take your pick. She was stealing and she got caught. Reputation shot. Lost the trust of everybody she worked with. Could have gone to jail. Or could be her husband found out about her affair. Or maybe Sam threw her over. I didn't know her that well and I'm not a psychiatrist."

"Any patients who got into disputes with Wendy about their bills, particularly any of Dr. Dee's patients?"

"Sisemore does not pad its bills, detective. In the few cases that went to court our invoices have stood up every time. If patients don't pay we turn them over to a collection agency. We don't keep a record of patients who whine about their bills but we have records of any formal complaints. I'll tell our accountant and our attorney to let you review them. Are we done here?"

"For now."

"Next time, detective, could you please not show up wherever I happen to be? Call my office and make an appointment."

Chapter 23

# Sheriff's Detective Carl Breuninger

I called Revett Cook, Sam's tennis partner, at the number Charlotte Dee gave me. We agreed to meet at The Athletic Club a half hour before he had a doubles match. Dee's friends had found a substitute to fill in for him.

It figured that Dee would belong to The Athletic Club of Bend, the top athletic facility in the county. Anybody with an athletic bent and the money to afford it was a member, more expensive and more exclusive than the city's swim and fitness center at Juniper. The club had basketball, racquetball, squash, a pool, and a weight room. Members could even get a massage or get their hair done. But the biggest draw was the seven indoor tennis courts, available winter and summer.

I met the man in the restaurant near the club's entrance. I was waiting for the greeter to come back and point him out to me. But I was in uniform, easy to identify. I watched a man in tennis whites, very traditional, very old-fashioned, leave his table and come to meet me. He was Revett Cook, a wiry dark-haired man in his forties.

"Come have a seat," he said. "Would you like something to drink? I'm having a Gatorade." I said thanks but no. He went on. "I don't picture this sort of thing happening to people I know. If it could happen to Sam, I suppose it could happen to anyone. Got any idea who killed him or why?"

"I hope you can help me with that. I knew Sam myself but I need to get a fuller picture of him and everything that was going on in his life."

"It's hard to imagine anyone with a reason to kill the man. He'd go out of his way for you. My labs were out of whack one time and the only appointment I could get with a kidney doctor was four weeks out. Sam knew the guy. Called him up and I was in to see the doctor the next day. Turns out Sam saved me from having serious problems. Only fault I ever found with Sam, since I suppose you're interested, was he didn't like to share the spotlight. Last year he and I won the club's doubles tournament in our age group. He told everybody about the best shots he'd had and how he'd won his serve every single time. He had a good serve but we won a lot of those points because I poached the return. I grumbled about his boasting a little, only to myself, and some guys said Sam was overdoing it. But I was a long way away from killing him. Didn't occur to me for a microsecond. Maybe he pissed off the wrong person at the wrong time."

"Anybody outside of tennis?"

"I suppose a dissatisfied patient but I don't know anything about that. I am not a doctor and Sam never discussed his patients with me. There was the whole Conclave thing but I don't think anybody actually lost money on it."

"The Conclave, that development out east of Redmond?"

"Yeah. Sam talked it up all the time. A Robert Trent Jones golf course, a terrific clubhouse, first class landscaping, and great views of the mountains from every lot. Sam was going to buy a lot and build a house on it himself. Wanted all his friends to do the same. We'd love it, he said, and we'd make a pile whenever we sold. Sam took some of us out there one time. It was bare land, rocky, uneven, and scrubby. It was available because nobody wanted it. Now I've seen poor land like that turned into nice-looking resorts, like Pronghorn and Brasada. You have to see it to believe it. But that Conclave land, as raw land, was the opposite of inspiring. I don't know why Sam took us out there.

"Now, of course, the thing's a bust. No water. Sam got some egg on his face from that one. Hasn't mentioned The Conclave again. I wanted to tease him about it but I felt sorry for him. He was so wrapped up in that place, wanted to retire there someday, surrounded by his friends, I guess."

"Did anybody lose money on The Conclave?" I asked.

"Nobody, at least nobody around here, nobody Sam gabbed to about it. The development wasn't close to selling lots. Hadn't mapped out the roads or the golf course, much less the lot lines."

"Why was Sam so excited about it?"

"Never could figure that out. I think he saw, well, we all saw, other resort communities built on land we'd assumed was worthless. Like turning lead into gold. Sam said we could each make a killing."

"Did you think he was right?"

"Not really. I've seen this show over and over. The developer counts on the buyer thinking the lot will appreciate after the sale. But the developer has already gotten most of that value. Unless the buyer wants to build a house for himself there and live in it, buying a lot is a sucker's bet. Well, that's my opinion. I never told Sam that. I rather enjoyed his enthusiasm."

I shifted my focus to see how visible Sam's drug use was, if it were visible at all. "Any problems with drugs or alcohol?"

"Not Sam. He'd have a drink but I never saw him get tipsy."

"Any women on the side?"

"I don't think so," he said. "Not for lack of available women. They adored him. But I would say he had more discipline and respect for his marriage than to go running around." I nodded my head as if to confirm Cook's impression. If Sam did have other women he kept it hidden.

"I'm getting a picture of Dee as a respected, decent man," I said. "Did he have any weaknesses, anything he indulged in?"

"Scotch whiskey," said Cook, "only one Scotch on the rocks at a time but always the most expensive, single malt if they had it. Scotch in the afternoon after tennis? We'd kid him about it. It's the last thing I would have wanted. And then he'd pay for it in cash, even if he was having a sandwich with it. Weird all around. But I can't imagine that's going to tell you anything about who killed him."

"Maybe not," I said, "but the strangest things turn out to be important."

Cook walked me out to the front door of the club and hurried back into the building to his tennis match.

When I checked voicemail on my phone at the sheriff's department Sarah Chatham had asked me to call her.

"How would you like a free trip to the Caribbean?" she said. "I think Sam Dee knew Wendy Whitlock was embezzling and he looked the other way. And I think she took a lot more money than Sam accepted as restitution to Sisemore. I've booked two tickets to the Cayman Islands to find out where the money went and I might find out more about who killed these people. I think the answers to both our questions, or big parts of them, are on Grand Cayman Island."

"Sam Dee said he went fishing in the Caymans. So he's been there."

"Interesting. I didn't know that. Maybe he did some fishing while he was banking. Anyhow, I could use your help, Carl. I want you to come with me and I'll pay for the trip."

"Well, I don't think Deschutes County is going to pay for it but I think it would be worthwhile. I'll go even if I have to take time off to do it."

"Do you have a passport?" Sarah asked.

"I do. My wife has relatives in Vancouver."

"Can you leave tomorrow?"

"I'll explain to the sheriff why I'm going. He won't say no."

"Redmond Airport, 5:30 a.m. flight to Denver then fly to Miami."

"No problem. See you there."

That was a quick turn of events. But in a promising direction. The crime lab report and the autopsy wouldn't be in until I got back. And though I'd learned a lot more about the good doctor I didn't have any leads I considered hot.

And then I did, maybe.

When my cell phone rang I expected someone from the sheriff's department. Hardly anyone else has my cell phone number. But I saw it was Dan Martinez, my fishing buddy from the Cascadians fishing team in the One Fly tournament. I answered it.

"Hello Carl," he said. "Amy has information about the shooting up the hill. Are you working on that?"

"If she's got something I want to hear it." Right away I heard Amy's young but forthright voice. She and Dan were an attractive couple, he six-foot-four and dark, she with curly sandy-blond hair and tall for a woman. Very athletic, the both of them. They had a new baby and were leading conventional, successful lives. But they both had grit when they needed it, especially Amy. She had saved a dozen women on a camping trip from a madman with a semiautomatic rifle. She stopped him with a cold-eyed pistol shot in the dim light of early morning. He fled the scene but we got him later.

"Hi, Carl. I saw something that may be related Sam Dee's shooting. When I was on my bike in the Pole Pedal Paddle a car drove really fast out of the sand station at the top of the hill. It almost hit me. I don't know when the shooting was exactly but maybe there's a connection. I slammed on my bike brakes and the car didn't even slow down. The driver was a man in a uniform wearing one of those hats with the fake fur that comes down over your ears and the back of your neck." She was trying to be as precise as possible.

"Make and model of the car?" I asked.

"I don't know. No idea. It was a small sedan. Dark gray."

"License plate number, even partial, just the letters."

"Sorry, detective. I was concentrating on the race. It could have been anything."

"Two door or four door?"

"I don't know. I'd say four but I may be wrong."

"And the guy? Age, build, hair color, race?"

"Middle-aged, I guess, medium build, white guy. Couldn't see his hair because the ear flaps were down. And I could be wrong about any of these things. I'm surprised I remember as much as I do."

"What time was this?" I asked. The answer took a while in coming.

"About 10:15," said Amy. "I can nail it down better once I see my splits and know what time I started the bicycle leg. And I can figure out who started right after me and might have seen the car too."

That was promising. "Anything else?" I asked.

"He was in a hurry. Didn't stop or slow down. Could have killed somebody."

"Can you come in and look through some mug shots? I'll be away but I'll set it up to have a deputy take you through them."

"How long will it take?"

"As much time as you can stand. The deputy will start you with white men about the right age who have been arrested locally in the past few years. Then we'll broaden it out geographically and back in time until you've identified ten or twenty men who are real possibilities. Or until your eyes start to glaze over. Your choice."

"I'll do my best."

I hoped Amy had a better picture of the man in her brain than Sean did, assuming it was the same man. But her description of the man's uniform and hat matched Sean's and her description of the car matched the one I found at Kapka Butte Sno-Park. My net around the killer had tightened another half-inch.

## Chapter 24

# Sarah Chatham

Carl and I changed planes three times to reach the Cayman Islands, two hundred and fifty miles south of Cuba. On that long day, at my age, and having the money to afford it, I wasn't going to fly anything but first class. If I didn't recover at least a hundred thousand from the two estates I'd pay for the tickets myself.

I imagined Carl, having traveled less than I had, might prefer to gaze out the window as we flew but he wanted the aisle because, he said, he might need to get out of his seat in a hurry. I didn't think a hijacking was likely but I was happy to accommodate him. There was plenty of leg room in both seats.

"Is there a gun in your luggage?" I asked.

"Nah. If you have a gun in the Caymans you have to keep it in a safe. The police can show up anytime demanding to see it. No concealed carry. No carry at all." I couldn't tell whether Carl approved of this law or not, very different from Oregon. I did think we'd agree, however, that the law represented how the citizens of a city, a state, or a country wanted to live. The law deserved obedience whether or not we thought it was good law.

"I did bring my badge, though. No legal authority there but it might get me some respect."

The nighttime taxi ride from the Grand Cayman airport into

Georgetown took six minutes, about the time it took to drive from my office to the Newport Avenue Market. The population of the entire country was about two-thirds of Bend's one hundred thousand. Our first-world hotel, with crisp clean sheets and dead-quiet air conditioning, confirmed this country was not poor. In fact, as I read on the airplane, it was the fifth largest banking center in the world.

The next morning we walked the short distance to the Bank of Cayman Brac. I'd set up an appointment with Nigel Buckhampton. He turned out to be a mixed-race man, like forty percent of the country's population, with English reserve and Anglo features in a light brown face. Carl and I sat across from his carved wooden desk while I reiterated our reason for the meeting—to determine where the cash cycled through Wendy's account had ultimately gone. Our host was cordial, businesslike, as though he fully expected that I would produce the necessary documents, he would answer what I asked, and he would readily transfer the funds I requested. I wondered if he presented a fiercer face to someone depositing their money for safekeeping, implying that he would defend their assets as ferociously as Cerberus guarding the dead.

I'd brought what I needed—Wendy's will certified by the probate court and her death certificate. For good measure I'd brought the same documents for Sam Dee, my power of attorney from Charlotte Dee, the bank statements from the Bank of Boise, and my own passport.

"That's all we need, Mrs. Chatham," he said with a smile. "I'll print you the past six years' transactions showing where the funds in the account came from and who they were transferred to. I'll be a few minutes." Thirty seconds after he left a woman came in and offered us coffee. We both said yes and she came back in minutes with coffee on a small cart with white cups and saucers, silver spoons, sugar and cream, and linen napkins. The bank's clients were treated well.

Buckhampton returned with a neat pile of reports. Simply glancing at the top page I got a shock. The account was in Wendy's name, no surprise. But the report, unlike the statements I'd seen online, showed who had signature authority on the account. The first name under "Signature Authority" was Wendy Whitlock's. No surprise. But there was one more name listed and the name was Samuel Dee. I showed Carl the report and pointed to Sam's name. Carl's eyes widened and he gave me a look to show he was as astounded as I was. We were both grappling with the implications of Sam's connection to, and even control of, the embezzled money.

"No wonder Sam was so eager to settle with Wendy's estate," I said. "He knew she was embezzling all along and he was getting a share of the money. Sam wanted Sisemore to forget about the stolen funds as quickly as possible."

I looked back through the reports. All the money coming into the joint account came from the same account at the Bank of Boise. A year ago one and a half million dollars was transferred out of the account to a name I'd seen before—Far Away Resorts.

"So Dee and Whitlock did have an investment in The Conclave," said Carl, like someone who has finally found a key piece in a jigsaw puzzle. "That's why Sam talked it up so much. They invested in The Conclave through this other company, this Far Away Resorts. Probably thought they'd make a fortune."

"And that's why Wendy listed an investment in The Conclave in her will," I said. My tone was dispassionate, professional, as though I were explaining how to solve a problem in trigonometry. Inside I felt more like I'd started a car with an almost dead battery on a cold morning. Triumph and relief. Buckhampton was not as animated as Carl and I were about our discoveries but he wasn't bored either. He smiled a reserved smile. His clients, or at least his clients' representatives, were getting what they came for and he was pleased about that.

"But what are all these other transfers out over time?" I asked the happy banker. "Five thousand here, seven thousand there, to a company called Kraken." None of us had ever heard of Kraken. I made a note to investigate that later.

"Aside from where the money went," I asked, "who authorized all the transfers of money our of the account? Was it Wendy Whitlock or Samuel Dee?"

Buckhampton turned to the computer on his desk and tapped in a query.

"It was Mrs. Whitlock for virtually all of them, including the large transfer to Far Away Resorts and the next to last transfer out of the account, three hundred thousand dollars to an account with the Bank of Boise. The only transfer authorized by Dr. Dee was the most recent one two weeks ago for twenty thousand dollars to Samuel Dee's personal checking account at the Umpqua Bank in Bend."

"So who owns the investments in Far Away Resorts and in Kraken?" asked Carl.

"You'll need to ask the respective companies," said Buckhampton. "Ownership will depend on how Mrs. Whitlock and Dr. Dee registered with the companies. It could be either of them or both of them together or even someone else."

"Do you have contact information for the companies? Will Cayman law and bank policies allow you to share that with me?"

"Yes." Buckhampton turned to his computer, found the answer, and recited it for me slowly so I could write it down. "Far Away Resorts. President Jake Sampson, North Coast Road, Little Cayman." Buckhampton gave me a number with a 345 area code. Little Cayman, I knew, was part of the Cayman Islands but much smaller than Grand Cayman, the island we were on.

"Can you tell me anything about Mr. Sampson?"

"Perhaps." Buckhampton turned to his computer again. "The population of Little Cayman Island is less than three hundred people. There is only one Jake Sampson and he is apparently a fishing guide. This is public information. You can find it online."

Carl summed up what we were all feeling. "Seems odd that a fishing guide would be president of a multi million-dollar company with an investment in The Conclave back in Oregon."

"In any case," I said, "I'll need to contact Sampson about getting any remaining assets in Faraway Resorts back to the heirs of whichever person they are registered to—Dr. Dee or Mrs. Whitlock or both. In the meantime I'll want to keep the account with the Bank of Cayman Brac. If Far Away returns any money to its investors it may take a lot less hassle to transfer the money back into the account it came from. Then we can distribute the money to the estates of Wendy and Sam."

"That won't take much time," said Buckhampton. "Our clients want to protect their money but they also want to make sure inheritance is a sure thing—quick, easy, and straightforward."

Chapter 25

# Sarah Chatham

"We need to go fishing," said Carl. We were standing on the sidewalk outside Buckhampton's bank. The sun was getting hot. Carl's approach was a more creative idea than I had come up with, issued almost in the tone of command. "We can catch this Sampson guy off guard. Out in a boat he can't get away. Start with a friendly conversation. Fishing guides are a talkative bunch anyway. Strongarm him if we have to. Bring a pen and a notebook. You know how to fish?"

"I fly fished for years with my first husband—trout, salmon, and steelhead—all over the Northwest. But never salt water. I don't even know what kind of fish they catch here. Marlin, sailfish, tuna?"

"Those are deep water fish. The catch here is bonefish. Shallower water—'flats,' they're called. Salt water about ten feet deep with a sandy or grassy bottom. Bonefish are long and silvery, almost translucent, bigger than a trout and very strong. But if you can fish for trout, you can fish for bonefish."

"You've fished for them?"

"Never. You know who told me about bonefish? It was Sam Dee. He was down here. That's probably how he got connected with this Jake Sampson fellow."

I searched for "Jake Sampson, fishing guide Cayman" on my cell phone and found he could be hired through a resort on Little

Cayman Island. Carl called the resort, the Southern Cross Club, booked us two rooms for two nights, and booked Sampson for a morning's fishing. Sampson would pick us up at the resort, drive us a mile to his boat, and take us out. He would provide all the fishing tackle but we had to bring our own fishing clothes.

Sport fishing was an important business in the Caymans and we found a shop that sold fishing equipment a short walk from the bank. I bought us lightweight nylon long pants and long-sleeved shirts to protect us from the sun, with vents built in to keep us from cooking ourselves. Fingerless gloves to prevent sunburn and hats with long bills. We needed sunglasses for sure but we had brought them with us.

The plane to Little Cayman was a sixteen-seater with an open doorway between the cockpit and the passenger seats. Our fellow travelers were tourists as far as I could tell. One man told us he was coming for the diving, not for fishing. The fishing flats were on the south side of the island—miles of shallow water that were home to bonefish. Diving was on the north side where the so-called "Great Wall" dropped a hundred feet a short distance offshore. The story, according to the airplane magazine, was that Jacques Costeau said it was one of the three best dives in the world.

We landed on a grass runway with no control tower and waited while the pilot and co-pilot unloaded our luggage. A light blue van, spotlessly clean but with dents and scratches from a long life, took us a mile. I said we should have put our luggage in the van and walked to the resort.

The Southern Cross Club consisted of fourteen brightly colored bungalows—yellow, pink, and green—strung along a beach with a common dining room and bar in the middle of the group. A long wooden pier stretched out into a bay of untroubled blue water. Hammocks hung under grass-thatched gazebos.

"You have to be pretty rich," said Carl, "to come this far and pay this much to lie in a hammock. You can always go to Lowe's back home and get a hammock for fifty dollars."

We sat outside on a patio for dinner, something of a curiosity to the other guests—a ruddy powerfully-built man in his fifties and a dark-haired woman fifteen years older, a woman either vain enough or deranged enough to wear a cocktail dress to dinner on the beach. Did they speculate I was a rich woman with a paid companion, maybe a bodyguard? Or a daffy old lady with a scoundrel who's after her money?

Carl had never been to the Caribbean before and neither had I. We were west coast people and it was a long way to go for vacation. We ordered local drinks to indulge in the spirit of the place, a Jamaican Red Stripe beer for Carl and a mojito for me. Our waitress was college-aged, very American, her fair complexion taking a beating from the sun every day. How did she like Little Cayman? It was a small place, she said, but she was here for the diving and that was fantastic. She was going back to school in the fall. We ordered conch stew for dinner. She pronounced it "conk." Neither of us had ever had conch before. She said it was good and we'd probably like it. She was friendly enough but half her mind was elsewhere. Off she went.

"Do you think Jake knows that Sam is dead?" I asked. "Does he know The Conclave is going bust?"

"We'll have to play it by ear," said Carl. "There are things Jake will tell us if he thinks everything is hunky-dory that he won't tell us if he knows there's trouble."

The conch or "conk" stew was very good and meatier than I expected. I'd seen spiral-shaped conch shells all my life and even heard a jazz musician play on them. I'd never given a thought to the animal inside the shells. It reminded me I could overlook the obvious.

Jake arrived during breakfast, a young man, not muscle bound but not an ounce of fat on him either. He wore his sunglasses indoors and hung his long-billed cap on a lanyard down the back of his white fishing shirt. He turned a chair around backwards to talk with us.

"You have sunscreen?" he asked. We said yes. He said he had water, beer, and Gatorade on ice and asked if there was anything else we wanted. Not a thing, we said.

"No bathroom out there," he said. "But you can always jump in the water."

"Sharks?" asked Carl.

"Nurse sharks. They won't bother you." They bothered me already but I didn't mention that. I'd never heard of a nurse shark.

Jake's boat was a white fiberglass skiff, low in the water, with a shallow cockpit in the middle wide enough for two anglers. There was a flat deck at the bow where one of us would stand to cast. Another deck at the stern had room for Jake and a large outboard motor. Above the motor, raised on metal struts, was a platform where Jake would stand to better spot the fish. Jake had a long white fiberglass pole to get us in position by pushing along the bottom. The outboard would take us out to where the fish were but noise from the motor would scare away the fish if we used it anywhere near them. Bonefish scoured the bottom in schools, heads down and tails up, to hunt for shrimp, worms, and small crabs. The sand they churned up would show us where the fish were and where they were headed. Fishing blindly to vast stretches of water would be pointless. You had to wait to see the telltale discoloration in the water. Jake called it a "mud."

We waded out to Jake's boat through quiet water. The ocean waves broke a mile away where the flats rebuffed the deeper ocean. In the blue sky above there were three cirrus clouds, their horsetails trailing from denser balls of white, streaming over the earth like massive comets.

I stood on deck first, nine-foot rod in one hand, the fly line in the other. The fly imitated a grass shrimp and would sink slowly in the water after my cast landed, softly if possible, on the surface. The fly was weighted so the hook pointed up where the fish wouldn't see it from below.

"Mud," said Jake from his perch in the back. "At two o'clock, coming our way." I could see the ruffled patch of dirty water he'd spotted coming right to left. Jake poled the boat forward to cross the path of the fish.

"Lead them by fifteen feet," said Jake, far more than I'd ever led a trout, "and don't make a sound." If I moved my feet only a little the fish would sense the vibration coming through the boat and the water. I raised my rod slowly and false cast it twice in the air before

I landed the fly, as gently as I could, in the path of the oncoming school. I waited. Nothing happened. My line lay peacefully in the water while the mud passed right by the fly and moved off. I reeled in my line and held the end of it, dangling the fly from my hand. Carl and I began to ask Jake about himself while all three of us watched the water for another school.

Jake was more than willing to talk about himself. He grew up in Montana, dropped out of college, taught skiing in Colorado, and lived year-round on Little Cayman with fishing trips back to the states, to South America and New Zealand, apparently paid for by very wealthy clients. He lived with a girlfriend who worked at a dive resort on the island. Telling his personal story was part of the service he provided, a story to make our day more entertaining. He didn't ask us about ourselves. We were his clients for only one morning. He saw so many people, he couldn't keep their stories straight. And, despite being friendly and attentive, he didn't really care who we were or where we came from.

I drew in a sharp breath when I saw another ripple of milky water moving in our direction. Jake, a good guide and host, must have seen it before I did but he wanted me to spot it. He gently moved the boat with his pole while I steadied myself at the bow. I got set, standing with my rod in one hand and my fly line in the other. As quietly as I could, I cast out ahead of the fish. The fly landed without a splash and began to sink.

I knew what a fish strike felt like and I recognized the tension when a bonefish took my fly. I lifted my rod tip to pull the line taught and embed the hook. Pull hard but not too hard. The section of the line closest to the hook, the leader, was transparent, long, and thin so the fish wouldn't see it. It was the weakest section of the line and the fish could break it if the fish and I pulled too hard against each other. My bonefish, well-hooked, took off like a burglar fleeing the police, faster and stronger than any trout I'd ever hooked. The line spun off my reel until the fish slowed down a hundred yards away.

"Reel in, reel in," yelled Jake. I cranked the reel furiously and got thirty feet in before the fish took off again. I held the line a little firmer this time and reeled more line in every time the fish took a break. The muscles in the fish almost outlasted the muscles in my hands. After a good long fight I got him next to the boat, at last more tired than I was. Jake scooped him up in a net.

"Four pounds," said Jake, "really good for your first bonefish. You fought him well." He unhooked the fish, held it in the water fifteen seconds, and let it swim away. Jack said bonefish were lucky they weren't good to eat. Carl took his turn and caught another good bonefish, a little longer and heavier than mine.

I volunteered we were trout fisherman from the Northwest—Bend, Oregon as a matter of fact—and we were in the Caymans for business. The business purpose implied, I hoped, that we might be skirting the law a bit ourselves, or at least the tax authorities at home. We thought we'd try flats fishing while we were here and we'd gotten Jake's name from a fishing acquaintance of ours, Dr. Sam Dee, and did Jake remember him?

"Good fisherman," Jake responded, "very competitive."

"That's Sam," said Carl, and launched into a story, all true as far as I could tell, about fishing with Sam Dee in a competition in Wyoming. I turned around to catch Jake's expression while Carl was talking. His eyes were scanning for fish but he seemed to be listening and enjoying Carl's tale. Ray, my first husband, always said that one of the principal joys of fishing wasn't actually fishing. It was swapping stories about fishing. I hoped the story deepened Jake's sense of us as fellow fishermen. I hope he trusted us more and, when the time came, he would tell us more about Sam and his investment in Far Away Resorts.

"Sam had a friend named Wendy Whitlock," said Carl. "Did you ever meet her?"

"She was here the first time he came. He said she was a business associate but they shared a room. She only went fishing one time. Most days she was on the internet or she read a book on her porch. She had dinner with Sam and the men he hung out with but she left when they lit up cigars. You know Cuban cigars are legal here and the men liked them. She got up early every morning to run while it was cool. One morning she ran all the way around the island."

"How far is that?" asked Carl.

"Little over twenty miles."

"How did Sam know these other men? Did they come from Oregon too?"

"Nope," said Jake. "He met them here. I introduced him to them. They knew each other from business they did up and down the east coast and came down in the winter. The fishing is good all year but people don't want to come in the summer. After that first time Sam came back the same week as they did in February."

"Sam could make friends with anyone," said Carl.

"Yeah. They liked Sam because he told good stories and he listened to them about their ailments. No time limit, no tests, no prescriptions. They liked talking to a doctor as a friend. Sam gave them good questions to ask their doctors back home."

"Who were these other guys?"

"Oh, I don't know. I don't keep track. Just guys."

"Any of them doctors?"

"Nah. Businessmen."

My turn to move the conversation forward. I was standing on the front deck watching for fish but I turned around so I could see Jake's face.

"Sam told us a little about an investment he had in something called Far Away Resorts. Did these other men have investments in it too?"

Jake locked on something in the distance, as though it were a school of fish that were far more important than Sam and Far Away Resorts

"Far Away Resorts?" I asked again.

"No. Never heard them talk about it. Never heard of it."

"The company had a share of a resort being developed back in Oregon called The Conclave. Sam talked a lot about it back home. Did he talk about it here too?

"I don't remember it," said Jake, gazing at the water with a "what does it matter?" shrug.

I matched Jake's off-hand tone. "Did you know The Conclave is stopping the project? They couldn't get water. Thirty million dollars sunk and the land is worth less than when they bought it."

Jake's jaw hung loose and his eyes widened. He hadn't known.

"You didn't know?" I asked.

"Did you have any money in the project yourself?" I asked.

"No, no, no," said Jake.

I followed up quickly. "Through Far Away Resorts?"

"No way," he said testily. "I told you I never heard of it."

"That would be strange," I said. "Because I learned yesterday that you, in fact, are the president of Far Away Resorts. We need to know who the other investors are."

Jake glared down at me from his perch. He was no longer thinking about fish or being our friendly host. "Who are you people? I'm not answering any more of your stupid nosey questions." Jake was confused, even in his own boat in his home waters. He lifted his head and regained his composure, standing tall on his platform, gripping the pole that rested on the seabed. "We're going in," he said, leaning on the pole while he jumped down to start the motor. Carl grabbed the front of his shirt and pulled him down until Jack was sprawled on the narrow deck, his feet hanging off the side of the boat. Carl had decided to skip over-friendly questioning and move into brute force, not my area of expertise. I didn't want to watch any more and I didn't want to testify about it later. I turned toward the bow and, pretending I didn't know what was going on behind me, I tucked my rod under my arm while I brought a small notebook and a pen out of my shirt pocket. I could hear the sound of rubber-soled shoes slipping over the fiberglass deck, a quick exhalation of breath, part sigh and part grunt, and the sounds of flesh and bones knocking against the hollow boat. Whatever Carl was doing was illegal. He could go to jail; maybe both of us could. But Carl knew how to operate this way and I did not. My legal training was about as useless as Jake's skiff without a pole or a motor.

"Now, Jake," said Carl, breathing hard. "You need to tell us who the other investors are, where they live, and anything else we need to know to find them."

"I can't. They'll kill me." This was followed by a groan and, "You're going to break my arm off." Another groan. There was muddy water about hundred yards off the bow. I didn't mention it.

"Did you know that Sam Dee was murdered? We might be doing his friends a favor. Might be doing you a favor." Carl's statement about favors had very little logic in it but it might get our guide to loosen his tongue. "We won't tell them who told us," Carl added.

"Okay, okay," said Jake. "Now let go of my arm."

"Name and domicile first." What a strange word to use in these circumstances. Maybe Carl used it to distract Jake from imagining the revenge these men might wreak on him.

"Elmer Russo, Mt. Kisco, New York. Fred Coppola, Miami. Benny Cozzolino, Newark. Billy De Rosa, Chicago. That's all of them. That's all I know. Now let me go."

"One more question," Carl asked, and it was a question more for my sake in following the money more than for Carl's sake in finding a killer. "Did Sam and Wendy invest jointly in Far Away or was it just Sam by himself?"

"Together. Jointly."

A joint investment would be interesting to explain to Warren Whitlock and Charlotte Dee. I'd try to leave out the part about Sam and Wendy sharing a room at the Southern Cross.

I heard another groan and then something like a whimper. I finished writing down the names and put the notebook back in my shirt. I still didn't turn around.

Carl spoke up as though nothing extraordinary had happened. "Sarah, why don't you make another cast and we'll go in. It's getting hot." I no longer saw any sign of fish.

"Forget fishing," said Jake. "I can't even lift the damn pole, thanks to you."

"Put some ice on your shoulder when you get home," said Carl. "You'll be fine in a day or two." I made a cast at empty water and waited. From the shore, if anyone were watching, it would seem to be a legitimate cast, as though nothing were happening in the boat but me fishing. I reeled in my line and stepped down into the cockpit for the ride back to shore. Carl and I had caught five fish between us. When we got to the beach Carl racked our rods on top of the van. Jake couldn't lift one of his arms above his shoulder.

"If you promise never to tell these men I gave you their names I'll promise not to tell the Cayman police you nearly broke my arm. That's assault."

"Assault?" said Carl. "Sarah, did you see me assault Jake here?"

"No, I never did. I could swear to it."

"And names? We got the names from some papers in Sam Dee's office. Jake Sampson had nothing to do with it." That was clever of Carl. He'd told me earlier Sam's home and office had turned up nothing about Far Away Resorts, Jake Sampson, or any Cayman Islands bank accounts. We were going to protect each other now, Jake and the two of us, an alliance of convenience after our recent confrontation.

Jake drove us back to the resort one-handed. He was not a happy man. He made us promise again to never reveal how we got the names of the Far Away investors.

With no flights until the next day, Carl and I spent another night at Southern Cross. We walked out to the beach before dinner to watch the sun set, faster at this latitude than in Bend.

"I think I can find out how much of their investment the partners in Far Away get back and see that Wendy and Sam's heirs get their shares. At least I can try," I said. "It will be interesting."

"And I got some new leads on who might have killed our friend Dr. Dee," said Carl. "I don't know if we learned anything more about the death of Wendy Whitlock. If it was murder it was long before anyone knew The Conclave was going to collapse. But I got a few more pieces to fit into the puzzle. We've had a good day. Made some progress and caught some fish."

I liked the sound of "we." I had grown fond of Carl. Not in a romantic way but as a fellow soldier on an unlikely mission, an adventurer in an unfamiliar land. It gave me faith, perhaps fleeting and illusory, that people from different backgrounds and different points of view could get along if they worked at it. We could accomplish great things if we tried hard enough. Clouds above us rippled through shades of red, pink, and purple as the sun went down. It was an exceptional sight in a place I'd probably never see again.

Chapter 26

# Sarah Chatham

I fell asleep on the plane coming home and, lulled by the constant low roar of the engines, I fell, as Alice did, into a vivid and troubling dream.

I was driving alone up a narrow mountain road, like the dirt road up to Paulina Peak near home where a car coming the other way simultaneously tests your sense of where your wheels are and your courage. The road in my dream only went one way and was narrower. I had died, I knew, and I was going to the next place. The car had a clutch on the floor and a gearshift on the steering wheel. How would younger people, who had never seen a clutch, ever make this drive? I was in some kind of Ford or Chevrolet. I wished I had my father's old Studebaker, the car I'd learned to drive in.

"I'll get there when I get there," I said, thinking that an all-powerful God surely could have built a better road.

The road ended in an oval parking lot like a scenic viewpoint. There were five cars in the lot and I parked carefully between the lines in a vacant spot. There were signs saying to leave the keys in the car, like returning a Hertz car, and I left my set of keys hanging from the ignition. I had nothing to take with me when I got out. The light on the rocks around me was soft like a summer evening and the air was warm. A faint earthy smell, I realized, was emanating from myself and I wished I had deodorant with me.

At the end of the lot, in an area leveled with crushed gray rock, a man sat at table made from a sheet of plywood laid over two sawhorses. He had a white beard, long white hair, and a body-covering white robe that had been through the wash many, many times. He resembled Jake, our fishing guide in the Caymans, aged forty years.

"Hello Sarah," the man said as I approached his table. "I'll be with you in a jiffy." He was writing in a lined notebook with a black cardboard cover and a sewn binding, the kind of notebook I sometimes used in college but bigger. The table was strewn with objects from my life but not the ones I would have counted as most important. There was a small doll from my childhood but it wasn't my favorite and I wasn't very much into dolls anyway. A receipt from Walgreens held down by a chunk of obsidian I discarded years ago. The set of car keys I had left in the car. A place card with "Bridget" on it from a party I'd given. A picture of me at Mt. Bachelor with my friend Elizabeth and her father. The oar from the scull I rowed with my college team extended over both ends of the table. I recognized the cover of a picture album from my wedding but when I opened it I found photos of an unfamiliar family on a trip to Crater Lake.

When I peeked upside down at the man's notebook I saw he was making lists in Greek. I could recognize the characters but I had no idea what he was writing. He lifted his head and smiled at me. "Just another minute."

Beyond the man, set into a cliff, rose two massive white wooden doors like the front doors of a mansion. There were no windows in the doors and the doors, while imposing, could have used a new coat of paint.

The man stopped writing, emitted a short sigh, and picked up a pocket calculator I'd thrown out years ago because the keys stuck. They still stuck and the man punched some keys multiple times. He got a result and entered it in the notebook.

"Door on the right," he said.

"Where does it go?" I asked. He seemed surprised at my question.

"Your destination," he answered, as though the answer were obvious.

Another car, newer and nicer than mine, drove into the parking lot. The Jake-like man stood up for the first time and walked to the end of the table. "Off you go," he said, looking me in the eyes and giving me a reassuring smile. He lifted the end of the tabletop and everything on it slid into a chute at the other end. I could hear it clattering down a pipe and glimpsed it flying out the side of a cliff into a deep canyon.

I walked up a dirt path that forked ahead of the doors. There was no one there to stop me from choosing whatever door I liked. I stepped to the door on the left, pulled it open, and peered in. A rocky gallery, like a pick and shovel mine, was lit by small light bulbs hanging from wires overhead. It led about three lengths of Jake's skiff to a turn I couldn't see beyond.

I closed the door and looked down the hill to where the man in the white robe was sitting with new objects on the table, talking with a woman who kept waving her hands. The man glanced up and flicked the back of his hand at me twice. I was meant to get on with it. Don't waste time. Stop dithering.

I went to the door to the right and peered in. Another rocky tunnel, no different from the first. The lights, however, were Christmas lights. Red, green, blue, and yellow. Some burned out. I stepped in. The air was cooler than outside. The door, on a pneumatic door closer, slowly shut behind me. I heard the latch click. There was no doorknob on this side, no lever, no crash bar, no hardware at all. The door felt as solid and immovable as a wall when I pushed on it. All I could hear was the slow drip of water over the rock walls. I stepped down along the tunnel. It was comforting, in a way, to no longer have a choice.

When I woke up Carl was still sitting beside me, earphones on, watching a movie. It was a scene in A River Runs Through It where Brad Pitt, or his double, stands in a rock-strewn river, throwing incredibly long and beautiful casts upstream.

"No one would actually fish like that," said Carl, stopping the movie and taking his earphones off. He'd seen me watching the screen. "You couldn't see the fish take the fly that far away and you'd have a devil of a time controlling him with all that line out."

"And you're casting past all that good water," I said. "You want to walk slowly up the river and fish every pocket."

## Chapter 27

# Sarah Chatham

"Why did Sam Dee suddenly transfer a traceable twenty thousand dollars from the joint Cayman Islands account to a plain old checking account in Bend after years of sending embezzled money in the other direction as secretly as possible?" That was the question I posed to Carl on our flight from Denver to Redmond.

"Good question. I'd like to know what he spent it on. Maybe he paid off a girlfriend. Or gambling debts. Or maybe he wanted to have some money that Charlotte didn't know about."

"But why transfer the money to Bend at the cost of blowing his cover? The IRS would eventually want to know how he earned that twenty thousand. His wife might get wind of it and she'd also want to know where the money came from."

"I don't think he told her about it," said Carl. "There may be a clue in the amount or in the timing. What could he want that cost twenty thousand dollars?"

I examined the bank statement again. "That was almost all there was in the account. It wasn't that he specifically needed twenty thousand. That was all he had. As far as timing, it was only two weeks ago. He could have taken that twenty thousand anytime after Wendy died or even before. Or anytime in the future. There was no hurry about it. The money was safe in the Cayman's account that only he and Wendy had access to. She was dead and nobody else was going to take it. I think he had a use for that money and the money had to be in Bend."

The Cascades, outlined by the bright sun behind them, inched into the airplane window, as the land below us grew darker. Scattered lights from lonely ranches assured us the plane was still high in the air and not about to clip the top of a mountain.

I turned to Carl. "The only way we're going to know what Sam Dee wanted that money for, and what he did with it, is to see the bank statement for the account in Bend. And the simplest way to get it, and skip using a subpoena, is to ask Charlotte Dee if she has the statements and if she'll show them to us. I'll give her a call tomorrow. Twenty thousand is not going to make or break her but I'm sure she'd like to get it if she doesn't have it already. And, of course, she'd like to find her husband's killer."

"Not of course," said Carl. "I don't think she cares. She thinks her husband was riding a tiger anyway, bound to get into deep trouble one way or another. If Person A didn't kill him it would be Person B. Or perhaps she herself was Person C. Even if she didn't have a hand in the actual murder, she might have an idea who it was and doesn't want to tell me. In fact, if you're going to pick up the bank statements from her I'd like to come with you. I might learn something."

The Redmond Airport seemed as much like home as an airport could. It felt as though all of us waiting for our baggage were less than two degrees away from knowing each other. Very likely we knew someone in common in Central Oregon. We'd driven the same roads, endured the same winters, hiked the same trails, been to the same movie theaters, visited the same lakes, probably been to a rodeo or the Deschutes County Fair, rooted for the same high schools, or their rivals, proudly celebrated Ashton Eaton from little old La Pine when he won the gold medal in the Olympic Decathlon.

Carl walked me to my car in the parking lot, not that it was a dangerous place and not, as my husband would have done for a woman, as some vestige of chivalric behavior, but as a well-practiced security measure. Friendly, though. He didn't hold the door for me but he wished me good night. I wanted to get home, to see what Bud had been up to, and tell him about my trip. It had been a long day and I was on Eastern time. Happy to climb into bed.

When I called Charlotte Dee the next morning she said she had two months of bank statements from a recently opened checking account in her husband's name.

"Surprise to me," said Charlotte. "There're only a few dollars in it but I haven't closed it because I thought there might be some checks still outstanding or there might be more money coming in. Sam never told me about this account and I don't know why he had it. You want me to fax you copies?"

"I'd like to come pick them up and I'd like to bring Detective Breuninger with me."

"Fine. I have some news for him." We agreed to meet at three o'clock.

I spent the rest of the morning on other business. We had a hemp farmer whose crop had been devastated by a hailstorm. Oregon had recently made it legal to grow hemp, not the same thing as marijuana but close. Hemp had been grown for centuries around the world to make rope but had been prohibited in most of the United States because people could get high smoking it. The new hemp didn't have the active, hallucinatory chemicals that marijuana had in abundance and traditional hemp had in lesser amounts. But the new hemp still had CBD in it that was known to alleviate aches and pains. So the farmers who first planted hemp stood to make a very good profit. Our client claimed the crop ruined by the hailstorm was worth what it could have been sold for at the time of the storm. The insurance company claimed the farmer had intermixed marijuana alongside it, which some farmers had done, that the farmer had therefore broken the law and had therefore violated the terms of the insurance policy. The insurance company claimed it owed our client nothing.

We had the insurance company inspector and our inspector walk the fields side by side. They reported that with the crop as damaged as it was, there was no way to tell whether there had been marijuana in the field or not. We negotiated an agreement with the insurance company for little more than the cost of planting, nowhere near what the crop was worth. Done. Final.

Then, to everyone's surprise, the wind-whipped hemp recovered. It stood up tall as though nothing had ever happened to it. It was, after all, a weed, a very tough weed. This was good news for the farmer, our client, until the insurance company found out. They said the farmer had not suffered a loss, was not entitled to insurance, and they wanted their money back. They wanted to negotiate a new settlement. I was writing a letter outlining our terms, reasonable but not generous. We had the upper hand. The settlement they'd signed earlier made no provision for the resurrection of the crop.

Carl was waiting for me in his car when I got to Charlotte Dee's house at three and we walked up to the door together. Charlotte, in Bermuda shorts and a light blue golf shirt, invited us in and asked if we'd like anything to drink—lemonade, Coca Cola, water, or anything else. Carl declined and I said I'd like some water. Charlotte took us to the living room, shades half down, blocking the afternoon sun and the view of Broken Top. She stepped out of the room and returned with a plastic bottle of Earth H2O water, chilled.

"Where are the kids and how are they doing?" I asked. Charlotte, as executor of Sam's will, was my client and I was here to pick up bank statements for the account Sam had opened in Bend shortly before he died. I didn't have any hard questions to ask and all I needed to do with Charlotte was maintain the client relationship and answer any questions she had about progress on the will.

"Brent went mountain biking with his friends and Waverly is taking a golf lesson. She rode her bike over to the range. They'll be home for dinner. I am trying to make their lives as normal as possible. They seem to be bearing up. Making a start on getting on with their lives. Me too, I guess. Anyhow, I have the bank statements you wanted. I kept copies so you can take the originals."

It didn't take long to see what happened in Sam's account at Umpqua Bank. There were only two months of statements. The account was opened with a hundred dollar deposit two months ago. Three weeks before Sam died twenty thousand came into the account. The statement didn't say where it had come from but I knew from the Bank of Cayman Brac that Sam and Wendy's account had been the source. Then a week before he died, Sam took the whole twenty thousand out in cash. He would have to have done that at the bank and Umpqua would have double-checked his identity before they handed him the money. There was still a hundred dollars in the account plus less than a dollar in interest.

"Have you ever seen the twenty thousand Sam took out in cash?" I asked Charlotte.

"I've never seen the cash and I've never seen anything that Sam bought with it. I don't know where it went. It might have been a gift to someone. Sam would have liked to be Mr. Generous to people. To be their savior in times of need. That's one reason I kept such a tight hold on our money."

"You told Sarah you had some news for me?" said Carl.

"I do. And it might help Sarah find out where the money went. I've had three women show up on my door claiming they had a very special relationship with Sam. That perhaps I didn't fully realize what an exceptional man he was and they wanted to make sure I knew. They hoped I would understand. Sam had understood them in a more profound way than anyone else ever had, more deeply than they had ever understood themselves, or had ever imagined they could. And they had understood Sam in a special way too. He had opened himself up to them as he said he could not to anyone else. Sam and each of the women had discovered they were soul mates, bonded together like coal compressed into a diamond. They hoped I would understand. And could they each come and talk with me about Sam sometimes. Could they come in and see where he lived, how he lived, the clothes that he had worn, the things that he had touched. One woman wanted a pair of his shoes. I told them all to go to hell.

"But I got their names and addresses first. Before I told them to get off my property and never come back, to never contact me again. And especially to never come near my children. Anyhow, detective, I think you should interview these women. And their husbands.

I can't imagine their husbands would be happy knowing Sam and their wives were soul mates."

Charlotte gave Carl a typewritten page with three names and address on it. He said he would investigate and to let him know if she learned of any other women in Sam's life.

"What about Wendy Whitlock?" Carl asked. "Do you think she considered Sam a soul mate?"

"She was too sensible for that," said Charlotte. "I dealt with her all the time, whatever had to do with Sam getting his share of Sisemore earnings. Or his benefits. Or anything related to the business. She was a smart woman. I don't know what was going on there. They were both attractive people. Maybe it was all about sex. I got along fine with her when she was alive but now…now I'm not exactly sorry she's dead."

"Don't go around saying things like that, Charlotte, especially not in front of a detective."

In the driveway outside I asked Carl whether he was going to talk with the women Charlotte had named.

"Got to," he said. "Unless Sam's killer walks into the sheriff's department and makes a full confession. No stone unturned. But I'm going to see what I can learn about the husbands before I decide to interview any of them. No point in driving around Central Oregon breaking up marriages if I don't have to."

## Chapter 28

# Sheriff's Detective Carl Breuninger

When I saw what was on my desk I rolled my eyes. More security footage, this time on DVDs. We'd had deputies collect all the security footage they could from retailers in Sunriver for three hours after the shooting. It had taken a while. It was a long shot, something we had to do to say we covered all the bases. What kind of idiot would stop at a store while escaping from a murder? They'd be on a nonstop drive to Eugene or Portland or California. Or they'd go home if they lived in Bend, or Redmond, or La Pine and pretend they'd never left.

What was worse, if I watched all these disks, what would I be looking for? The men Sean described wouldn't stand out from the local population, a thin man in a Forest Service uniform and a heftier man in clothes Sean couldn't remember. No Mohawks, facial hair, or shaved heads. The Forest Service uniform was for outdoors in winter. If the guy who wore it didn't have the brains to change out of it at least he would have taken off the hat in the car. There were fifteen DVDs, each labeled by retailer, camera location, time period covered, and the name of the deputy who had collected it. Hours of watching perfectly innocent people march into stores and march out of them. My mood improved when I saw one of the DVDs had a yellow Post-It on it.

"Carl. Watch This. Forest Service pants 10:55 am." The DVD, in color but with no sound, came from a small grocery store and deli on the road down from Bachelor. Most of that road went through vacant Forest Service land and this store, shortly before you crossed the river and got to Sunriver, was the first place you could buy anything. If the killers stopped here they were idiots. I watched the video as much to honor the work all the deputies did as in hopes of spotting a killer.

I started the video three minutes before the time written by the deputy. The camera was above the store's entrance door and pointed down toward a short porch and steps leading up to it. Not the best angle unless you wanted to find a missing hat. No view of the parking lot or the road beyond it. I watched a man come out of the store with a small brown paper bag. A minute of nothing happening went by before the man that the deputy wanted me to see came up the steps to the store.

The man had no hat or jacket and wore a heavy long-sleeved gray shirt that might or might not be part of a Forest Service Uniform. But his trousers were a brownish green with a wide flat pocket right above the knee. I'd seen Forest Service rangers wear pants like that and use that pocket for maps. The store had height markings on a post at the top of the steps and I could see the man was about five foot six. He was thirty-five to forty with brown hair cut short. Medium build, vaguely familiar. I might have seen him before somewhere. I stopped the video and stared at the man for two minutes, trying to let my mind drift into a corresponding image from my memory. But nothing came to me and I had no idea who he was.

The man left the store minutes later with something in his hand I couldn't recognize. I saved the best still of the man coming in at the top of the steps. I couldn't send out a "Be On the Lookout" notice based on the man's resemblance to Sean's description and my gut level feeling about him. But I sure wanted to talk to him, whoever he was.

I sent the photo to a friend of mine with the Forest Service to see if he recognized the man. I didn't want to waste time finding a Forest Service Ranger who had nothing to do with shooting Sam Dee. I also sent a text to the deputy who had put the Post-It on the CD to thank him for the help. He'd saved me hours. Sooner or later I'd want his help again.

I had a text from Amy Martinez saying she'd thumbed through mug shots from all over the state and found ten men who resembled the man she saw. She gave me their record numbers and I pulled the photos up on my computer, along with their names, last known addresses, criminal records, and other information Amy hadn't seen. She had only seen the photographs. Two of the men were in jail and one was dead. Two of the photos were ten years old and the men would now be in their sixties. None of the remaining five had a last known address in Central Oregon but all five of them, with some adjustments for aging, haircut, weight gain or loss, and maybe hard living, could have been the man I saw in the video. The feeling that I'd seen the man in the video somewhere before did not strike me again here. I didn't know any of these men. I transferred Amy's mug shots to my laptop and copied the convenience store video to it as well. I was hoping Sean could pick a winner.

Also on my desk were the medical examiner's report from Kristen and the crime lab report on what Susan had found at the scene. The shooter had scraped a cavity in the pile of crushed rock and buried his gun in it. Good for Susan! How the heck had she even guessed she should look there? It was a Sig Sauer P365 semiautomatic, a popular and common gun, easy for the shooter to conceal in a pocket, if he cared about that. The lab had traced the gun's serial number to a gun show in Nevada three months ago. The man who sold it said the buyer paid cash and gave the name Harry Smith. The seller didn't offer more information because Nevada didn't require a background check for private sales at a gun show. He said he couldn't remember what the man looked like. He was probably lying but I let it go. I had no way to challenge him.

Kristen's report said a bullet had entered Sam's chest on his left side between his fourth and fifth rib, passed through his heart, and exited out his back. Sean's bullet entered higher on his chest where it was stopped by a rib and lodged in his muscle. I could tell Kirsten and Susan had cooperated on their reports because they both contained the same sentence: "Findings are consistent with a single shot transiting Victim 1 (Dr. Dee) and maintaining its trajectory until intersecting Victim 2 (Mr. Wray)." I knew what the duplicate sentences meant—neither of them had enough information in their report to say for sure the same bullet had hit both men but they both believed that was what happened. Susan went on to say she'd found only one casing on the ground and the magazine in the gun was full except for one bullet. The lab said the slug dug out of Sean matched the gun. With some hemming and hawing their best scenario of what happened matched what Sean had told me. I flipped through the supporting data, reading less and less while thinking more and more.

Sam Dee had Oxycodone in his blood according to Kristen's report. A substantial amount, "indicative of habitual use and addiction." I sure wouldn't have wanted Sam—drowsy, moody, and feeling no pain—operating on me. I expected his surgery outcomes were getting worse. Sisemore and Sam's insurance company wouldn't answer that question without a subpoena. I might need that.

From Sisemore's accountant and attorney I'd gotten records of patients' formal disputes with Sisemore over the past five years. There hadn't been many. All settled out of court, no cases pending. None of the patients were the right age or the right gender to match the descriptions I had from Sean of the shooter or his accomplice. I would hunt these people down and interview them anyway. At least that was my plan until my memory surprised me with a quicker way to find the shooter, or at least the man in the Forest Service uniform.

Chapter 29

# Sheriff's Detective Carl Breuninger

I was taking my morning shower when I remembered where I'd seen the man in the store video before. The memory was so fleeting I stopped where I stood, the bar of soap against my shoulder, to make sure I didn't lose the image. I've learned often enough that when I have a flash of memory or insight, like finally remembering a line in a song, I have to go over a few times or it will be gone again, like trying to remember, sixty seconds later, the dream you were having before you woke up.

I saw the man way out in Hampton, in the east end of the county, at a ranch rented and occupied by a motorcycle gang called the Warriors of Odin. To get themselves fired up they claimed a mixed bag of political priorities—freedom to choose what drugs they carried, gun rights, white supremacy, sovereign citizenry—which pretty much amounted to a broad resentment of government and law enforcement.

With water running down my back I went over that day in my mind so I wouldn't lose the image. I had been out there looking for a totally different man, a gang member who was a suspect in a murder. The whole gang stood in a half circle facing me while their leader told me the guy I was looking for wasn't there. One of the guys over to my right that day, cradling a shotgun, was the same narrow-faced guy I saw in Forest Service pants in the video.

I didn't know the man's name or where to find him. But I knew the gang leader's name and I knew exactly where to find him, less than a hundred yards from my cubicle. He was in the county jail. Possession with intent to sell. I called the jail to set up a visit with Lloyd Fancher. A visit would be simple if he agreed to see me. If he didn't want to see me it would take a whole legal rigmarole to get an interview. Fortunately I wasn't the one who arrested him.

"Tell him I'll try to get his time reduced if he'll help me with an identification." The jail called me back fifteen minutes later to say Fancher was willing to see me and the jail could set it up for four o'clock that afternoon. That gave me time to go ask Sean if he recognized any of the men in Amy's mug shots. The hospital had discharged him so I called his home and got Grace. She said he was housebound for at least another week, bored and frustrated, and would be happy to see me.

One thing Sean had that other people didn't, was an armed security guard standing in his driveway. I could understand why. Sean had been the sole witness to a murder and possibly an intended target. Whoever shot him might want another crack at him. Sean could have afforded a squad of ex-Marines but maybe didn't want to alarm his kids.

Grace had told the guard to expect me but he asked to see my identification anyway. I could have flashed my badge and told him to get lost but Sean had hired the guard to do a job and I let the guy go through the motions of what he was supposed to do. Grace opened the door before I got my wallet back in my pocket.

"He's watched The Martian three times. He says it's one of the few sci-fi movies where the science really makes sense."

Sean was lying on a couch in his living room when I got there. His bathrobe was some luxurious silk thing with dragons on it in rich yellow, red, and gold colors. It didn't fit with the laid back, geeky, old shoe kind of guy I knew.

"Nice outfit, Sean. Thinking of opening a bordello?"

"Opium den," said Sean. "The customers are easier to handle."

Sean and Grace had a great view in a neighborhood on Awbrey Butte. But their house, built on a slope with a half-size lower level, didn't seem as luxurious as the neighbors'. Sean told me they didn't need a grand house and didn't want their children to think they were special. But inside the house I could see some indulgences—a tall wind-up clock with dials for the sun and moon, a model train that ran around the family room on the highest bookshelves. It disappeared behind a chimney and reemerged on the other side. If you don't care whether your bathrobe costs thirty-five dollars or thirty-five hundred dollars, you can buy something you like on a whim. But the couch, the rug, and even the drapes didn't seem any more special than what Estelle and I found at the Old Mill.

"No wonder people get hooked on drugs," said Sean. "I stopped taking Percocet as fast as I could tolerate the pain. But I kept thinking how nice it had been not to hurt. I asked Grace to take the pills back to Safeway for disposal. I may be a little grumpy but I think I'm clear-headed. What can I help you with?"

I showed him all ten of the mug shots one at time. We went through some noes and maybes.

Then: "This looks like the guy. When I saw him he was wearing a fur hat with the earflaps down and he had a scarf up to the bottom of his chin. But the face is the same. He's the guy who flagged us down. Not the one who shot us."

"A hundred percent?"

"Ninety percent."

Ninety percent might or might not be enough for a judge and jury but it was more than enough for me.

Sean had a question for me. "Any idea yet who this guy is and why he and his buddy wanted to kill either one of us?"

"We're making progress on the shooter's companion but still don't know who the shooter was or why Sam was shot. Remember anything new from that day?"

"Nothing to do with the killers but I did remember a few things. I remember I didn't have any idea we were in danger right up to the minute we were shot. Sam might have been a little nervous but he didn't say anything and he seemed totally ready to help the person who was supposedly injured. You never found anybody there who was injured did you?"

"No."

"I was going to pull over anyway but Sam said we should stop and see what the man wanted. I mean the man in the Forest Service uniform, the man you showed me. As I told you before, the ranger—or I guess he wasn't a ranger—said there was an injury up around the other side of the sand pile. Sam said we had to help and that made sense to me. When we got there he told me to park in front of the car that was there. Then he told me to stay in the car. He was very emphatic about that and I said I would. He was the doctor. This was an emergency. I was sure there were procedures, ways of responding, that I didn't know about. Or he didn't want me to complicate the situation. But in the rearview mirror I saw the other man, the beefier one I told you about, get out of the passenger side of the other car and stand there. I decided if this guy was injured it wasn't very bad and I couldn't do much harm in finding out what was going on. I was curious. So I got out of the car and walked around the front and then I got shot. I wonder if I'd stayed in the car they wouldn't have shot me. What do you think?"

"You weren't the target. They never intended to shoot you, not even for being a witness. It seems like they didn't think you'd be able to identify them. If you hadn't been standing behind Sam you probably wouldn't have caught a bullet at all. We're pretty sure the same bullet hit you both. It went right through Sam and lodged in your shoulder."

"That's some consolation if they didn't start out wanting to kill me. But now I've seen them. Will they come after me or am I safe now?"

"Probably safe. They think they hid their identities well enough you can't finger them. And they have to consider that getting anywhere near you exposes them more than they already are. Still, no harm in protecting yourself. Keep the guard out front until we catch these guys."

"You think you will?"

"Think so. You've helped." I left to go meet Lloyd Fancher at the jail.

Driving up Jamison Street I was struck again by what a clumsy tool the law was. Fancher was more or less a career criminal, as much as he tried to muddle his criminal history with rants about sovereign citizens versus a government trying to take away the God-given rights he and other citizens were born with. He was in jail for ninety days. Roland Lightfeather, who I drove to prison, was a law-abiding citizen until he killed a proven murderer. He was in for five years. Society would be better served if the sentences were reversed. Keep Lloyd Fancher out of circulation for as long as possible.

The procedure was to do all jail visits by video. Family members and friends could visit for thirty minutes twice a week but they couldn't be in the same room with the inmate. No sexy clothes or sexy acts. My visit wouldn't count as one of Lloyd's social visits. I sat in a small room at the jail where countless wives, girlfriends, other friends, and family members had sat to talk with inmates. Lloyd Fancher scowled at me from the screen on the wall.

"You gonna get me out of here?"

"I'll do what I can if you tell me what I need to know. You can speed my case along and save the county a lot of man hours. I'll tell the district attorney that and I know he will appreciate that." It wasn't Lloyd's first rodeo. He knew I could make a difference.

"If you try to trick me into saying something that will make me worse off I'm going to have my lawyer get your sorry ass fired."

"This has nothing to do with your case, Lloyd. I'm not going to ask you anything about yourself."

"What's your question?"

"I'm going to show you a photo. I want you to tell me if you know the man in it, what his name is, where he lives, and everything else you know about him."

"We'll see," said Lloyd. "Show me the picture." I held the 8 x 10 up to the camera and waited. "You're not going to tell this guy that I identified him, right?"

"Right," I said. "And you won't have to testify. I only need to find him."

"His name is Roger Babits. Called him Rogee. Never been in the military and can't shoot straight. Likes sixteen-year-old girls."

"Where's he live?"

"Don't know. His mother lives off Neff Road somewhere."

"Still with the Warriors of Odin?"

"Nobody paid their dues. That's gone. Rogee was a half-assed member anyway. Didn't show up half the time."

"Work?"

"Construction. But not steady. You could ask contractors around town but there's no one he stays with."

"Hangs out?"

"He liked to go up to the community college and loaf around. Watch the girls. Security kicked him out a couple of times. Goes to the brewpubs on Galveston. Same story."

"Who does he pal around with?"

"Used to see him with a guy named Skip McNulty. Drinking beer, riding around town, worked together sometimes."

I tried not to show Fancher any reaction to the name McNulty. Inside, though, my brain was racing like a hawk's when he's spotted his prey. It took a moment to remember where the name came from. Skip McNulty was Wendy Whitlock's brother. Did that fit together somehow? Or was it a coincidence?

"What can you tell me about Skip McNulty?"

"Hardly knew his name. Never hung around with the Warriors. He never rode."

"Okay. Ever hear the name Samuel Dee? Sam Dee? Dr. Dee?"

Lloyd put his hand to his cheek and had a think. First he tried to place the name and, when he couldn't, he tried to think of something that sounded plausible, something that would show he was trying to help me. At least that was what I imagined was going through his head.

"Doesn't he own a gun shop or something?" Lloyd was guessing. He'd never heard of Sam Dee. Didn't even recognize the name from the TV news about Sam Dee's murder. Just as well for Lloyd, I thought, that he'd convinced me he didn't know anything about the murder in advance.

"Okay, thanks. You've been helpful. I'll talk to the district attorney."

"How much time do you think I'll get off? I'm thirty days into ninety here."

"I don't make that decision. I'll do what I can."

I went back to my cubicle and called Jocelyn Nelson, Assistant District Attorney. I told her Lloyd Fancher had been helpful to the police and deserved some consideration.

"How much did he save the Deschutes County taxpayers?"

"Maybe three to five days of my time," I answered.

"So I'll give him three days off his sentence."

"Gee, I thought my time was worth more than that."

"No point in your catching 'em if we can't keep 'em locked up."

I disagreed on that point but I let it pass. "We might not solve the Dee murder at all without Fancher's help," I said.

"Five days then. And call me again when you find out more."

I told her I would. I left a message for Lloyd that he was getting five days off his sentence.

Skip McNulty had been arrested twice for public inebriation. That was it. Not a habitual offender. No assault. No robbery. Not even driving under the influence. I took his mug shots up to Sean.

Sean was glad to see me, even so soon again. "Wish we could sit out on the deck and have a beer. I'd need help getting up off this couch though, and the doctors have forbidden me alcohol."

"And I'm on duty, much as I'd like a Bear Hunter. I think we can make this quick. I have mug shots of other men you might recognize." I went through five mug shots of men who more or less resembled Skip McNulty and one mug shot from twelve years ago of McNulty himself. Sean held each photo in front of him for five seconds and then laid it in his lap.

"I'm not sure. I can't tell."

"The photos are twelve years old. Imagine what he'd look like now." Sean picked up the mug shots again and squinted.

"Don't you guys have some imaging software that ages people?" he asked without looking away.

"I can't get it without a special requisition and a tech to run it."

Sean squinted some more. "This one could be him," said Sean, showing me McNulty's photo. "That could definitely be him. The man who shot Sam and me. He's heavier now, I'd say. And his face looks like he's had a hard life. In the mug shot he looks kind of blissed out. But he didn't seem drunk or stoned when I saw him at the sand station. Stone cold sober and all business. Do you know who he is?"

"Best procedure is not to say. Someday there will be trial and you'll testify to what you saw and heard."

Sean nodded and I took the mug shots back.

Skip McNulty was not in the phone book or in any place online. I called Warren Whitlock, Wendy's husband, to see if he knew where to find Skip.

"You can try the D&D and a few other bars. I don't know where he's working now if he's working at all. He lives in a camper. You know Sarah Chatham was looking for him? The camper belonged to Wendy and Wendy left it to Skip in her will. I don't know whether Sarah ever found him but you might ask her."

"Got a license plate number?"

"I don't have it written down and I don't remember it. Sarah, as Wendy's executor, took the registration and title so she could transfer the truck to Skip. It's a red Ford 350 with a Lance Squire camper on the back. The bed's over the truck cab."

When I called Sarah she said she hadn't found Skip yet or his camper. But she gave me the registration number. "If you find McNulty, let me know. I need to transfer title to him."

I could put out "Be On the Lookout" notices for Roger Babits, Skip McNulty, and Skip's camper RV. But before I got the entire sheriff's department chasing BOLOs, I decided I'd check out two locations where homeless people who had RVs, or people who chose not to pay rent, could park their vehicles for free. The first was a church parking lot. It didn't have the showers and waste collection facilities of even the worst RV Park in Bend. But it cost nothing and had portable toilets. You had to have the church's permission to park there. If you couldn't behave yourself they would make you leave. I cruised through and didn't see the RV that Skip had supposedly inherited. The other likely place was a street that ran through a beat-up patch of juniper trees and sagebrush people had been driving over and dumping trash on for decades. After five hundred yards it turned into a dirt track. The street was built for the expansion of a shopping center, with a wide roadway and a sidewalk on the east side, but with no businesses or houses on it yet.

Halfway down the dead-end road, trying to catch what late afternoon shade two junipers could give it, I found the RV I was after. The paint was faded but the tires were brand new. There was an aluminum table by the side of the RV with two lawn chairs next to it. No sounds from inside. I knocked on door of the camper. Still no sounds and the RV stayed as level and still as when I first approached it. I didn't try the door. I didn't have a warrant. I could have deputies add the camper to their patrols until Skip came back. I hoped he wouldn't drive away without a deputy seeing him.

Under a lopsided juniper ten yards off the roadway sat a dome-shaped green camping tent. Chained to the juniper was a Harley Davidson Fat Boy motorcycle. Even as old and beat up as it was that Harley was not a cheap machine. Not the kind of thing a guy in a tent would own.

"Hello the tent," I called out. Someone behind the screen in the door flap peered out at me. I had my uniform on with my badge and gun. He knew I was the sheriff, or at least with some kind of law enforcement. "You know the guy who has the RV over there?"

"I seen him around," came the answer from a male voice, more annoyed than nervous.

"Could you tell him he needs to move that picnic table out of the roadway?"

"What for?"

"It'll get in the way of the snowplows." There wouldn't be any snow for another five months. But people hassled by the police tended to assume the law wasn't rational in the first place.

"I'll tell him."

"Nice bike," I said. "That's yours?"

"One hundred percent. Registered and insured."

"I see the tag is up to date. Can I see your papers?"

"Sure can," said the man, almost eagerly. For once he was on the right side of the law and pleased as punch about it. The man unzipped the tent flap and crawled out, papers in his hand. He stood up when he handed them to me. I recognized him from the surveillance photo, Roger Babits. He smelled like cigarette smoke. His registration and insurance certificate had his name on it and the address of a church in Bend. Both documents were less than a month old.

"Thanks," I said, as though now that I'd seen his documents we understood each other. We were on the same side of the law. As I handed the documents back to him I shot a glance into the tent. There was a gun, a revolver, half exposed under the edge of a sleeping bag. "Any idea when the owner of the camper will be back? Is he at work?"

"Don't know. I'll tell him about the picnic table. You don't need to come back."

"You'll be sure and tell him?"

"For sure," said Roger.

"Fine then. Thanks." I gave him a reserved, sheriff-issued smile before I walked away.

Now that I'd found them, did I have enough to arrest Roger and Skip for murder? I was close. I had the surveillance photo of Roger at a time and place consistent with the murder. I had Sean's identification of the two men at the scene of the murder. I could file an affidavit with the evidence I had and ask a judge to issue a warrant. I could get Jocelyn Nelson, assistant DA, to help me with the affidavit, especially how to include what I called "leftover facts," stuff that didn't prove guilt but supported the case that Skip and Roger had murder on their minds—the fact that Skip was Wendy Whitlock's brother, that he already believed her death was a murder, that he was going to lose his thousand dollars a month with Wendy gone and that Wendy worked for Sam Dee's clinic and the two were in league on an embezzling scheme that Skip might have known about. Also the fact that Skip and Roger had suddenly come into money for tires and motorcycles, source unknown. Even the fact that Sam Dee took twenty thousand in cash out of the bank and no one seems to know where it went.

"Let's keep it simple," Jocelyn said when we met. "When a judge signs a warrant he knows the police might have made a mistake. He accepts the risk. But if there is a mistake he doesn't want it to seem like he got seduced by some juicy details that don't necessarily support probable cause. You can still investigate your so-called leftover facts after you have these guys in jail." Our affidavit was short and to the point. Both Sean and Amy had identified Roger and a man resembling Skip as being at or near the scene of the crime. We also had the surveillance tape of Roger at the convenience store at a time consistent with the crime. We got our warrant.

Neither man was a model citizen. I would not be handcuffing them in their living rooms while they told their wives to call their lawyers. They'd been violent enough to kill Sam Dee and I'd seen a revolver on the floor of Roger Babit's tent. I told the sheriff we needed a SWAT team to make the arrests. Body armor and overwhelming force.

"You better be right about these guys," the sheriff said when he signed the requisition and handed it to me.

We got a team scheduled for five o'clock the next morning. To make sure Skip and Roger were actually there we sent an unmarked car down the road twice. Lights were on in the evening and both vehicles, the RV and the Fat Boy, were still there at 3 a.m.

We went with eight deputies in the department's military surplus armored truck. A passenger van would have been easier and cheaper. I knew damn well part of the reason to use the truck was to justify having it in the first place. It cost a lot of money and wasn't used very often. But part of the reason for the truck was psychological and even, faintly, rational. We were sending deputies into a situation where they might get shot at. They wouldn't even be in the truck if and when that happened. But the department needed to show it was doing everything to protect them. And that this was serious business.

The plan was to park a hundred yards away from the RV and the tent and surround them both as quietly as possible on foot. The trickiest part could be other people coming out of their RVs and cars to see what was going on. We wanted to minimize the numbers, to zero if possible, and keep down the noise. Two deputies were assigned to lag behind the others and tell anybody who showed themselves to get back inside and keep quiet. We could arrest them for interfering with a law enforcement operation but we didn't want to tie up deputies doing that.

We'd go for Roger Babits first because we could get inside the tent with one slash of a knife. I took that duty because I could recognize him and he could recognize me. If he thought some freak was going to rob and kill him he'd be more desperate, more likely to reach for his gun and use it. I crept up to his tent, deputies on either side of me, flashlights pointed at the ground. Not a sound from the tent. I held my tactical knife near the top of the tent to the right of the door flap, stabbed in and slashed down to the ground. The deputies switched on their high-powered flashlights. With my free hand I pulled half the panel away.

"Roger, this is Sheriff's Detective Carl Breuninger. I need you to keep quiet and slowly put your hands where I can see them." Roger was lying in his underwear in a half open summer sleeping bag. The deputy on my right slashed open the next panel to the right and shined more light into the tent. Roger didn't move a muscle. He could have been dead, drugged, or in a very deep sleep. I decided he was scared stiff.

"We're not going to hurt you. We're going to arrest you. So sit still and slowly show me your hands." His hands slipped out from beneath him and poked up into the light. They were empty. The deputy next to me dropped his light, grabbed Roger's left hand, and slid Roger completely out of the tent onto the bare ground. He turned Roger over and, in a practiced maneuver almost quicker than I could see, handcuffed Roger behind his back.

"Stay quiet," I hissed. "Roger Babits, you are under arrest for the murder of Samuel Dee. I need you to stay with the deputy and stay quiet. Do you agree to do that?"

"Okay, okay, okay," said Roger, forcefully nodding his head, panic and confusion on his face.

"Is Skip in the camper?" I asked. Roger needed time to answer the question. I grabbed him by the back of the neck and squeezed. He hunched his shoulders.

"I guess so. I think so. I don't know."

"Anybody with him?"

"Not that I seen. I don't know. I don't know."

No light or sound came from the RV and the team moved in closer, keeping lights pointed at the ground. A deputy sidled up to the back and tried the handle on the screen door. He laced his fingers together to show us that it was locked. Another deputy handed him a treble grappling hook. Two deputies held the rope while the first deputy stabbed the hook through the screen and pulled it tight against a cross-brace in the door. The two deputies tensed the rope and then pulled the screen door off the camper. Another deputy with a black metal battering ram broke the lock on the solid door behind the screen door with one good slam, leaving the door hanging and twisted. The first deputy charged in with a light on his helmet and his pistol drawn.

"Deschutes County Sheriff. Hands up. You are under arrest." I was glad not to hear a gunshot. Skip was too sleepy, or too sensible, to fight. The deputy brought him out and another deputy handcuffed him.

We had a Miranda party for the two of them outside the RV and started them off to separate patrol cars.

"What about my camper?" asked McNulty.

"We're going to impound it. Where are the keys?"

"On the counter next to the bed."

"While we're at it, we'll collect the tent and everything in it. We'll impound Mr. Babit's bike too, for safekeeping."

"I better get it back," said Roger.

"You won't need it," I said.

# Chapter 30

# Sheriff's Detective Carl Breuninger

Jocelyn and I knew taking Roger Babits and Skip McNulty to trial with the evidence we had would leave too much room for acquittal. The two weren't about to make a deal either. While I hoped the lab would come up with DNA evidence putting them in the getaway car, that would take two weeks and might come up negative. That left us interviewing these guys while trying for a breakthrough, some little slip or some little piece of information that could crack open the door to evidence we could convict on. My questions would have to seem innocent, oblique, and even irrelevant to the case at hand.

McNulty had the brains, and somehow the money, to hire a good defense attorney. We'd interview him second. Babits had the wit to get an attorney but no money to hire one. He got a public defender straight out of law school. Jocelyn said the young man was good on the law but not experienced in the wily ways of law enforcement. And, of course, the poor attorney was overloaded. He'd be excited to be defending a suspected murderer but the longer we stretched out the interview the more anxious he would get about his other cases.

The sheriff's department had interview rooms designated "hard." Steel tables and chairs and no decoration on the walls. Then we had "soft" interview rooms with stuffed chairs, a low round table, and color photos of nature on the walls. We decided to interview Roger in the soft room. Get him to relax. I took out the coffeemaker so he couldn't hit us with it.

I let Roger stop for a smoke in the parking lot between the jail and the sheriff's building. I brought a pack of Marlboro's and let him pick one. I even lit it for him. He relaxed immediately and even smiled. I knew that whatever he told me in the parking lot would not be admissible in court—no recording of it and his attorney was not present. But I might learn something useful.

"That's a sweet bike you have," I said. "How does it ride?"

"Like a dream," he said. He took another puff.

"Soft tail. I bet your girlfriends like that."

"Yeah, they like it. It's an easier ride."

"Trade in?"

"Nah." I knew it wasn't a trade-in. I found the bike in the DMV database. Roger had bought the bike two weeks ago, private sale, from a guy in Redmond. When I called the man he said Roger paid cash. Hundred dollar bills.

"I took it to the bank as soon as he left," the man told me over the phone. "I didn't want his buddies to think I had five thousand dollars in my pocket."

Roger took another suck on his cigarette.

"How long did'ya save up to get it?"

"Got lucky at the casino," said Roger. It was a lie but it was great progress. He admitted that he'd suddenly come into some money. At the same time he'd lied to me, an officer of the law, a crime in and of itself.

"I wish I could get that lucky," I said. "If you've got any cash left you can post bail and be out by tomorrow."

"Maybe."

We met Roger's attorney in the lobby of the sheriff's department and I showed them both to the interview room where Jocelyn was waiting. Roger and his attorney had met earlier at the jail to get their story straight. I was counting on Roger to have completely blown that opportunity. He should have told his attorney the truth from beginning to end so the attorney would know what he was up against, know what facts we were likely to have and what the weaknesses in our case might be. But I expected Roger told the attorney the same baloney he was planning to tell me.

I stated the interview was being recorded with video, gave everyone's name for the record—Roger, his attorney, Jocelyn, and me—and stated the case number and description. I announced Roger was under arrest for the aggravated murder of Samuel Dee, the attempted murder of Sean Wray, and the conspiracy to murder them both. I noted that Roger had been read his Miranda rights and I didn't deliver them a second time. We sat back in the upholstered chairs, all four of us with our legs crossed. A deputy sat behind a one-way mirror in the wall. I took Roger's handcuffs off but I couldn't offer him a cigarette. No smoking in the building.

I told Roger and his attorney about the surveillance video of him at the convenience store but I didn't tell them that Amy and Sean had identified him in mug shots. I insisted that whether or not Roger was involved in the murder, we hoped he knew something about it, he must have seen something. If he could tell us what he saw we might be able to make this whole thing go away for him—no charges, free to go.

Roger didn't even look at his attorney. I was a better pal now than his attorney was. "We was there. We went to see the race, maybe help some racers if they needed it. The uniform was to make sure we could get where we wanted to go. We parked beside a building in the sand lot and just got out of the car when a little gray car pulled in. We thought the guy looked suspicious so we watched him around the corner of the building. He din't see us, not a bit. All of a sudden this Hummer pulls in ahead of the gray car. Two guys get out of the Hummer and start walking back toward the little car. Might have had guns. I couldn't see. The guy in the little car is already out of the car and he caps them both right then and there. Down they go, boom. The guy wipes the gun off and sticks it in the sandpile. Then he gets in his car and takes off."

"Toward Bend or up the mountain?"

"Couldn't see. He went out the exit towards Bend but we were at the back of the sand station and you can't see the exit from there."

"And you didn't call 911?"

"Wish we had. We shoulda. But we didn't know what was going on. We didn't want that guy after us next. He looked like a rough son-of-a-bitch. Typical criminal type."

I could have torn that story apart but I held off. Roger's attorney clearly believed him and I didn't want the attorney to tell Roger to shut up. I wanted more information, truth preferred but lies accepted, if it would give me ammunition for Skip. I thought of asking Roger what the shooter looked like. But he'd make something up and I would learn nothing from it.

"What kind of gun did the shooter have?

"Sig Sauer," said Roger.

The attorney rolled his eyes. "I've told you before," he said. "Don't answer any questions until we talk about them." It would be hard for Roger to know what gun the shooter had if he were peeking around a building from a distance. He'd know, however, if he and Skip brought the gun to the scene.

"Was it a robbery? Did the shooter take anything from the men he shot?"

"Yeah," said Roger, "it was a robbery sure as shootin'. The man that got shot handed something to the guy with the gun. I don't know what. How could I tell?"

"How many shots were fired total?"

"Two," said Roger.

"You sure?"

"You got two men down, right?" Roger was acting impatient with my thick-headedness. But I knew he was wrong about the two shots. He skipped over what he actually saw to give me lies that fit the story he was telling.

"We're done here," said the lawyer.

"Yes," I said. "I think we are."

Chapter 31

# Amy Martinez

I'd come in third among Pole Pedal Paddle women 25 to 29. I'd won a mug. I expected I would keep the mug forever. Even if I lost it somehow I would keep the memory of winning it. Not the most important achievement in my life but perhaps the one that took the most focus, the most dedication, and the densest concentration of hard work and determination. Natasha had come in fourth and didn't get a mug. I felt sorry for her but I would never, ever want our standings to be reversed. Natasha would get another chance if she wanted it, probably multiple chances. I might or might not.

To train for the PPP I'd gotten a used Nordic Trak through Craig's List and set it up in the bedroom we used as an exercise room. It was an old wooden model that I folded up and leaned against a wall to make room when I wasn't using it. I liked listening to Beethoven's seventh symphony while I was on the Nordic. I'm not a classical music buff but the music was lively. I imagined I was improving my musical sensibilities. I still listened to Beethoven after the race, working out less, and working on getting a new job.

My search was focused. The job had to be in Bend and, if at all possible, in bioscience. I'd majored in biology and my only job in Bend had been with a company that made a medical device, a tiny chip that got inserted in pills and would let you and your doctor keep a record of when and whether you actually took the pill. Good for busy people, forgetful people, and people who definitely should not take more pills than were prescribed.

Bend, remote as it was, had about a dozen bioscience companies. Most were small and added only a few employees a year. They didn't have a lot of job openings at any given time. I updated my LinkedIn profile and responded to the few job openings there were. That took almost no time at all and I decided to build what relationships I had in the industry, always making sure not to hound people or give them a negative impression. I called the people I knew in the industry and wrote to the officers of companies asking them to keep me in mind. I could do lab work, organize product trials, and do marketing and sales. I could fall into something or the search could take months. I read up on all the companies and their technology. When and if I got a serious interview I could show off how interested and informed I was.

There was no better proof of preparation leading to luck than my job search. It took a week. A venture-backed ten-employee company had been developing a new drug for years, were close to getting FDA approval, and needed someone to market the drug and get a larger drug company to buy it. The marketing director, a title I was excited to think of having, would have to learn the technology and present it in a factual, clear, but more compelling way than the researchers could. I'd have to develop documents and presentations for high level management and finance people and for deeply technical people. The product's effect was to tamp down panic and nervous conditions while leaving the brain sharp and alert. The story behind it was attention-getting if not always reassuring. The chemical formula was discovered in a South African scorpion and it was actually a poison. The scorpion used it to kill very small animals like earthworms and insects and to defend itself. A good sting, untreated, could kill a linebacker. In the right amount, though, tests showed it had a highly predictable effect on human anxiety with minimal side effects.

They offered and I accepted. I liked my new boss. A woman, super technical and very smart. Not very strong on human relations, I judged, but that was fine with me. As long as she was responsible and honest I wouldn't need her to hold my hand. The salary was more than my last job and I had an office to myself with a view of Pilot Butte. My fifteen-minute commute would go past the market on Newport Avenue and other places I'd want to go. I could buy bananas on the way home.

Chapter 32

# Sheriff's Detective Carl Breuninger

Skip and Roger couldn't make bail, neither one of them. So they sat in jail while Jocelyn and I worked up the case against them. We hoped to find their DNA in the getaway car but we didn't think we had to. The techs weren't sure they could find it among all the DNA-loaded junk in the car. We told them to take their time. If they came back with no match to Skip and Roger it would nudge the scales of justice toward a not guilty verdict and we didn't want that. We especially didn't want it before we negotiated a plea bargain.

I knew we'd have a battle on our hands when Skip McNulty hired Tod Morgan to be his defense attorney. Tod got his clients off by throwing sand into the prosecution's case. He was more focused on tripping up detectives and the district attorneys on proper procedures than he was on proving his clients were innocent. But he was effective. If I were charged with a crime, Tod is the attorney I would hire. Especially if I were guilty.

Skip, Tod, Jocelyn, and I met in a conference room in the district attorney's office next to the courthouse. The fake wood tabletop and the leather swivel chairs seemed more suited to business negotiations in a manufacturing plant than to plea bargaining. Tod wore a suit and tie. I was in uniform. Skip was the odd man out in his county-issued jumpsuit. Bright orange. Jocelyn wore a Navy blue skirt and a long-sleeved blouse with a complex multi-color pattern on it. In her late thirties, she wore no jewelry except a watch and a wedding band. She was a professional, on the job, and she was going to run the meeting. People said she had the right personality for a district attorney, able to switch from warm and sympathetic one minute to freezing cold the next. This morning she started like a sheet of ice sliding off a roof.

"Mr. McNulty, you are charged with aggravated murder, not second-degree murder, for the reason that you committed this murder for hire. Either charge will bring you a life sentence but aggravated murder includes the possibility of a death sentence and means it will be thirty years before the state will consider whether you have been rehabilitated and might be released. Our offer is to knock the charge down to second degree in exchange for a full confession and a guilty plea. Second degree would take the death penalty off the table and require the state to consider releasing you after twenty-five years instead of thirty. You could make a good start on your quest for rehabilitation by making a clean breast of the crime and saving the county the cost of a trial." Jocelyn glared at Skip while she said this but if Skip had any brains and self-control he would let his lawyer respond. Skip buttoned his lips and Tod answered.

"Murder of any kind is absurd. You're likely to lose a jury trial and you know it. Reasonable doubt doesn't begin to cover it." Tod spoke calmly and confidently, scoffing at the offer—more to impress his client than to shake Jocelyn's resolve. She quickly reviewed the evidence.

"We have an eyewitness who survived the shooting and has already identified you in a photo lineup. We have a video showing you and Roger Babits driving through the ski area parking lot shortly after the murder and a video of Roger stopping at a store along the escape route. We have a video of you stealing the car you used to leave the scene. Roger himself has already stated you and he were at the murder scene at the time. We can offer Roger a separate plea bargain for a fuller confession and his testimony against you. We can show that you received a substantial amount of cash at the time of the murder. Our case is very strong." Skip took this with a stony face but Tod got more and more restless as Jocelyn spoke.

"Phony baloney," said Tod. "Your eyewitness suffered a trauma and was rendered unconscious during the shooting. Roger Babits is a flake, totally unreliable, and the jury will see that. The video from Robberson Ford shows a man in a hat who could be a million other people. Any tie to Wendy Whitlock's death is purely speculative. A judge may not even let you mention it at trial. You don't know the source of the cash Skip and Roger received around the time of the murder or how or why they received it. There are so many holes in your case you don't stand a chance with a jury. We'll tear your case apart. You should be asking the judge to reduce bail before we do."

I had to admit that was sobering. My faith in a conviction ebbed a little but Jocelyn's did not.

"Our witness, whom the defendant shot, has perfect eyesight. He's an upstanding citizen and highly credible. If we can determine who gave you the cash to kill Samuel Dee our case will only get stronger and you'll wish you had taken our offer. We do know that Dr. Dee persuaded a group of known criminals to invest in The Conclave and their losses gave them a reason to hire a hitman. They are all under investigation by our office and the FBI. It's credible, given your need for cash, that they would hire you." Three of us were battling for Skip's emotions, Tod trying to build up Skip's confidence in getting an acquittal so the two of them could negotiate a better deal, Jocelyn and I trying to weaken his confidence.

I wondered if Jocelyn would mention we still had a chance of pulling Skip's DNA out of the Ford Focus. Maybe she wasn't sure the lab would ever find it. I thought if they spent enough time on it they eventually would.

Tod's next salvo in the battle for Skip's confidence was something Jocelyn and I already knew well. "This will be a high profile case and the press will be all over it. Voters will remember if the DA's office goes to trial and fails to convict." We sat stone faced, as though we only cared about right and wrong. "Make Skip a better offer, a much better offer, or let's set a date for trial."

We left the room without a plea bargain.

The FBI knew all the names Jake, the fishing guide, had given Sarah and me of the people who had invested in The Conclave through Far Away Resorts. Gangsters. Organized crime. The FBI had Far Away Resorts, Jake, and even a mention of Sam Dee in their files. But the whole Conclave connection was small potatoes, not worth the FBI's time.

"Not everything gangsters do is illegal," a supervising agent told me. "They make legitimate investments too."

I told the agent how Sam had persuaded his Little Cayman buddies to invest in The Conclave and how they had lost all or most of their money. "Would they kill Dr. Dee for misleading them?"

"If he swindled them they might. But from what you're saying Dr. Dee didn't personally get any of the money these men put into this Conclave thing. They might be mad at him but they're businessmen. Some investments go bust. If they kill anybody it's usually some other criminal who has robbed them or betrayed them to law enforcement. They don't go around killing regular citizens for revenge on bad investments. Might have scared the bejesus out of your Dr. Dee, though, just for good measure."

So how did Skip and Roger suddenly come into some money right around the time they committed a murder? I had a wild idea. Wendy Whitlock. She'd been siphoning money out of the joint account that she and Sam had at the Bank of Cayman Brac. Maybe Sam had discovered it or was about to discover it. It hadn't occurred to me she could be that greedy or that willing to kill. So she hires her brother Skip and his buddy Roger to bump off the good doctor. Pays them in advance. When Wendy dies suspiciously Skip decides Sam Dee is responsible. Or something. And Skip, loser that he is, decides that the one promise he can keep to Wendy is to kill Sam Dee. And she's already paid him to do it.

And where would Wendy get the money? From the funds she shunted out of the Bank of Cayman Brac into the Kraken company I'd never heard of. I called Sarah to see what progress she'd made on tracing the money that went to Kraken and whether she'd seen any of it come back to Bend. Her admin said Sarah was finishing up a call and wanted me to wait. I said I would. I neatened up my cubicle and filed some papers in the desk while I waited. I'd been putting it off for days. When Sarah got to the phone I asked what she was working on.

"Another hemp farmer," said Sarah. "Sorting out what happens to his sales agreement when his crop is barely legal and the buyer's afraid the THC content in his hemp will rise to illegal levels when it dries out. What's new with you?"

I told her about arresting Skip and Roger and my attempts to find a cash transfer from one of Sam's fellow Far Away Resorts investors in payment to Skip for murdering Sam. Then I told her my idea that Wendy might have hired them. I asked what she learned about Kraken and whether Wendy had taken any money back from the company.

"Kraken is not a company. It's a crypto currency exchange for buying digital money. She was buying Bitcoins."

"So she was trying to launder the money like a drug dealer. Do you know who has these Bitcoins now? Could some of them have gone to her brother Skip?"

"Bitcoins are all new to me. I've asked Dan Martinez to see what he can find out. He's the most tech savvy person in our office."

# Chapter 33

# Sarah Chatham

I knew almost nothing about Bitcoins and what I did know about them made no sense. Bitcoins had no intrinsic value and no government stood behind them. What you owned, apparently, was a long string of numbers. Totally worthless as far as I could see but the dollar value of a Bitcoin kept going up and up.

I asked Dan whether we could learn who had Wendy's Bitcoins now and he said maybe. He asked whether I knew the number of the first wallet Wendy transferred money into from the Bank of Cayman Brac.

"Wendy left a note for me with a very long number in it, with letters mixed in with the numbers. The number was much longer than a bank account number."

"Let me see what I can learn from that." He left my office and came back fifteen minutes later. "There are no Bitcoins in that wallet now. They've all been transferred to other Bitcoin wallets. There are too many for me to track but we can hire a service that uses a computer program to follow the money through multiple transactions and Bitcoin wallets. There's a ledger on the internet, open to anyone, that shows every transfer of Bitcoin funds from one wallet to another. The service I've found searches through that ledger to follow the money. If the money is still in Bitcoin we can find out what wallet or wallets it's in. To get the money out, though, you have to have the password for the last wallet."

"But," said Dan, "if Wendy converted the Bitcoin into a dollar account at a bank we can get a court order to find out where the money went from there. So should we hire this service to follow the money?" The price Dan quoted seemed like a bargain to me given the hundreds of thousands of dollars we were pursuing.

Dan came back to me a week later with what he called a "Chain Analysis Report" from the service company he hired. The news was not good. Wendy was definitely trying to hide the money. From the wallet where she initially bought Bitcoins she transferred the money into ten other Bitcoin wallets. All legitimate and traceable. Then all these wallets transferred the Bitcoins into a mixing service called a "tumbler." The tumbler mixed up Wendy's money with hundreds of other people's and over time transferred Bitcoins out to wallets its customers had set up anonymously. Not even the government could trace where each customer's money went.

I gave Dan a copy of the paper I'd found with all the strange numbers on it. He came back a day later.

"I didn't need the passwords. These are the same legitimate wallets the Chain Analysis Report gave us, wallets the money went through before it went in the tumbler, not the wallets the money wound up in. Wendy, or somebody, has to have those addresses and passwords or the money is locked up and gone forever."

The money had not reappeared in any legitimate account I could find, not in her savings or checking. Warren Whitlock didn't know where the money might be and he let me examine his bank statements and the statements for his landscaping business. No really big deposits and what deposits he'd made in the business matched up over time with expenses and a modest profit. I supposed the money was probably still in a Bitcoin wallet somewhere. It belonged to whoever had the wallet address and the password.

Sitting in Oxton's conference room, on the speaker phone with Carl at the sheriff's office, Dan and I explained what we'd learned. Carl wasn't much more familiar with Bitcoin than I had been.

"As I understand it," said Carl, "it's kind of what Silk Road did for drug dealers. It made it easy to hide money transfers and launder money. The Silk Road guy went to jail for life."

"Technically this was different," said Dan. "Silk Road ran on the so-called dark web and mostly handled drug transactions. Every account ..."

"Let's stop there," I said. "There's no end to the technology and we don't need to understand all of it. The bottom line is Wendy hid her money and, as I understand, there is no way that the service we hired can find it or seize it. All we can hope is that someone connected to Wendy will suddenly have more money than we would reasonably expect them to have. Then we can investigate where it came from."

"Could she have transferred some of it to her brother and to Roger Babits for killing Sam Dee?" Carl asked.

"Could have. But she would have transferred the money before she died. And once they had the money and she was dead, why would Skip and Roger go through with the murder and risk getting caught?"

"They decided to be men of their word, for once. Or Skip figured the good doctor had a hand in Wendy's death and he wanted revenge. And the dummies thought they were so smart they would never get caught." Carl might be right. He had more experience with the vagaries of the criminal mind than I did. But I had another avenue to pursue.

"While we're talking about money moving around, you should know that Sam Dee transferred twenty thousand dollars from the Cayman Island bank back to a bank account he set up right down the street at Wells Fargo. No Bitcoin involved. This was a week before he died. He never transferred any money back here before. Anyhow, as soon as the money got to Sam's new bank account here in Bend he took it all out in cash. Charlotte's been searching for the cash ever since and Dr. McGrath's having people scramble through every inch of Sisemore Orthopedics for a trace of it."

"Interesting," said Carl.

Dan offered up three theories, "Was somebody blackmailing Sam? Was Sam buying something, like drugs, he didn't want Charlotte to know about? Was he paying a woman to go away?"

"All possibilities," said Carl, tilting his head to the left and shrugging his shoulders. He had thought of something he wasn't ready to share with me.

"There's something you're not telling me, isn't there?"

"Maybe," said Carl.

"We've come this far together, Carl, and I've helped you every step of the way. I may be able to help further. You should tell us what you know and what you're thinking. We will keep it confidential."

"All right. It's only fair. I am fitting some of the pieces together and I have a theory. I'll need Skip to confirm parts of it but my theory goes like this. Sam's life is about to fall apart and he knows it. His gamble on The Conclave is about to go bust. His fellow investors and all the people he bragged to about The Conclave will only laugh at him if he's lucky. The investors may be angry enough to kill him or his family. On top of that his fellow doctors are threatening to kick him out of the partnership because his drug use exposes them to liability. He could lose his license to practice medicine. No more 'Doctor of Record' for the Pole Pedal Paddle, or for anything else. And he could lose easy access to the drugs he needs. He'd need money more than ever to buy drugs and would have to ask Charlotte. If he doesn't have the money and position to seduce all of his 'soul mates', one of his women might expose him to Charlotte or to all his friends, patients, and the entire city of Bend. So here's a guy, hero of the community, loved and respected by all, including his children and his long-suffering wife. It's all about to come to an end. For someone who cherishes his image this is a tragedy like in a play.

"What's his solution?" Carl went on. "Go out at the top. Victim of a sensational murder. And, it so happens, he knows where to find a willing murderer, somebody who hates him enough to kill him anyway and whose source of income recently dried up. Someone desperate for cash. And who is the perfect recruit for this job? The culprit I have in jail for the murder."

"And that's where the money went," I added. "Sam took the twenty thousand leftover in the Cayman Islands, transferred it to Bend and took it out in cash to pay Skip and Roger."

"Came up with the plan as well," said Carl. "Gave Skip and Roger the stent retrieval tool to fish the keys to the car they stole."

Chapter 34

# Sheriff's Detective
# Carl Breuninger

Jocelyn and I hauled Skip McNulty over to the district attorney's office for a second round of plea negotiation. Skip and Tod, his attorney, had not accepted our earlier offer and probably expected us to make a more generous offer than we had the first time. Maybe manslaughter instead of murder, a ten-year minimum sentence instead of twenty-five for second degree. They were in for a surprise.

I stared Skip straight in the eye to press upon him the weight of what I was about to say. Neither the expression on my face nor the tone of my voice would make any impression on Tod. Tod would only listen to the words.

"Skip, your attorney hopes we won't convict you of Sam Dee's murder because we couldn't say who hired you to kill him. Now we know who it was and we can prove it. It was Sam Dee himself. We found his fingerprints on hundred-dollar bills in your camper—the bills you hid in a metal water bottle with a hidden compartment in the bottom. Our eyewitness will testify that he saw Sam Dee hand you the money before you shot him."

"You can't prove it wasn't a robbery gone wrong," said Skip.

Tod put his hand on Skip's arm to remind him not to say anything. Skip had just admitted he was at the scene. Even if we couldn't repeat his statements in court, anything he said might help us understand the facts better and present a stronger case. We all knew the "robbery gone wrong" idea wouldn't fly but Tod didn't look down or roll his eyes. He waited for Jocelyn's response.

"How did you and Roger know Sam would be there and what car he would be in if he didn't tell you? How did you know he'd be carrying all that cash? Why did he hand you the envelope with the money in it without you saying a word to him, as our witness will testify? How did it happen that you used a doctor's instrument to steal the car you drove to and from the scene? And why would Dr. Dee have twenty thousand dollars in cash if not to give it to you? He hired you to kill him and you did it, Mr. McNulty. No jury will give credence to the 'robbery gone wrong' idea."

"It was assisted suicide," said Skip, "legal in the State of Oregon."

Tod slammed his hand on the table. "Skip. Don't say anything more. Not a word."

Jocelyn did not go into a long explanation. "What you did does not meet the standard for assisted suicide. Not even close. Our offer stands. Plea to second degree murder in return for a full and complete confession." Skip sat back, shaking his head, and waited for his lawyer to speak.

"We might have something to offer in return for manslaughter instead of murder," said Tod. I had my doubts but waited to see what was coming.

"The county has not made much progress investigating death of Wendy Whitlock." That was insulting but true.

"Mr. McNulty can give a full accounting of his sister's death, who caused it, and how it happened. He is in no way involved in her death himself. In fact, he would have gone to great lengths to prevent it."

"Let's hear the story," said Jocelyn.

"No way," said Tod. "Change the plea deal to manslaughter and you get the truth, the whole truth, and nothing but the truth. It will be enough, along with evidence we believe you and Detective Breuninger have, to charge Wendy's killer with murder, in my professional opinion."

"And convict the killer?" asked Jocelyn.

"You never know. But I will promise you not to defend this person myself."

"And how does your client know how Ms. Whitlock died? Was he present?"

"Before I answer that question, are you open to this deal—manslaughter instead of murder in return for the complete story of Wendy Whitlock's death?"

"I need to confer with Detective Breuninger." Jocelyn and I left the conference room for her office and closed the door.

"I didn't see this coming," said Jocelyn. "Where do you stand with the investigation? Is this a deal we should take?"

"We've pushed the limit of the forensics and our investigation into Wendy Whitlock's financial shenanigans. I don't think we'll ever prove what happened without Skip's testimony."

"So we should take the deal?"

"Actually, no," I said. "Skip's offer in itself tells us who the murderer was. The killer was not some thug who might have bragged about it. Wendy's killer was clever and careful. So why did the killer tell Skip how he killed Skip's sister? He wanted Skip angry at him, mad enough to kill him. The person who wanted Skip to kill him was Samuel Dee. The twenty thousand wasn't enough. The chance for revenge pushed Skip over the edge to murder."

"We can't convict a dead man," said Jocelyn.

"Exactly. Skip's testimony will satisfy our curiosity but it won't advance the cause of justice." I expected Jocelyn was pondering what she would tell her boss, the District Attorney, and what he would tell the press and the public. I was pondering how I was going to tell Warren and Ethan Whitlock what we discovered and why we would be halting the investigation into their wife and mother's death.

"Okay," said Jocelyn, "we'll tell Skip McNulty we're not interested in his testimony. He pleads to second degree murder or he goes to trial for first degree."

Skip eyed us suspiciously when we came back into the conference room. When Jocelyn told him what we decided he put his head in his hands and his elbows on the table.

Tod said we were passing up a good offer and predicted we would live to regret it. I think he said that to make his client feel better. He didn't believe it.

Chapter 35

# Skip McNulty

I am not a bad guy. I'm really not. I'm trying to turn my life around, seriously. I am going to stop drinking so much. Get a job. I'll tell you that my sister's death, Wendy's death, made me take a good hard look at my own life. No more lounging through it, living one day to the next, only getting by, spending too much time in bars getting sick on vodka and talking with idiots. Passing out and getting rolled. Walking home to my camper in dirty clothes and collapsing on my bed. That camper smelled awful sometimes. I was done with all that. I had a real grubstake that would see me through to a steady job. I didn't spend that money on partying like I had been doing every time I had a little. First thing I did was go down to Les Schwab and buy a new set of tires. Went to the carwash and the laundromat. Bought some decent groceries.

I made a plan to go online at the library the next day and search for job openings. I could work hard, as hard as anybody. Come to work every day. Be responsible. It was time to grow up. Past time, I had to admit. I was thirty-five.

Then the goddamn sheriff shows up and I'm off to prison. Twenty-five years. No time off for any reason. I spent all my money on a lawyer and wind up in jail anyway. But goddam Dee hired me to kill him! I told my lawyer over and over it was assisted suicide. I didn't do a damn thing Dr. Kevorkian didn't do. This Sam Dee, Dr.

Samuel Dee, knew I was going shoot him and he stood there and took it. Paid me the money right there on the spot. If that wasn't suicide I don't know what is.

"That's the way the law works," my lawyer tells me. "The court doesn't want to get tied in knots over who said what to whom, or what they really meant, or how the other person understood it. Or who might have had second thoughts at the last minute." I am listening to this over a video channel at the Deschutes County Jail. "For assisted suicide they want papers filled out with witnesses and a prescription from a doctor for legal medication. The suicide guy has to have a terminal illness already and has to wait fifteen days between his first request to a doctor and his actually getting the medicine." It's all bullshit. If a guy wants to die, the guy wants to die. He's a grownup.

Sam Dee came to me. I didn't seek him out. I hardly knew who he was. And he tells me a story that makes me mad enough to kill him on the spot. But that's what he wanted. See? We were sitting in my camper, over that tiny table. You have to arrange your knees so you're not bumping into each other. He says he understands how I feel. He wants me to kill him. But he wants me to get away with it. Doesn't want for me to get caught. He wants to die, he says. And he'll pay me to do it. Twenty thousand dollars. He has a plan. A good plan. A smart plan. The guy who killed my sister would be dead and I'd have twenty thousand dollars. Well, I'd have to give Roger something and I gave him six thousand. Told him I was getting twelve thousand and I was splitting it with him.

The only person who cared about me consistently, not some charity one-off "pat-yourself-on-the-back" act of mercy, was my sister Wendy. She was three years older than me. From the time I was ten we lived in foster homes and in hotels rented by child welfare services. The kids we lived with were all sad and many were deranged, I mean certifiably crazy. Some beat up other kids and some killed themselves. The only thing that got Wendy and me through, mostly me with her help, was that we had each other. She saved my life. She got a high school degree and she learned bookkeeping. She got a job with a lumber company in Roseburg. Then she married Warren Whitlock and started to live a normal life. Had a child, Ethan. They moved to Bend and she went to work for Sisemore Orthopedics, first as a bookkeeper and then as an administrator.

I got a high school degree and started work stoking the burner in a lumber mill. But I didn't have the backbone Wendy had. I started drinking and carrying on. It got to where I couldn't go for long without drinking. I lost my job. I lost a whole string of jobs. I moved in with Wendy and Warren for a while and I helped them by watching Ethan when he was younger. But they couldn't stand my drinking or the hours I kept. They couldn't depend on me to stay with Ethan and they said I was a bad influence on him. Bad role model. Hell, I was a bad role model for myself. Wendy bought the camper for me to live in but she kept the title and paid the insurance.

"Don't come by without calling and don't come unless you're stone cold sober." This was my sister but she was right. Wendy gave me some money at first when I asked for it. But then we both got tired of me begging for it and she wrangling with how much to give me. So she made up this arrangement where we had a joint checking account except we never printed any checks. On the fifth of every month she put a thousand dollars in it and I could take it out with a debit card. Warren didn't even know about it. A thousand dollars a month was not chump change for them. I couldn't take more than two hundred on any given day. When I asked for money after that Wendy said no every time. "Get a job," she said. I got some jobs but, of course, I couldn't keep them. She told me to go to AAA but I hated that, bunch of stupid platitudes for losers. My only friends were drunks or, like Roger, idiots.

When Wendy died I knew the money would stop coming and sure enough, the next month there was no money in the account. Warren wanted nothing to do with me. Hung up on me. Ethan did too. They put up No Trespassing signs and when I went to their house, mostly sober, Warren called the sheriff on me and I had to leave.

Then this guy, movie star looking guy, parks his Range Rover next to my camper and offers me twenty thousand dollars to kill him. Foolproof plan. No one will know it was me. I think this is the screwiest thing I've ever heard. If he's serious why doesn't he just off himself?

Insurance, he says. His life insurance won't pay out if he kills himself. Also, he says—and this is the craziest thing—he's got a reputation to uphold. People respect him, he says. He doesn't want them to think he's a quitter. I'm thinking, who cares about their reputation when they're dead?

Then he asks me would I like to kill the man who killed Wendy? Now he wants me to kill people and I'm thinking I don't want any part of this. The guy is crazy. I want him to get out of my camper and never come back.

"I killed Wendy," he says. Tells me over the table, barely two feet from his face to mine, that he's a doctor at Sisemore Orthopedics where Wendy worked and the two partnered up to steal from the company. Wendy handled hiding the money and together they got the inside track to invest in The Conclave, a super-luxury resort that was going to get built near Redmond. Except that this guy found out that Wendy had been taking money out of their partnership for herself. And what's more, the embezzlement was about to be found out. So, he says, Wendy and he decide the only way out is to commit suicide. Both of them together.

"Then I thought about Wendy stealing part of the money for herself," says the doctor. "I was mad about that and I also figured out she was the only person who could testify that I was in on the embezzling. If she were dead I'd never get caught.

"We were going to hang ourselves in the Whitlock barn. Threw two ropes over the steel beams holding up the roof and put one of Warren's pruning ladders under each of the ropes. But they weren't close enough for us to hold hands when we jumped the way we wanted to. I said I would move my ladder but as soon as I got to the ground I lifted up one leg of your sister's ladder and tipped the whole thing over. She managed to yell 'No!' and reach for the rope but it was too late. I wiped down everything I touched and I left. Took her cell phone with me to erase the record of the calls between us. Killing

Wendy was wrong and I've regretted it ever since."

I didn't believe the guy when he said he regretted it. And I seriously thought about killing him on the spot, right in my camper. But we were face to face and we'd been talking for twenty minutes, the longest sober conversation I'd had in months. I thought about the bloody mess it would make to kill him in my camper, starting with my fists and finishing with a knife. Then I thought about the twenty thousand dollars I might get if I killed him his way.

"How the hell is this supposed to work?" I asked

He'd planned it all out. How we'd do it in the middle of the Pole Pedal Paddle when everyone was paying attention to the race. How we'd steal an untraceable car from Robberson Ford with a special tool that he had. He'd hand me the money and I could see it in the envelope before I shot him. He'd paid cash for a pistol at a gun show in Nevada. It couldn't be traced to either one of us. I had to shoot him up close, right in the heart, to make sure he died from it. I should wear gloves and hide the gun in the sand pile once I shot him so I couldn't get caught with it.

He told me where to stand at the ODOT sand station and made sure I knew where it was. I did. He told me what car to watch out for and told me another man would be driving but Dr. Dee would tell the other man to stay in the car. The guy would never get a good look at me. And I should wear a parka with the hood up.

"Where's the second car going to come from? The one I get in after I ditch the one that's stolen?"

"Can your camper make it up the hill?"

"The engine and tranny are good but it needs new tires. Can't afford to get a flat driving either direction."

The doctor wasn't used to dealing with people who didn't have any money. So he reaches in his pocket and pulls out a wad of hundred-dollar bills. He peels off ten of them and tells me to get new tires.

"And a full tank of gas," he said. As if I wouldn't think of that. "You're going to need another man to get two cars up there. Have you got somebody who can drive one while you drive the other?" I picked Roger. I could talk him into anything. I'd have him drive the stolen car up the mountain while I drove the camper. And I'd have him wave the doctor's car down so I didn't have to huff it up the driveway of the sand station to where we'd be out of sight. I'd have to give Roger some of the twenty thousand and that pissed me off from the start.

Then the damn guy driving the Hummer was supposed to stay in the car. The doctor said he would but he didn't. He got himself shot for it. Served him right. Then Roger has to stop for cigarettes, right when we're getting really clear of the whole thing. 'Course he wants to smoke one right away and it stinks up my truck. If we hadn't stopped for his damn cigarettes we would have gotten away with the whole bloody thing.

I hear that Sam Dee's wife is having the devil's own time getting his life insurance to pay off. The insurance company says it was suicide and they don't pay on suicide. She says if the State of Oregon put me in jail for murder then it was murder and they should pay. I asked Tod Morgan if a court decided the insurance company didn't have to pay because it was suicide, then it was suicide, not murder, and could I get out of jail? He said there wasn't a prayer of that happening. Of course by that time I'd given Tod all the money I had and he wouldn't get any more money if he tried to help me. He turned me over to a public defender.

When I get out I'll be sixty years old. They say it should give me something to hope for. Strange to call it hope because it is so far away. Strange because I have no view of how my life will be any better when I get out than it was before I went in. Strange to feel any hope at all after being out of practice with it virtually all my life.

The only person who came to see me was Ethan. He wanted to know how his mother had died. What he really wanted to know was if she planned to kill herself. He'd had two shocks already, his mother dying and then his discovering she was a criminal. And in a conspiracy with a man who wasn't her husband. Poor kid had to wonder if he knew his mother at all.

"Was she in love with Dr. Dee?" he asked me.

"I don't know," I said, which was the truth. "But I think she was happy with your father, happy to have you, and happy to have a family. She was no fool. I mean Sam Dee was handsome and sophisticated and a doctor. But she would not have believed any promises he made. Too many people made too many promises to her growing up." I didn't say she might have volunteered some recreational sex to seduce Sam Dee into helping her steal. But she wouldn't have done it for fun or romance or some sense of adventure. She wanted money and she wanted Ethan to have a better life than she had. Sam Dee was a necessary partner in crime, not a partner in upsetting the family she'd managed to pull together.

"As far as killing herself, I don't think she ever would. Dr. Dee told me the two of them thought their crime was about to be found out and they agreed to commit suicide. But he planned all along to kill her and make it look like suicide. Then he could blame all the embezzling on her and she couldn't testify against him. The man had no conscience. He got her up on that ladder with a noose around her neck and then pushed the ladder over. That's what he told me.

"But I don't think she ever planned to jump. She got up on that ladder expecting the doctor to jump. God knows he had reason to jump. Not only was he going to be caught embezzling, he was going to lose his doctor's license and get kicked out of Sisemore for being a drug addict. The big reputation he had in the community was all going to go in the other direction. Maybe his wife was going to find out about all his girlfriends. I think Wendy thought Dee would jump and she wouldn't. But the man was a rat and a coward. In any case, he wanted your mother dead and he killed her. Your mother would never have left you voluntarily. You've got to believe that for her sake."

Ethan's eyes were still on the screen in front of him, the screen where my face appeared. But he wasn't registering me anymore. My words were turning over in his head, like rocks being polished in a rock tumbler.

"Makes sense," he said.

I was relieved. Ethan believed me. I didn't know whether I truly believed what I'd said but that didn't matter. I hoped Ethan would believe what I told him for the rest of his life. It might be, I knew, that this was the last time I would ever see Ethan. He might never come back to see me again. There was one more thing I wanted to make sure he understood.

"Do you remember I said that your mother gave me a thousand dollars a month for years to keep me going? She'd transfer the money into a checking account in her name and I used her debit card to take the money out in cash at an ATM." Ethan's interest was tailing off but I had to get across to him something a teenager would rarely think about, if ever. "Do you know who came after her wanting to know where that money was coming from? It wasn't the police. It was the IRS. They considered it income no matter where it came from and they wanted to tax it. Didn't care whether it was stolen or not. Just wanted their share. Wendy put them off somehow. Maybe she actually paid taxes on it. But I kept getting my thousand dollars. My point is, and this is important, if your mother left you any money hidden away anywhere, you want to be very careful about getting your hands on it. Even if she settled with Sisemore the government is going to want their cut of whatever you get. Either find some way to hide that you're getting it or get a good tax attorney or something."

Ethan didn't say anything but his eyes said he was paying attention. I knew Wendy had put a lot of money into Bitcoin and no one could trace it. But I knew damn well where it had ended up. The kid on my screen could be a millionaire whether he knew it or not. And he would understand all that online stuff—block chains, digital currency, the dark net—all of it. He would figure out a way to channel that money to where he could use it. I didn't know how but I knew he would find a way to do it.

"Gaming," he muttered. "Online gaming." I hoped he would be luckier, or smarter, than his mother and his uncle.

# Acknowledgements

I am lucky to have friends who have competed in the famous Pole Pedal Paddle and who helped me immensely with their stories and ideas: Dick Arnold (three mugs, two as an individual), Dave Duerson, Phil Northcote, and Kim Rogers. Many thanks to all of them and to Molly Cogswell-Kelly, Events Director of the Mt. Bachelor Sports Education Foundation and organizer of the Pole Pedal Paddle race. All helped me make this a richer and more true-to-life book.

My deepest gratitude to Tom Montgomery, friend of many years, phenomenal fisherman, teacher, and photographer (*The Nature of Fly Fishing*). Tom inspired some of the fishing scenes in the book and improved the accuracy and realism of all of them. Any wind knots or other errors are my own.

I am immensely grateful to the editors and commenters who made this a much better book than I could have created without their efforts: Jessica Powers, Kristin Weber, Cindy Davis, Jared Haynes, and my ever enthusiastic wife, Joan Haynes. I am also much indebted to Lynn Stegner and my fellow students in her Novel Writing Class who steered this book, and my writing, in the best directions in the early stages of the project.

# Fact and Fiction

Bend's premier sporting event, the Pole Pedal Paddle, began in 1977 and has run every year except 2020 and 2021, typically with over two thousand competitors. Pole Pedal Murder attempts to represent the race as accurately as possible without confining it to a specific year. The competitors in this book are all fictional but the names of past year all women's teams (e.g. "Miles to Martinis") are real. For photos of the 2022 Pole Pedal Paddle see www.tedhaynes/ppp.html.

The Jackson Hole One Fly fishing tournament began in 1986 and the description in this book closely follows the actual competition. The anecdote of the elderly lady who finished first among women on day one of the tournament is true. She was my friend, Elizabeth McCabe, and she was ninety-nine years old. I didn't use her age in the book because my friend Tom said, "Nobody will believe it."

The Deschutes County Sheriff's Department is over one hundred and forty Oregonians strong, twelve of whom are detectives. For the sake of this story, *Pole Pedal Paddle* mentions only Carl Breuninger.

The Cayman Islands truly are the fifth largest international banking center in the world and are renowned, as described in the book, for protecting their clients' identities and assets. I may have bent their rules and procedures a little to serve the cause of fiction. The Bank of Boise and the Bank of Cayman Brac are fictional but Umpqua Bank, in spite of its unlikely name, is very real.

The Fort Rock Indians are fictional but the description of their pow wow closely follows the traditional American and Canadian pow wow program and builds on my visit to Straight Out of Auburn Big Time Pow Wow in 2018.

Sisemore Orthopedics is fictional but Sisemore Street in Bend is very real, its name taken from John Sisemore, an early settler of Bend and its first postmaster.

The Conclave resort is fictional but luxury golf communities have been regularly carved out of the desert in Central Oregon. There is an enormous aquifer with consistently good water a thousand feet below ground. Finding bad water, as The Conclave did, is a flight of fiction.

Facebook (now known as Meta) does have an enormous data center in Prineville, a city smaller and more remote than Bend about forty miles away. If you are a Facebook user, it is virtually certain there is a copy of your profile in Prineville.

## About the Author

Ted Haynes is the author of both history and fiction set in Central Oregon. He and his wife first visited Bend in 1975 and built a log house on the Little Deschutes River in 2007. Ted is a fisherman, golfer, and competitive master swimmer. He has studied fiction writing with Hillary Jordan, Lynn Stegner, Nancy Packer, and Martha Conway. He is a member of Mystery Writers of America and a founding board member of the Waterston Prize for Desert Writing, located in Bend.

## Books by Ted Haynes

**The Northwest Murder Mystery Series**
*Suspects*
*The Mirror Pond Murders*
*The Mt. Bachelor Murders*
*Pole Pedal Murder*

*On the Road from Burns – Short Stories from Central Oregon*

*The Dot.Com Terrorist*

*Vandevert – The Hundred Year History of a Central Oregon Ranch*
(non-fiction, co-authored with Grace Vandevert McNellis)

For the latest on books by Ted Haynes, see
www.tedhaynes.com
or email Ted at
publisher@robledabooks.com